Sherlock Holmes and The London Majestic

A Case of Poison, Performance, and Peril

A Sherlock Holmes – Victoria Watson Adventure

By Joni Lambert

Hardcover ISBN 978-1-80424-768-6
Paperback ISBN 978-1-80424-769-3
ePub ISBN 978-1-80424-770-9
PDF ISBN 978-1-80424-771-6

Published by MX Publishing
335 Princess Park Manor, Royal Drive,
London, N11 3GX
www.mxpublishing.com

Cover design by Joni Lambert

The misty veil of a London morning clung to the cobbled streets as Victoria Watson stepped off the train at Paddington Station. She paused for a moment, breathing in the dense, damp air and letting her eyes adjust to the gray light so unlike the bustling brightness of New York. The sharp clip of boots, the rustle of newspapers, the shouts of porters—it was London in all its chaotic glory, yet it felt almost like meeting a long-lost relative: familiar in feature, but not yet intimate.

At her side stood Daisy Dawn, her ever-loyal assistant. Daisy, a woman in her early thirties with chestnut curls tucked under a modest hat, had been with Victoria for four years. Their friendship had begun when Victoria, searching for a costumer for a last-minute production, had stumbled upon Daisy—desperate for work, newly abandoned by a cruel husband, and sleeping in a boarding house with barely a cent to her name. Victoria hired her on the spot. What began as a necessity turned to loyalty, and soon Daisy became confidante, assistant, and family.

"Will Londoners find my American accent dreadfully scandalous?" Victoria asked, her voice lilting with amusement as she surveyed the sea of bowler hats and umbrellas.

Daisy raised an eyebrow. "You mean the accent you got after your American friends teased you for sounding too British?"

Victoria grinned. "Touché. I suppose I belong nowhere now."

"Or everywhere. Like a true actress," Daisy retorted.

As the station swirled around them, Victoria's eyes softened with memory, and her hand clutched the handle of her carpetbag just a little tighter.

She spotted a man in the crowd who took her breath away. No, it can't be him; he's gone. The flash of William Wallace's smile came to her mind.

They had met backstage at a charity gala on a rainy spring evening in Manhattan. The event was to benefit a children's hospital, and Victoria had just finished her number, still in costume and flushed with the thrill of performance. As she stepped into the wings, she collided with a tall, well-dressed man holding two glasses of champagne.

"Oh!" she had exclaimed, steadying herself.

He had smiled—warm, gentle, with dimples and thoughtful hazel eyes behind wire-rimmed glasses. "I was just looking for the soprano who sang 'Moonlight in May.' That was you, I presume?"

She'd raised an eyebrow playfully. "That depends. Did you enjoy it?"

"I loved it," he replied handing her one of the champagne glasses. "Even if the orchestra struggled to keep up with you."

She laughed, and in that moment, something shifted.

He was a young investor and an avid patron of the arts, always quietly supporting the theater but never demanding the spotlight. With blonde wavy hair always slightly tousled, an old-fashioned pocket watch, and a wardrobe of muted grays and blues, William Wallace looked more like a thoughtful professor than a businessman.

They exchanged letters at first—his as polished, poetic notes on stationery slipped into her dressing room while she was on stage. He brought her editions of Jane Austen and Keats, always inscribed with a line that seemed to say more than the books themselves. He never demanded, never presumed, only waited patiently for her affection to deepen into love.

Their courtship was a slow, golden bloom. Walks in Central Park. Candlelit dinners. Afternoons spent reading plays aloud by the fire. He kissed her forehead as if she were something rare and precious. And one snowy evening beneath the gaslight outside The Fifth Avenue Theater, he asked her to marry him.

They were engaged within a year of meeting. Plans were drawn up for a house near New Rochelle with ivy-covered trellises and French windows. Her career flourished in those years—theater producers courted her, critics praised her grace and expressiveness, and she was called "the English rose of the American stage."

But tragedy came without warning.

William had left his office to head to the theater to see Victoria's performance and take her to dinner afterward. He declined the offer of a carriage, preferring to walk the familiar, lamplit route through Midtown. On his way, a startled horse pulling a heavy delivery cart broke free from its driver. As the cart careened down the street, it struck a carriage and overturned, throwing debris and wooden planks in every direction. William was caught at the worst angle, struck by a wooden beam.

The crash was fatal. He died instantly, without suffering—but without the chance to say goodbye to his love.

Victoria had been backstage, finishing her makeup, when the theater manager knocked softly on her door, his face pale. At first, she couldn't understand his words. She stared at him, uncomprehending, as if he were speaking a foreign language.

But as the sounds of the overture reached her, instinct carried her forward. She performed—every note, every gesture—flawless, mechanical.

Only when the final curtain fell and she had returned to her dressing room did it hit her. She opened the door expecting to find William waiting in his usual chair with a rose and a quiet smile. But the chair was empty.

Her knees gave way.

Daisy caught her before she hit the floor, holding her as sobs wracked her body.

William's mother, Martha Wallace, had always been kind but reserved. The type of woman who showed love through pretty table settings and quietly stocked pantries. After William's death, she clung to Victoria—not with desperation, but with a quiet, mutual grief that softened both of them.

One evening, weeks after the funeral, Victoria sat with Martha in her parlor. The older woman's skin was paper-thin, her voice soft but steady.

"You shouldn't stay," Martha said. "You're young and beautiful. The world is still opening for you."

"I'm exactly where I need to be," Victoria replied gently, taking her hand. "You're family. I'm not leaving you alone."

Martha's chin trembled, and for the first time, she wept in Victoria's arms.

From that moment on, Victoria gave up the stage and devoted herself to caring for the woman who had no one else.

It was a year of decline—fading breaths, soft soup, and lullabies at night when the pain wouldn't let Martha sleep. When she passed, Victoria was prepared for grief, but not for what came next.

The will was read in the library of the Wallace home, a dark and somber affair. Sunlight filtered weakly through heavy curtains, casting long shadows on the walls lined with aging books and quiet memories.

Victoria sat stiffly in a high-backed chair, the faint scent of lavender and paper lingering in the air.

Across from her sat Mr. Gainsworth, the family's longtime solicitor. He was a thin man with spectacles perched on the end of his nose and a voice like dry parchment. He shuffled the pages in his leather-bound folder, cleared his throat, and began.

"To Miss Victoria Margaret Watson," he said, "I bequeath the entirety of the Wallace estate."

Victoria blinked. "I...I beg your pardon?"

Gainsworth adjusted his glasses. "The house, all properties, investments, bank holdings, and personal effects are to pass solely into your name, effective immediately."

"I didn't know," Victoria murmured. "She never spoke of the estate, or of any money at all. I thought perhaps, maybe a keepsake or a letter."

Gainsworth gave a small, patient nod. "Mrs. Wallace was a very private woman. She confided in me some years ago that she had once placed her trust in family who betrayed her—nieces and nephews who manipulated her kindness. She resolved then to leave her legacy only to someone who proved truly loyal."

Victoria's voice caught. "But I never did anything to deserve this. I stayed because I loved her, and for William."

"Precisely," he said gently. "She saw that. She said that you reminded her of herself in her better years. Fierce in conviction and gentle with the weak. Devoted without seeking reward."

She looked down, overwhelmed. "It doesn't feel right."

Gainsworth offered a rare smile. "She made her decision clearly and without hesitation. If it comforts you, she amended her will less than a month before her passing. Her only concern was that you might refuse it."

Victoria didn't speak for a long time. Then she lifted her gaze and said quietly, "I'll honor her. I'll make sure it means something."

That evening, as the fireplace flickered low, Victoria and Daisy sat together in the parlor of the Wallace home. The silence between them was heavy with unspoken things until Victoria finally broke it.

"I've written to Father. I need to see him, to be with him. I want to go home to England."

Daisy set down her tea. "Of course. I thought you might."

Victoria hesitated, her hands twisting in her lap. "I will miss you terribly."

Daisy looked down at her hands. "How can you miss me when I will be with you?"

Startled, Victoria took a deep breath. "But I can't ask you to give up everything. I know you've built a life here, and—"

"Victoria," Daisy said firmly, "don't. I came to you with nothing, remember? And you gave me a reason to start over. I've no family here. No ties. You are my only family, my sister. Wherever you go, that's where I belong."

Victoria blinked, eyes shining. "But I don't want you to feel obligated—"

"I'm not," Daisy cut in. "I want to go. I need a new beginning just as much as you do. I still have many bad memories here."

There was a long pause, the air between them settling.

"I suppose we'll both be starting over," Victoria said, her voice thick.

Daisy reached over and took her hand. "Then let's start over together."

Victoria looked at her, heart full, and finally said, "I think it's time to go home."

"Victoria!"

The sound of her father's voice pierced the fog of memory.

She turned sharply, and through the swirling crowd of coats and hats, she saw him.

Dr. John Watson stood at the edge of the platform, searching, his eyes scanning the crowd until they landed on her. In that instant, his face broke into a wide, almost boyish smile. His mustache twitched, and his eyes shimmered with unmistakable emotion.

Victoria's carpetbag thudded to the platform as she ran the last few steps toward him. He opened his arms, and she nearly collided with him, throwing her arms around his shoulders.

"Father," she whispered, her voice trembling.

"My girl," he murmured, his arms tightening around her.

For a long moment, neither spoke. It was the kind of reunion made possible only by years of longing and love carried over distance. He pulled back to look at her, hands cupping her face, drinking in the adult woman who still had the same curious eyes and the same determined chin.

"You're even more beautiful than your photographs," he said.

She smiled through tears. "You've more silver in your hair than yours."

He laughed, brushing a hand down her cheek. "Just a sign of wisdom—or worry."

Behind them, Daisy wiped her eyes and smiled.

They turned and embraced her too, bringing her into the fold of the moment.

It was only the jostle of a porter's cart and a sharp whistle that reminded them they were standing in the middle of a busy station. With one last look of warmth, Watson grabbed the bags and led them toward the waiting cab.

"Let's go home," he said.

The cab ride to Baker Street was filled with catching up, half-finished sentences, and shared smiles. Dr. Watson listened with pride as Victoria spoke of her theater career in New York and how she had cared for Martha Wallace until her passing.

"She left me everything," Victoria said quietly, still disbelieving. "She never told me how wealthy they truly were. Mr. Gainsworth said she had even sworn William to silence about it until after the wedding. She told him that she wanted me to love them without expectation."

Watson looked at her with tender admiration. "That speaks more of your character than hers. And now you're home, my girl. You've come full circle."

He glanced out the window, then back at her, his expression softening.

Both women looked at him, then Daisy said, "Doctor, I know we've just met, but I almost feel as if I know you after reading all your adventures with Mr. Holmes. And Victoria has told me so much about you and her childhood here in England."

"Ah, my little Victoria. Those were happy times. She was born in the spring," he said, his voice dipping into memory. "Her mother, Margaret, was seventeen. I was just a year older, headstrong, and in love. We married quickly—her father was a cruel man, and she needed a way out. We were young, foolish perhaps, but we had each other. And then we had you." He looked at his only child lovingly.

Victoria turned toward him, listening in silence. Watson took her hand.

"You were eleven years old when I was called to Afghanistan. A military surgeon. I knew it might be years before I returned. I couldn't bear the thought of leaving you both alone in London, especially with the fever spreading through the East End. So, I sent you and your mother to America to live with your grandmother. It seemed the safest and kindest choice."

He paused, pain flickering across his features. "Your mother died not long before I returned. Some illness that took her too swiftly. You were thirteen. I was injured and half-broken when I came home… and not fit to care for a child on my own. You stayed in America with your grandmother. I thought it would be temporary. But life…"

"Life changes plans," Victoria said gently.

He nodded. "When I moved in with Holmes at Baker Street, it was just meant to be a stop along the way. Then came the cases… the writings. And you… you grew up and had made a life for yourself in America. Your letters always brought me such joy. Even when I wasn't there, I felt connected to you."

"I never doubted you loved me," Victoria said. "Even when we were apart."

He smiled at her. "You were only sixteen when you joined that little theater company. Your letters suddenly turned into playbills and press clippings. I kept them all."

"I know," she said with a fond smile. "You told me every time."

The cab turned a corner and slowly came to a stop.

"You're home now," Watson said, placing his hand over hers. "Whatever time we lost, we'll make up for it."

Mrs. Hudson opened the door to 221 Baker Street with her usual bustling energy. She took one look at Victoria and let out a delighted exclamation.

"Oh, so this is Dr. Watson's little girl! Welcome, dear. We've been tidying up flat C just for you. Well, I say 'we,' but really it was me. And I didn't touch Mr. Holmes's corner of the hall, don't worry."

Victoria laughed, charmed. "Thank you, Mrs. Hudson. I'm so glad to finally meet you."

Watson led her up the stairs. "Your flat is directly across from Holmes. Number 221C. The former tenants were a lovely, elderly couple who decided to move out of the city. Now it's yours."

Mrs. Hudson had placed a small table next to the doorway with a simple floral arrangement. The flat was surprisingly spacious—an abundance of natural light, a fireplace, and a tiny balcony overlooking the street. Victoria walked slowly through the space, taking it all in. Mrs. Hudson had clearly gone to great effort. Fresh wallpaper with delicate rose patterns graced the walls—"something fitting for a fine lady," she had said. The wood floors gleamed, recently refinished to a warm, honeyed sheen. Built-in bookshelves flanked the fireplace, their empty spaces already sparking ideas in Victoria's mind. There was a principal bedroom with lace curtains and a small but charming guest room just off the hall. Her familiar trunks and carefully packed furniture were stacked neatly, having arrived a week ahead by steamer.

"I love it," she whispered.

Watson smiled. "Capital! Mary's preparing a proper welcome home supper. I'll go help. Be sure to bring Daisy. Come around at seven?"

She kissed his cheek. "We'll be there."

Later, dressed in a casual blouse and long skirt suitable for moving boxes and hammering nails, Victoria set to work. She and Daisy had the door propped open to invite the breeze while they unpacked. Books were stacked on the floor, linens folded, trunks thrown open.

"The men should be here shortly to get your trunks and take them to your new flat," Victoria said, "we should keep an eye out for them."

"I'm very excited to see my new home." Daisy beamed, "I'm so grateful to your father for finding it for me. And it's only a short walk from here."

"I want the skyline over the fireplace," Victoria said, lifting a large canvas painting of New York at sunset.

"Your friend Mr. Church did a fine job with this one," Daisy said.

Victoria stepped onto the ladder, carefully aligning the wire with the hook she'd nailed in earlier. Daisy guided her to see that it was straight, saying, "A bit more to the left."

A soft clearing of the throat made them look toward the hallway.

Sherlock Holmes stood in the doorway.

He looked every bit the legend—tall, lean, with eyes like flint and a presence that filled the frame. His coat hung open, a leather folder tucked beneath one arm. His gaze moved swiftly from Victoria's precarious position to the half-unpacked chaos of the room.

"Miss Watson," he said, tone even. "Welcome to Baker Street. I trust your journey was manageable."

Victoria, startled and embarrassed by her disheveled appearance, steadied herself and flushed. "Mr. Holmes. Yes, thank you. Very manageable."

His eyes lingered a second on the smudge of dust across her cheek. "I see you've wasted no time settling in."

"Idle hands," she said, recovering her poise.

Holmes's eyes shifted to Daisy, and in a tone more curious than condescending, he said, "You left Pittsburgh five years ago. You worked for a man in costuming and left under difficult circumstances. You've worked with Miss Watson for four years."

Daisy blinked. "I...I beg your pardon?"

Holmes tilted his head. "Your accent—western Pennsylvania. Your blouse has faint chalk lines consistent with garment marking. The way you cut that twine suggests tailoring work, not stage work. The labels on your trunk show your pattern, departing Pennsylvania, going to New York, where you met Miss Watson, and traveling with her along a well-known theater circuit in America."

Daisy stared, mouth agape. "Well. You're not wrong."

Then Holmes turned to Victoria. "Your father tells me you are a classically trained soprano—your breath control and posture confirm as much—but your phrasing suggests musical theater rather than opera. During your temporary retirement from the stage, you never lost your passion for the arts."

He glanced around the flat. "You do not decorate like a transient. Your belongings arrived ahead of you. You intend to stay. And yet—there's something more."

His gaze sharpened. "You've come back to reconnect with your father, yes, but that is not your only motive. The blueprints on your writing desk are for the old London Majestic theater— in need of restoration but rich in potential. You intend to purchase it but have not yet told your father."

Victoria's eyes widened. "What?"

Holmes offered the faintest smile. "A thin layer of graphite on your fingertips from architectural sketches, smudged only recently, shows you have been examining the plans."

Victoria narrowed her eyes. "And my father doesn't know."

Holmes inclined his head. "Not yet."

"What makes you think Father doesn't know?" Victoria inquired with slight anxiety.

A thin smile crossed Holmes's lips. "He would have told me."

She crossed her arms but smiled despite herself. "Well. That was invasive."

Holmes's mouth twitched, almost imperceptibly. "But accurate."

"May I trust you to keep my secret for now?" Victoria asked, "I don't wish him to know until I'm entirely sure I will proceed with the plan."

"Of course," said Holmes, "I would never betray a lady's trust."

Trying to muffle a sigh of relief, she asked, "Will we be seeing you at dinner tonight at Father and Mary's house?"

"I'm afraid not. The case I've been working on has reached an unexpected turn. I'll be out most of the evening."

"Of course. The game is afoot," Victoria said with a smile.

He inclined his head, "Quite. Good day."

And just like that, he vanished into his flat across the hall.

Daisy peeked around the doorway, eyes wide.

Victoria, brushing her hands on her skirt, said. "Well. That was... brief."

"And yet, oddly intense," Daisy murmured. "Are you all right?"

Victoria gave a small smile. "Of course, silly girl. Wait- I think I hear your movers. We'd best go meet them at the door."

The evening air had turned crisp, but the walk to her father's house filled Victoria with a sense of warmth and anticipation. Gaslights flickered in the fading daylight, casting gentle shadows on the cobbled streets. Daisy walked beside her, arms tucked close for warmth, both women wrapped in woolen shawls and soft conversation.

Victoria clutched a parcel containing a belated wedding gift for her father and Mary.

"I hope she'll like me." she asked, her voice light but tinged with uncertainty.

"Mary Watson? Please," Daisy said. "She's written you letters for months. Anyone who saves newspaper clippings of your shows clearly already loves you."

Victoria smiled, reassured. "It's strange. I feel like I know her already, but tonight still feels like a debut of sorts."

"Everything's a debut with you," Daisy teased. "But this time, there's no curtain."

As they rounded the corner to the Watsons' home, a golden glow spilled from the windows. Victoria felt her breath catch—this was no audience, no stage, and yet it felt just as significant.

Watson opened the door before they could knock, eyes bright and voice booming. "There they are! Right on time."

Mary greeted them with joyful hugs. She looked into Victoria's eyes saying with heartfelt warmth, "My dear, I'm so delighted to finally have you here with us."

Victoria felt her concerns dissolve as Mary's heartfelt warmth wrapped her like an embrace. Handing her the gift Victoria said, "I brought this for you from America – a belated wedding gift. Welcome to the family!"

Mary called her husband to her, and they opened the gift together. They gasped together, almost as if rehearsed, delighted at the exquisite silver platter discreetly stamped "TIFFANY & CO. STERLING" on the back.

"Oh, my dear! It's beautiful!" Watson said, carefully turning the platter to admire the engraving, 'Dr. & Mrs. John H. Watson – 1889.'"

Mary and Victoria, eyes brimming, embraced with the joy of newfound family.

Inside, the dining room was softly lit with flickering candles. The table was set with a simple elegance with lace-edged napkins, delicate stemware, and at Victoria's place, a plate she hadn't seen in years: white porcelain ringed with painted violets, foxes, and rabbits in a flower-filled meadow.

She let out a quiet gasp. "Father... my plate!"

Watson was beaming. "It is. You used it every morning for breakfast when you were little. You loved it from the moment I gave it to you—said it looked like something fairies would use for a garden tea."

Victoria touched the plate reverently. "I never forgot it. I used to pretend the animals would talk to each other when no one was looking."

"And I could never bring myself to pack it away," Watson said simply. "Some things are too precious."

Dinner was a lively affair. Mary asked thoughtful questions about Victoria's time in the theater, while Watson chimed in with small anecdotes of her childhood that made everyone laugh. Daisy relaxed quickly, charmed by Mary's quiet humor and the way she and Watson moved with such ease together.

At one point, the conversation turned to acquaintances.

"Do you remember Dr. Stamford?" Watson asked.

Victoria furrowed her brow. "Only vaguely. He worked in the medical offices, didn't he?"

"Yes," Watson said. "He's the one who introduced me to Holmes, actually. Good man. We served together at Barts. He's come under some scrutiny lately accused of poisoning a government official." Victoria blinked. "Dr. Stamford? But why would—?"

"No clear motive," Watson said, his tone darkening. "The evidence is circumstantial, but troubling."

Mary steered the conversation to lighter ground, but the name lingered in Victoria's thoughts.

Later, in the parlor, Victoria and Mary found themselves seated side by side with teacups in hand, while Daisy and Watson chatted in the kitchen while getting dessert.

Mary's voice lowered with affection. "I can't tell you how long I've waited to sit beside you like this. John and I kept every letter you sent. And the newspaper clippings, photos, even those old playbills. He'd bring them home like treasures. We were so proud."

Victoria felt her chest tighten. "I always wondered how different life would have been had the circumstances allowed us to be together when I was younger."

"Your father longed for you every minute you were apart, dear," Mary said. "He sent you away to keep you safe and with family."

Victoria replied, eyes misty, "Yes, I know he was doing what he felt was best. Who knew things would happen the way they did? Even so, I have always felt close to him. I missed his hugs the most."

Mary took a sip of her tea and smiled softly. "I met John during a case, you know. *The Sign of the Four.* Not the most conventional start to a romance, but it was very… him. Dangerous and noble. And I was just foolish enough to say yes to a man who smelled like gunpowder and medical tinctures."

They laughed, and Mary's gaze grew wistful. "Love doesn't always arrive the way you expect. Sometimes it sneaks up on you, even when you think your heart is closed."

Victoria arched an eyebrow. "Is that a general sentiment, or is there a specific point you're hinting at?"

Mary chuckled. "I'm just a hopeless romantic. My dear, I know you've been grieving, but I hope you won't give up on love."

Victoria gave a polite laugh. "My focus now is on my career. I have no time for romance."

"Mm," Mary murmured, unconvinced but gracious, "that's when it typically sneaks up on you."

The warm aroma of baked apples and cinnamon drifted through the Watsons' cozy kitchen as Daisy set a platter of apple tartlets on a tray beside a pitcher of cream. Dr. Watson was carefully plating slices of treacle pudding, humming contentedly to himself as he reached for a serving spoon.

"Mary is the perfect hostess," Daisy said, arranging the tartlets just so. "Her food was wonderful. I'm not sure I can move, let alone carry all this in."

"That's the mark of a proper welcome," Watson replied, placing the last dessert on the tray. "Now let's see if we can get this into the parlor before Holmes turns up and declares sugar a distraction from logic."

Daisy smirked, but her smile faded a touch as she hesitated. "Speaking of Mr. Holmes…"

Watson glanced at her, curious. "Yes?"

She took a breath. "I don't know how to feel about him. He was… impressive. But also, rather—startling. He looked straight through me."

Watson gave a knowing smile. "Yes, he does that. It's rarely personal."

"It felt personal," she said. "Like he had already formed a dozen opinions about me before I even spoke."

"He had," Watson said with a soft laugh. "But that's Holmes. He observes, deduces, and files you away before most people remember your name."

Daisy folded the linen napkins as she thought aloud. "I wasn't prepared for it. One minute I was helping Victoria hang a painting, the next I felt like I was being dissected."

Watson set down the pudding dish and leaned slightly against the counter, his voice kind. "Holmes is… unique. But I can promise you, he's good. Underneath the sharp edges and odd habits, he's the most dependable man I know. If he respects you, he'll show it in his own way."

She looked up at him. "You really trust him?"

"With my life," Watson said simply.

Daisy absorbed that, her brow still furrowed but her shoulders softening. "He's not what I expected."

Watson chuckled. "He rarely is."

They exchanged grins and stepped out of the kitchen together, carrying the sweetness of the evening with them.

In the front hall, Watson and Mary stood arm-in-arm as Victoria and Daisy donned their coats.

As the door opened to the night air, Watson gave Victoria a hug and kissed her cheek. "I'm thrilled your home, my girl. And even more thrilled that your sister has come, too."

Daisy laughed, blushing. "I've never had a sister before."

"Well," Watson said, "you do now."

Victoria smiled at them both. "Goodnight. And thank you—for everything."

"She'll thrive here," Mary whispered.

"She will," Watson agreed, his voice low. "But I worry sometimes. She's endured more than most women twice her age. Heartbreak, grief, responsibility. She's so strong, but I don't want that strength to become a prison. I want her to find joy again. Real joy."

Mary looked up at him with warmth and certainty. "She will. Because she's not doing it alone. She has you. She has me. And she has that young woman beside her who'd follow her to the ends of the earth."

Watson gave a soft laugh. "Yes, she does. And she's always been a girl of strong faith. So often in her letters during that difficult season, she would tell me not to worry because she felt our prayers and knew her Savior walked with her."

"As long as she knows she's loved," Mary said, "she'll find her way."

The London air had cooled, and gas lamps shimmered softly on the slick stones. Victoria and Daisy walked shoulder to shoulder in companionable quiet.

After a few paces, Victoria broke the silence.

"Daisy, I never said it properly, but thank you."

Daisy glanced at her. "For what?"

"For staying. For holding me up when I couldn't stand. For giving up your life in America without a second thought."

Daisy's voice softened. "You don't have to thank me for that."

"I do," Victoria said. "I don't know how I would've managed any of it without you. Losing William, caring for Martha… even now. You've been more than a friend. You're the reason I made it through. You are my special blessing from God."

Daisy was quiet for a moment, then she slipped her arm through Victoria's. "And you're the reason I had anything worth building again. We saved each other, Victoria. That's what sisters do."

They walked in silence for a few more moments before the shout of a newspaper boy broke through the evening calm.

"Government Official Still in Peril! Poison Suspected! Parliament on Edge!"

Victoria slowed. Her brow furrowed as she looked toward the headline.

"That must be the case Mr. Holmes mentioned… the one keeping him away tonight."

Daisy tilted her head. "Do you think it's serious?"

"I think," Victoria said slowly, "he's trying to prove someone innocent. Someone important."

She paused, connecting the dots. "Dr. Stamford. It has to be."

Daisy blinked. "The man who introduced your father to Holmes?"

Victoria nodded. "He's on Parliament's medical staff now. If anyone had access…"

She glanced ahead toward 221 Baker Street, where one window glowed faintly in the upper flat.

"I think Holmes is already three steps ahead of everyone."

After seeing Daisy to her door, Victoria continued to Baker Street and glanced up toward the darkened windows where the detective was surely still awake, piecing together some quiet puzzle.

Murder and mystery—those were Holmes' affairs. Hers, she told herself firmly, were on the stage.

And yet, she couldn't help but wonder.

That evening, as golden light spilled across the rooftops, Victoria curled into a comfortable armchair by the window that had once graced her New York flat. The room was far from finished, but it already felt like her own. A steaming cup of tea sat beside her. She opened a soft leather journal, worn at the edges and filled with years of thoughts.

She wrote:

It is strange to feel like a stranger in the place I once called home. London is heavier than New York—older, quieter, yet alive in a different way. Father hasn't changed much. It is a relief and a comfort. And he seems proud of me. I hoped he would be.

She paused, the ink pooling slightly on the page.

Holmes is… unlike anyone I've ever met. There's something unspoken in his presence. A silence that isn't empty but searching. He barely looked at me, yet I felt entirely seen. It's unsettling.

She closed the book slowly, pressing her palm to the leather cover.

Tomorrow would be a new beginning.

Tonight, she was home.

Late the next morning, a knock at Victoria's door drew her from unpacking. She opened it to find her father, freshly shaven and smiling, his coat collar dusted with the remains of fog.

"Lunch?" he asked. "Mary insisted you might enjoy a break from unpacking. She's at the café waiting."

Victoria laughed and reached for her shawl. "How could I refuse?"

As they descended the stairs, Watson paused at Holmes's door. "I should see if he's in. Just for a moment."

Victoria followed, curious.

Watson rapped twice before letting himself in. Holmes, coatless but waistcoated and alert, stood near the window, violin resting across a side table among scattered papers.

"Watson," Holmes greeted, nodding. "Miss Watson."

"Holmes," Watson returned, stepping inside. "We're off to lunch, but I thought I'd check in. Any progress on the matter you mentioned yesterday?"

Holmes's eyes flicked momentarily to Victoria, then back to Watson. "Progress, yes. But the political sensitivities require... delicacy."

"Of course," Watson said, glancing at his daughter. "Delicacy."

Victoria narrowed her eyes slightly, catching the awkward attempt at vagueness. Her voice was gentle, but direct. "This wouldn't have anything to do with the Parliament case, would it?"

Holmes didn't answer, but the faintest lift of his brow acknowledged the question.

She continued, "And the accused... It's Dr. Stamford, isn't it?"

Both men looked at her.

Watson blinked, surprised. "Victoria—"

"It's only a guess," she said, raising a hand. "But it fits. He's on Parliament's medical staff. And he was a dear friend to both of you."

Holmes crossed his arms, studying her. "That was a well-reasoned deduction, Miss Watson."

She gave a small smile. "It was hardly genius. It's the only thing that makes sense. From what I've learned about you from Father's stories, you don't usually involve yourself unless something isn't adding up— and you don't risk your reputation on a stranger."

Holmes gave a faint nod of approval. "Your instincts are formidable."

Watson smiled, proud and a bit astonished. "You've always been sharper than I."

Victoria chuckled. "No, just less distracted."

Holmes turned to the window, gaze distant. "If Stamford is innocent, the proof will be in the details. That's where truth hides."

Victoria's smile faded slightly. "And if he's guilty?"

Holmes didn't answer.

Victoria hesitated, then spoke softly, "I don't remember much of him. Just fragments. But I do remember that when I was small—maybe four or five—Father brought me to his office once. I had a sniffle and insisted on tagging along. He gave me a plush rabbit. It had a blue ribbon around its neck."

Watson smiled at the memory. "That would have been his office on Gower Street."

Holmes gave a short nod, expression unreadable. "A generous man, in small ways. Not always understood in larger ones."

Watson cleared his throat. "We'll leave you to it. Come along, Victoria, before Mary fears we've fallen into a case ourselves."

As they stepped into the street, Victoria glanced once more up at the windows of 221B.

"I don't think he's as cold as he lets on," she murmured.

"No," Watson said quietly. "But the world taught him to be cautious. You'll see, in time."

Over lunch at a quiet café near Regent's Park, Victoria stirred sugar into her tea and studied her father's face.

"You're worried," she said.

"I'm a doctor. I'm always worried," he replied with a smile that didn't reach his eyes. "But yes. About Stamford. About the truth. And about you."

"Me?" she asked, lifting a brow.

"You've come back from great loss," he said gently. "And I wonder what your plans are, now that you're here."

Victoria hesitated. "I'm still sorting things. There are a few possibilities I'm considering."

Watson smiled knowingly. "Such as buying a theatre, perhaps?"

Victoria's mouth dropped open. "He sold me down the river!"

"Who did what?" Watson asked, perplexed.

"Mr. Holmes!" she said, exasperated. "I knew it!"

Mary looked equally confused. "Sold you down what river, dear?"

Watson looked at his daughter blankly. "Yes, I admit I don't follow."

Victoria paused, then laughed. "It's an American phrase. It means betraying someone."

Mary laughed. "Oh! How dreadful."

Victoria waved a hand. "It doesn't matter. Mr. Holmes clearly told you."

"Actually," Watson interrupted, "he didn't say a word. But Daisy might have mentioned something about 'plans for a stage' last night while passing the pudding. She didn't specifically mention your plans, but you have mentioned in your letters over the years that you dreamed of owning a theater."

Victoria groaned. "Oh, Daisy…"

Mary looked intrigued. "Is it true then?"

Victoria set her teacup down. "Yes. I've been looking into the London Majestic. It's been dear to me since I was a child, when you and Mother took me there, Father. I remember the chandeliers, and the velvet curtains. I don't know why, but I always dreamed of making it mine."

Watson looked at his daughter slowly, his eyes misty. "She would be proud of you."

Mary reached across the table and squeezed Victoria's hand. "It's bold and wonderful. I hope you do it."

"I will," Victoria said quietly. "But I'll need help. There are contracts, negotiations, repairs... It's more than I can handle alone."

Watson straightened. "Then I'll help with tradesmen and attorneys — anything you need."

Victoria looked at him, eyes warm. "Thank you. I can't tell you what that means."

"You don't have to," he said. "You're home now, and your family is behind you."

She smiled gratefully, then tilted her head. "Now that I've answered your question, it's my turn."

Watson lifted a brow. "Oh?"

"The Stamford case," Victoria said. "Tell me what you can."

Watson hesitated, then agreed. "Only what's already known. A member of Parliament collapsed after a dinner hosting high ranking officials—violently ill. He survived, barely. Lab results later showed traces of a toxin in his wine. Stamford was at the dinner."

"I don't understand why that should make him a suspect," Victoria said. "I'm sure many other people had the opportunity to poison the poor man's wine, too."

Watson sighed. "The victim and Stamford had a long-standing professional rivalry. Disagreements on medical policy, access to certain clinics, even accusations of favoritism in appointments. They weren't exactly friends."

Mary added, "And the press is ruthless. And politics makes enemies."

"Exactly." Watson agreed.

"Do you think he did it?" Victoria asked.

"I don't," Watson said. "Neither does Holmes. Stamford was there for me after the war. He introduced me to Holmes. He may have his faults, but I owe him more than one debt of gratitude. Holmes does too, though he'd be less likely to admit it."

Victoria thought for a moment. "Then the answer will have to come from somewhere unexpected. Something everyone else missed."

Watson gave a half-smile. "That's why Holmes is on the case."

"And why you're worried."

"I trust Holmes," Watson said. "But I know how quickly a good man's life can unravel if truth doesn't arrive in time."

Victoria could see the concern for his friend in her father's eyes. "Then we'd better hope he finds it fast."

Though both Victoria and Holmes were swept up in their own responsibilities, the rhythm of life on Baker Street made it nearly impossible not to cross paths. Holmes, often in and out at odd hours, usually appeared with a flurry of a coat, case notes, and clipped urgency. Victoria, for her part, was deep into meetings with contractors, scanning theater archives at the public library, and arranging financial details for the purchase of the London Majestic.

Their paths crossed most often in the hallway, Holmes locking up as Victoria was returning, or Victoria descending the stairs as Holmes swept through the entry. Their exchanges were brief but cordial: polite nods, the occasional "Good evening," or "All well, I trust?"

She never asked about the case. It wasn't easy. Victoria followed each newspaper report closely, clipping articles and circling names. She pressed her father gently for updates—though he offered only what was already public knowledge. Despite her curiosity, she remembered Holmes's words: *The political sensitivities require delicacy.*

And so, out of respect for Holmes, for Stamford, and for the truth still struggling to surface, she kept her questions to herself.

One late afternoon, as the golden light of sunset angled down the narrow stairwell, Victoria hurried up with a sheaf of notes in hand just as Holmes descended with an armful of folders.

They collided at the landing.

Papers flew. Documents fluttered like startled birds, tumbling down around them.

"Forgive me," Victoria said, already kneeling.

"No harm done," Holmes replied, crouching opposite her. Their hands moved quickly, brushing once as they both reached for the same slip of paper.

Victoria stole a glance at the heading of one of his documents— Toxicology Report: Ricin Derivatives—before returning it swiftly to the stack. Holmes, meanwhile, paused at a folded ledger in her hand.

"Theater schematics," he remarked. "London Majestic?"

Victoria raised a brow. "You deduced that from a half-folded sketch?"

"I also glimpsed the name in bold at the top," he said dryly.

She laughed. "So not deduction, just eyesight."

"Even I am not above reading."

They straightened together, each holding their reclaimed piles.

Holmes continued, "Also the wire transfer this morning—to a private holding company suggests you intend to purchase the Majestic outright."

Victoria blinked. "You read my bank records?"

"I read *movements*," he said coolly. "Your banker left your flat at half past nine. Judging by the ink on your right cuff and the pace of his departure, I inferred he had been asked to expedite a sizable international transaction. The transfer receipt—partially visible in your folder now—confirms it."

She tilted her head, half amused, half resigned. "Yes, no investors. It was important to me."

"A bold move," Holmes said. "Expensive, risky, and very independent."

"I've had enough of people telling me how things must be done," she replied, meeting his gaze.

Holmes said nothing for a moment. He looked at her and said, "Then it suits you."

Victoria hesitated, then added softly, "You haven't asked about my plans."

"I suspected. But I would not presume," he replied. "Though your efforts have been thorough. Permit applications. Staff vetting. Restoration contracts." He glanced at one of her annotated pages. "And a lighting schematic, if I'm not mistaken."

"I'm impressed," she said, half-smiling.

"Merely observation."

There was a pause.

"I remember Dr. Stamford, you know. Just a little," she said. "He seemed very kind."

"Holmes's expression didn't shift much, but his voice was gentle. "He had moments of compassion. Fleeting, but sincere."

She casually touched his arm. "I hope you find something. Something that clears him."

"If there is something to find," he said simply, "I will find it."

Victoria stepped back with a nod of thanks. "Good evening, Mr. Holmes."

"And to you, Miss Watson."

They continued in opposite directions—two currents moving through Baker Street, each with secrets yet to surface.

Later that afternoon, Daisy let herself into Victoria's flat with the ease of someone already at home. She carried a small leather folio, a pencil tucked behind one ear, and a scone she hadn't had time to finish on the way over.

Victoria looked up from the writing desk. "You're a sight for sore eyes—and organizational ruin. These papers are breeding."

Daisy stepped over a stack of architectural sketches and dropped her folio onto the table. "I bring order and crumbs. And I come with questions about our grand theater."

Victoria smiled and gestured to the table. "Sit. Let's sort this mess."

As they took their seats, Daisy opened the folio and pulled out her notes, but paused, frowning at the pages in Victoria's hand.

"Good heavens," she said, lifting the wrinkled stack. "What happened here? These look like they were trampled by a newsboy and his cart horse."

Victoria laughed. "Close. I had an encounter on the landing with Mr. Holmes. We collided—papers everywhere. The man is like a storm cloud with legs."

Daisy gave her a knowing smirk. "Did he say anything interesting?"

"Only about my paperwork," Victoria said with a shrug. "And he made a rather accurate observation about my financing."

Daisy lifted an eyebrow.

"He deduced that I had just completed a sizable wire transfer and that I'm buying the theater outright with no investors." She exhaled. "It was impressive, really."

"And what about the Stamford case?" Daisy asked gently.

Victoria hesitated. "He didn't say a word about it. And I didn't ask."

Daisy raised her brow. "That doesn't sound like you."

"I know," Victoria said, tapping her pencil against her lip. "But he asked for delicacy, and despite how fascinating it all is, I want to respect that. Besides, Father's been giving me crumbs here and there."

"You're sure you're not getting too caught up?" Daisy asked, then motioning towards the theater plans. "This is the dream, Victoria. You've worked toward this. Don't let yourself get tangled in a mystery investigation."

Victoria looked at her friend. "You're right. I know you're right. But it's hard not to be curious. Dr. Stamford was kind to me as a little girl, and seeing him involved in something so sinister..." She trailed off.

Daisy softened. "I just want you to keep your eyes on the goal. This theater isn't just a building—it's your future."

"I haven't forgotten," Victoria said. "Speaking of which, let's talk staff."

Daisy perked up. "I was hoping we'd get to that."

Victoria leaned forward, her eyes gleaming. "I want you to track down people who worked at the London Majestic before it closed—ushers, box office staff, stagehands. If any of them would consider returning, we'd be starting with people who know the space and the work."

Daisy tapped her pencil against her notebook. "I can try the theatrical associations and see if I find any names. There's a costume shop that might have kept in touch with some of them. Also, there's a fellow I met who works at the Adelphi. He might know who worked the Majestic before it shuttered."

"That's perfect," Victoria said. "If we can find a few key players, the rest will fall into place. If we can find the stage manager and he's of good reputation, that could make a huge difference."

"We'll need to start thinking about auditions eventually," Daisy added. "Are you still planning on staging an original work first?"

"Yes," Victoria said. "But we'll need to finish the renovations first. That ceiling plaster isn't going to patch itself."

Daisy scribbled furiously. "I'll start with the former staff. Maybe someone who worked front of house. Someone people remember."

"Good," Victoria said, her voice warming with excitement. "I want to keep some of its soul. It's not just about profit—it's about reviving an antique from the past that meant something to people."

Daisy looked up. "I love that perspective."

Victoria smiled. "Ever since I was a little girl. I still remember the first time Father and Mother took me. I was five. I wore a red ribbon in my hair and insisted on a lemon drop during intermission."

"That explains a lot," Daisy said with a grin.

Victoria glanced down at the theater ledger and sighed. "This is going to be harder than anything I've done before."

Daisy reached across the table and squeezed her hand. "Then it's a good thing you're not doing it alone."

They sat for a moment in the soft hush of the afternoon, the weight of the past behind them and the shimmer of possibility ahead.

Evening had fallen on Baker Street, casting a warm amber hue through the fog-dimmed glass of 221B. A low fire crackled in the hearth. Holmes, legs crossed and pipe in hand, sat in his well-worn chair. Across from him, Watson leaned forward, elbows resting on his knees, his brow furrowed in familiar concern.

"So," Watson said at last, "how dire is it?"

Holmes exhaled a slow stream of smoke, eyes narrowed. "Three principal points threaten Stamford's case. Any one of them could prove damning in court. Together, they form a narrative the prosecution will be eager to exploit."

Watson sat back, already dreading what he was about to hear.

Holmes raised a finger. "First, motive. Stamford and the victim, Lord Percival Mornay, had a known animosity. Letters between them, intercepted from Mornay's estate, include accusations of professional incompetence against Stamford, veiled threats, and formal complaints lodged to the Home Office."

"He loathed Stamford," Watson said grimly.

"Precisely. And Stamford did little to disguise his contempt in return. A physician with a sharp tongue and a shorter temper—hardly a model of discretion."

Holmes lifted a second finger. "Second, access. Stamford was one of only five individuals allowed in the private dining suite where the incident occurred. The poisoned wine glass belonged to Mornay. All guests drank the same wine, yet only his was tainted."

"That proves opportunity, but not guilt." Watson said defensively.

Holmes paused before answering. "True. But circumstantial evidence, layered thickly, can suffocate reason."

"And the third?" Watson asked, bracing himself.

"Means," Holmes said simply. "The toxin used was derived from *Ricinus communis*—castor bean extract. Refined into ricin. It's rare, lethal, and very specific. Stamford, as a medical officer, once published a research paper regarding exotic poisons, including ricin."

Watson let out a long breath. "So, to sum up – he had reason, opportunity, and the knowledge to make it happen."

Holmes leaned back, fingers steepled. "It's damning. But..."

Watson perked up. "But?"

Holmes reached for a folder resting on the table between them. From it, he drew a folded sheet—handwritten notes in his spidery scrawl. "There's a detail the police have underestimated. The decanter used to serve the wine tested clean. No poison traces. No fingerprints. As if it had never been touched at all."

Watson interjected. "But the victim's wine glass contained the poison."

"Exactly. Which tells us something vital," Holmes said, tapping the page. "The wine itself was not tampered with in bulk. The dose was introduced after the pour—targeted, not careless."

Watson's brow knit. "Meaning someone laced the individual glass, not the entire decanter. That takes precision and opportunity."

"And intent," Holmes added. "The decanter was almost certainly handled during dinner, yet it yielded no prints. That is not typical. Either someone wiped it deliberately or used gloves, both of which imply forethought."

"Removing fingerprints from the decanter while putting the poison in the glass seems odd," Watson murmured. "Perhaps they were trying create confusion."

Holmes tapped the arm of his chair. "Indeed. I'm having the cabinet where the decanter and glasses were stored examined for prints. Lestrade sees little use in the exercise, but I find that the truth rarely rewards the lazy."

Watson shook his head in disbelief. "I can't believe it's come to this. Stamford—a man who's devoted his life to saving lives is now sitting behind bars."

Holmes's tone softened slightly. "He is no murderer."

A silence fell between them for a moment before Holmes added, "Your daughter has keen instincts."

Watson glanced up. "Victoria?"

"She deduced Stamford's identity without being told. Used logic and deduction. And I daresay, sentiment."

Watson smiled. "She always had a mind for piecing things together. She took after her mother in that way."

Holmes said nothing, but the corner of his mouth twitched.

Watson stirred. "She's taken a strong interest in the case."

"I've noticed," Holmes replied, "But she's restrained. A rare quality, especially in a woman."

"That won't last long," Watson said with a chuckle. "Curiosity burns in her. It's only a matter of time."

"Perhaps," Holmes said, "but for now, we let her focus on her theater."

Watson nodded slowly. "She told me about her plans. She's thrown herself into it. She has vision."

Holmes tapped his pipe against the ashtray. "She also has very wrinkled schematics. We collided on the stairs yesterday."

Watson laughed aloud. "You didn't frighten her off, I hope."

"On the contrary. I believe she attempted to examine my papers as much as I examined hers."

Another quiet chuckle passed between them before Holmes reached for a second file.

"I need you to visit Lestrade," he said. "Scotland Yard has the set of anonymous letters—typed, not handwritten—that denounce Stamford's integrity. I want you to examine them. Check their typeface. Lestrade won't mind. And his assistant, young Murdock, owes me a favor."

Watson's brow lifted. "You think they were valid?"

"I think they were manufactured. Mornay had enemies—powerful ones. One of them could be stirring the pot."

"And I'm to poke around and see what boils over?"

Holmes offered the folder. "Precisely. Ask about any other suspects dismissed too easily."

Watson accepted it with a nod. "You believe someone else was present that night."

"I believe someone wasn't meant to be seen and yet managed to leave their mark. Perhaps more than one."

The fire crackled. A clock chimed the hour.

Watson stood, folder under his arm. "I'll go in the morning. You'll have something before lunch."

"Be thorough," Holmes said. "And discreet."

Watson smiled. "Discretion is my specialty."

As he moved toward the door, Holmes called after him, "And Watson—"

The doctor turned.

"Your daughter may not be a consulting detective, but I suspect she'll find her way into the heart of this mystery nonetheless."

Watson gave a rueful nod. "God help whoever tries to stop her."

The door closed behind him, leaving Holmes alone with the music of his violin and the haunting question of innocence tangled in a web of deceit.

Dr. Watson arrived at Scotland Yard early-morning, the clamor of the street giving way to the heavy, bureaucratic stillness of the station's interior. The scent of ink and damp wool clung to the air. After a brief wait, he was shown into Inspector Lestrade's office—a narrow space cluttered with case folders, and a teacup balanced precariously atop a stack of reports.

Lestrade looked up from his paperwork, his expression guarded but not unfriendly. "Dr. Watson," he said, standing to shake his hand. "It's been a while. Still trailing after Holmes, are you?"

Watson smiled. "In this case, I'm more of a courier. He sends his regards—and his questions."

Lestrade gestured to the worn chair across from him. "Sit, sit. I suppose this is about Dr. Stamford."

Watson took the offered seat. "You know he's an old friend to both of us."

Lestrade sighed. "I do. And I'm sorry for it. But that doesn't change what's in the reports."

"He's not the man they're painting him to be," Watson interjected.

"No, maybe not," Lestrade agreed, lacing his fingers. "But the evidence is damning, and now, there's more."

Watson blinked. "More?"

Lestrade opened a folder and flipped to a stapled set of papers, his finger running down the typed lines. "We received a statement, anonymous initially, now confirmed with a name attached. A witness claims to have seen Stamford introduce something into Lord Mornay's glass the night of the incident."

Watson's stomach tightened. "Who?"

Lestrade hesitated, then sighed. "I shouldn't be telling you this but given how many times Holmes pulled my neck from the noose, I'll make an exception." He glanced at the door, then leaned in slightly. "Her name is Anne Godfrey, a maid employed by the hosting family. Says she was refilling water pitchers in the service corridor just outside the dining suite."

He tapped the page. "Her statement: 'I saw Dr. Stamford lean over Lord Mornay's place setting while others were engaged in conversation. He held something small in his right hand and reached near the wine glass. I didn't think anything of it at the time. Later, when the lord fell ill, I remembered.'"

Watson raised an eyebrow. "Was the door open?"

40

"Just a crack, she said. Enough to see but not enough to be noticed."

"Why wait to come forward?"

Lestrade shrugged. "Fear, maybe. Or guilt. She claims it was the headlines that spurred her. Thought someone should know."

Watson studied him. "Do you believe her?"

"I believe she saw something. What she saw, that's harder to say."

"Could it have been a handkerchief, a note, anything else?"

"Could've. But that's for the courts to decide. You're the first outside the Yard I've told about this," Lestrade confessed.

Watson rose, reaching for the folder Lestrade had left open. "May I relay the contents?"

Lestrade hesitated only a moment, then agreed. "Tell Mr. Holmes what I told you. But tell him to be careful. If this girl's lying, someone's pulling her strings."

"Or she's telling the truth," Watson said softly.

Lestrade's eyes narrowed. "And then Dr. Stamford's in real trouble."

Watson folded the notes carefully and tucked them into his coat. "Thank you, Lestrade. Truly."

"Just don't make me regret it, Doctor."

Watson paused at the door, then turned back. "One last question—have you spoken to this maid yourself?"

Lestrade nodded. "I interviewed her personally. Frightened girl, but calm. Said it all like she rehearsed it in her mind a hundred times. That's the part that troubles me."

Watson offered a faint smile. "You're not the only one troubled, old friend."

As Watson stood to leave Lestrade's office, the inspector held up a hand. "Before you go, there's one more thing. You might want to speak to Murdock. He's in Records—just down the hall, second door on the left. He's been cataloging those anonymous letters related to Stamford. Might let you take a look, considering he owes Holmes a favor."

Watson raised an eyebrow. "Murdock?"

Lestrade gave a wry smile. "Holmes once caught the man who blackmailed Murdock's sister. Quiet affair—kept it out of the papers. Murdock's been quietly grateful ever since."

Moments later, Watson found himself knocking on a worn wooden door marked "RECORDS—EVIDENCE INTAKE."

"Come," a voice called.

Inside, Murdock sat at a cluttered desk piled with files. His eyes lit up when he recognized Watson.

"Doctor! What a surprise," the young inspector said as he stood and extended his hand.

"I was told you had something that might help us. The anonymous letters about Dr. Stamford?"

Murdock stood, retrieving a slim folder from a drawer. "Typed, not written. No fingerprints. They were sent to the Home Office, the press, and even a few political rivals. All within the last month."

He handed over the file. Watson opened it and began to read.

Watson leaned in. The letters were concise, clinical—almost sterile in tone.

To whom it may concern,

Dr. James Stamford has a long history of unethical behavior. Those in power may wish to believe otherwise, but he is not to be trusted. His proximity to the Parliament physician staff is a matter of convenience, not merit.

The second letter was bolder:

Do not let influence blind you. Dr. Stamford has ties to foreign agencies. He should not be trusted with national secrets or men of rank. Look closer. Follow his steps. You will find dirt.

The third was more chilling:

The man is dangerous. He has long trafficked in deceit, covering errors in diagnoses and falsifying reports for profit and favor. His proximity to recent events is no coincidence. Search his past, and you'll find the poison Dr. Stamford wields is not only chemical. If action is not taken, someone will pay the price. This is your final warning.

Watson read them again, this time with Holmes's voice echoing in his mind: *The devil is in the detail. Don't look for drama. Look for fingerprints of motive, access, and execution.*

Watson checked the margins—uniform. He turned over the pages—no imprint, no watermark. No scent, no smudge. But something nagged at him.

"Were they delivered by post?" Watson asked.

"Yes, Doctor. Delivered in plain envelopes, no fingerprints or distinguishing marks. Postmarked from different boroughs but dropped in-person at sub-stations with no security."

Watson picked up the second letter again and frowned. "This paper stock, it's heavier than the others."

Murdock tilted his head. "You noticed?"

Watson, still deep into his examination said, "And look here—this typeface. Slightly off-alignment. The 's' in 'secrets' is slightly raised. That could indicate a faulty typebar, or perhaps the machine had been poorly maintained."

"You've learned a few tricks from your friend."

Watson smiled faintly, "Not nearly enough."

He paused, tapping the final letter. "This phrasing— 'someone will pay the price.' That's not a warning. That's a prediction. Or perhaps, a threat?"

Murdock's brow furrowed slightly. "That's how we read it. But we can't trace it to anyone."

Watson took out a small notebook and scribbled a few notes. "There's something else I'll mention to Holmes. Though it may be nothing." He held up the envelope from the second letter. "This stamp is half a millimeter misaligned. Subtle, but consistent on all three. Could be something—or just sloppy pasting."

Murdock leaned back in his chair. "You're thorough. I see why Holmes keeps you close."

Watson gathered the letters carefully. "It's less about closeness and more about loyalty. Holmes believes Stamford is innocent. And if there's a thread to pull—we'll pull it."

Murdock gave a nod of respect. "Well then, Godspeed. If anything else crosses my desk, I'll let you know."

Watson carefully reassembled the pages and thanked Murdock, who added quietly, "For what it's worth, Doctor, I don't believe Stamford did it. Not the man I knew. But the evidence…"

"…is stacked against him," Watson finished.

With a nod of thanks, he left the Records room with another piece of a puzzle he hoped Holmes could fit into place.

The comforting clatter of dishes accompanied the warm scent of roasted meat and bread as Mrs. Hudson swept into the sitting room at 221B Baker Street. Balancing a tray with practiced ease, she set lunch before Holmes and Watson, who sat across from one another, their places hastily cleared of notes and case files.

"If you don't eat more than scribbles and suspicion, Mr. Holmes," she scolded, her Scottish temper flaring slightly as she set down a bowl of stew, "you'll waste away into one of your own shadows."

Holmes offered a distracted smile. "Thank you, Mrs. Hudson."

She turned on Watson with equal force. "And, Doctor, your daughter's as bad. Working herself to the bone, skipping meals. Between these two, I'll be running a hospital ward out of my kitchen."

Watson chuckled, lifting a spoonful of stew. "I'll speak to her. I promise."

"See that you do." She bustled off with a huff, but the corners of her mouth twitched with fondness.

Holmes waited until the door shut behind her before leaning forward, eyes keen. "Now. What did you learn from Lestrade?"

Watson set down his spoon. "Plenty. First, he's convinced of Stamford's guilt, but not without some discomfort. He shared something new. A witness has come forward. A maid who claims to have seen Stamford poison the wine."

Holmes's brow furrowed. "Anne Godfrey?"

Watson blinked. "You knew?"

Holmes gave a small shrug. "Her name surfaced earlier in a separate inquiry I made regarding the event's guest list and staff assignments. She was added to the household only a fortnight before the dinner. Curious timing."

Watson squinted in thought. "She was frightened but oddly composed. Lestrade said it was like she'd rehearsed the story a hundred times."

Holmes's lips thinned, "Too clean."

Watson gave a slight nod. "He also sent me to Murdock. He never forgot how you helped him out once."

Holmes waved a dismissive hand. "Blackmail case. A quiet affair."

"Well, your quiet affair earned us access to those anonymous letters. Three of them—all typed, not handwritten. No fingerprints. All delivered to various recipients—the Home Office, press, and political enemies."

Watson handed over the folder containing the letters and pulled his notebook from his coat and flipped to a page of neatly written notes.

Holmes read over the details in silence, then narrowed his eyes. "The phrasing... calculated. Cold. But something desperate here, too."

Watson pointed to a particular line in his notes. "The second letter was on heavier paper. Slightly misaligned type in one paragraph—the 's' in 'secrets' rides high."

Holmes looked up sharply. "A faulty typebar."

"Exactly. And I noticed the stamps were slightly off, likely pasted by hand."

Holmes stood abruptly. "That settles it. I was uncertain of the connection, but this confirms the trail. The author of these letters is William Enoch Trask."

Watson stood as well. "Who?"

"A former colleague of Stamford's. A junior chemist named Trask. He was once respected in medical circles. Not for his bedside manner, which was nonexistent, but for his theories on institutional design. Sanitation flow, ward configuration, staff movement. He was a man obsessed with control over healing spaces. He believed architecture could cure disease."

Watson looked up thoughtfully. "I recall something of that. Didn't Stamford mention once that Trask helped plan the Aldersgate Wing at St. Bartholomew's?"

"He did. And Stamford was the one who exposed the flaw in its ventilation system. Patients in the recovery ward were being exposed to infectious air. It was a devastating report, quietly buried in the press but catastrophic for Trask's career. Since then, he's written under pseudonyms, attacked medical professionals in various journals and always with a particular venom reserved for Stamford."

"Upon my soul," Watson murmured to himself.

"Trask shifted fields soon after. Reinvented himself as a private consultant in hospital design, then architectural planning in general. But he never regained the prestige he lost. And he never forgave Stamford."

Watson's brow darkened. "So, he didn't just want revenge. He wanted poetic justice."

Watson asked, "Have you met him?"

"No. But I've encountered his name repeatedly, always in the margins. He never confronts directly. He manipulates others. This maid, Anne Godfrey, may be connected to him."

Watson glanced down. "And the letters?"

Holmes crossed to his desk and retrieved a slim folder. "Months ago, I began to suspect a pattern. A series of anonymous letters submitted to fringe medical journals—attacks on various doctors. The tone was clinical, bitter, and always skirted libel by the slimmest margin. I requested access to the original submissions from the publishers, claiming scholarly interest in anonymous medical critiques."

He laid out several typed pages. "All of them were typed, not handwritten. And in each one the same mechanical flaws, including a slightly raised 's.' It was subtle, but consistent. At the time, I didn't know the identity of the author."

Watson rested his chin on his hand. "So how did you link them to Trask?"

"One of the editors recalled corresponding with the writer under the pseudonym 'E. W. Nash.' Payment for the letters was sent to a local bank. I followed the trail through a forged signature and an abandoned mailbox and found the name William Enoch Trask behind it."

Watson gave a low whistle. "And now the same typewriter has turned up in the letters to the Home Office."

Looking at his friend, Holmes replied, "The machine is the link. He thought anonymity and intermediaries would shield him. But it's that same typewriter, his own flaw, that will unravel the rest."

The street was narrow and gray, tucked behind a row of coal vendors off Camden High Street. Number 14 was an aging brick building with chipped lintels and a stoop that creaked as Holmes and Watson stepped up to the door.

A stout woman with sleeves rolled to the elbows and a dusting cloth in hand opened it partway. Her eyes narrowed as she took them in. "Yes? What's your business?"

Holmes offered a courteous nod. "Good afternoon, madam. We're seeking information about a former tenant of yours—Mr. William Enoch Trask."

She peered at them sharply. "And who are you?"

"Sherlock Holmes," he said simply, "and this is Dr. John Watson."

Her entire posture shifted. "Wait... *The* Sherlock Holmes? And Dr. Watson, as in the stories?"

Watson gave a polite bow of the head. "One and the same."

"Well, I'll be..." she muttered, flustered as she stepped back. "I didn't recognize you straight off. Do come in, Mr. Holmes—Doctor. I'm Mrs. Havers. I was just cleaning his flat."

She led them up a narrow stairwell and pushed open the door to a small, musty room with a worn rug and a view of the alley. "Trask lived here until three nights ago. He left in a hurry and took most everything."

Holmes surveyed the sparse furnishings. "He gave no notice?"

"None. Rent was paid through the week, and then he vanished."

"May I ask," Holmes said casually, "what kind of work did Mr. Trask do?"

She puffed out her cheeks. "He told me he was a manager. Some big industrial production plant on the East End, I think. He never said which one. But he was organized—*very* organized. Everything in its place, not a scrap of paper out of line. He said they loved him at work because he could keep any mess in order. Seemed proud of it."

Holmes gave a quiet hum of interest.

"And the typewriter?" he asked next.

She shook her head. "Gone. Heavy thing, too. Black Remington, with those old brass keys. Clacked a bit funny when it hit certain letters. He always made me use it."

"You typed for him?"

Her lips pressed tight. "I did. He didn't want anything in his own handwriting. Dictated the letters to me like I was his secretary. Wouldn't even let me see his notes."

Watson glanced at Holmes. "Letters sent to the Home Office?"

She hesitated, then looked down. "Yes. Said they were warnings. He said people needed to know what Dr. Stamford was. At first, I thought it was politics, but the things he said. The way he said them. It started to give me a chill."

"Did he mention Stamford by name?" Holmes asked.

"Not often. Just called him 'that snake,' or 'the deceiver.' Said he ruined lives. Said he'd see justice done one way or another."

"And you never saw where the letters went after?"

"No. He sealed and put the stamps on himself. His anger made him shake like a madman. I wasn't upset to see him leave my house. He'd stuffed them in his coat and disappeared."

"Did he leave anything behind?" Holmes asked.

She disappeared into the hall and returned moments later with a torn scrap of paper. "I found this under the dresser. Don't know what it means, but I kept it."

Holmes took the scrap and examined the typing: *"Never forget who built the stage. They owe me."*

There was no watermark. It had the same thick stock as the letters Watson had inspected.

Holmes folded it neatly. "Thank you, Mrs. Havers. If Mr. Trask should return—"

"Oh, I'll be sending word straight to Baker Street," she said, with a smile toward Watson. "I've read all your stories, Doctor. Got 'A Study in Scarlet' in my sewing basket."

Watson blinked, flattered. "That's very kind."

She gave a satisfied nod. "I always said, if anyone could sniff out rot like that Trask, it'd be the pair of you. Strange man, he was. Always watching people out the window like he was keeping score."

As they stepped back out into the late afternoon sun, Watson said, "So he didn't even dirty his own fingers with the letters."

"No," Holmes replied grimly. "He hides behind others, such as this landlady. Perhaps the maid, too. He's a coward, but a calculating one."

"You're certain he's central?"

Holmes turned to him saying, "Absolutely. And now we know one more thing."

"What's that?"

"He's gone to ground. And men like Trask don't vanish unless they believe someone's closing in."

The next morning, the scent of fresh paint mingled with dust as Victoria stood inside the London Majestic Theatre. Light filtered through high, grimy windows, falling in slanted beams across the ornate but aging interior. The stage creaked beneath her boots as she surveyed the skeleton of what had once been a thriving performance hall.

A voice echoed from the front entrance. "Miss Watson?"

She turned to see a man entering with cautious confidence. He was tall, broad-shouldered, and perhaps in his forties, with streaks of silver at his temples that gave him an air of experience.

"Yes?"

He stepped forward, doffing his cap. "Name's Samuel Lawson. I heard you're hiring for the renovation—someone to oversee the construction crew. Came recommended by a chap named Peters who did some masonry work for you last week. Said you might be looking for a foreman."

Victoria offered a polite smile. "We are. Walk with me?"

She led him through the dusty rows of seats, up the stage stairs, and backstage where wooden flats and old props lay stacked like forgotten dreams.

"Tell me about your background," she said, pausing by a half-collapsed dressing room door.

"Been in construction for twenty-odd years," Lawson replied. "Worked restoration on three older theaters—St. Edmund's in Kent, the Queen's Marquee off Charing Cross, and the Gaiety. I know the quirks of these old places—where they tend to rot, where the pipes run too close to wiring, that sort of thing."

He tapped a nearby support beam. "This one's solid but warped from water damage—likely from that roof collapse years back. I'd reinforce here, maybe add sister beams rather than replace the original structure. Maintain authenticity."

Victoria raised her brows. "Impressive. Most would suggest tearing it out."

"That'd affect your acoustics. I figure a theatre's not just walls—it's sound and soul."

His insight was disarming, and she felt her confidence grow with each step. Still, she hesitated.

Now, walking the length of the stage, Samuel Lawson paused, eyeing the rigging above. "That counterweight system is mismatched. You've got brass weights on the left and cast iron on the right. That'll pull crooked every time. Could be dangerous if someone doesn't fix it before the lighting crew arrives."

Victoria blinked. "You spotted that in less than ten seconds."

He offered a modest smile. "Well, it's the sort of thing you get an eye for after a while."

He seemed to drift into memory as he continued, "There's something noble about these places, don't you think? The way they gather people together. When I was young, my sister used to sing in chorus lines. I used to watch from the wings when I could. The smell of sawdust and greasepaint always stuck with me."

Victoria softened. "That's very touching."

Lawson shrugged. "Theater's not just glamour. It's work, timing, and structure. You need someone who sees the art and the angles."

"I do," she agreed. "And frankly, I'm impressed. But this is a significant position, and I'm not an expert in renovation. I'd feel better having my father meet you. He'll be at my flat on Baker Street later this afternoon. Would you mind stopping by?"

"Not at all. I appreciate the thoroughness." He removed his cap. "I look forward to it, Miss Watson."

As she escorted him out, Daisy emerged from the wings, arms folded, and eyebrows lifted.

"Well," Daisy said with a grin. "If you don't hire him, I might."

Victoria rolled her eyes. "Daisy."

"What? He's clever, capable, and just weathered enough to be interesting. Did you see those hands?"

"I was more interested in his brain."

"I noticed both," Daisy said, her smile teasing. "But truly, he seems like a good find."

Victoria concurred, though her thoughts were already racing ahead to the meeting that afternoon.

Later that afternoon, the scene shifted to Baker Street. Watson grunted as he maneuvered a rolled-up carpet through the doorway of Victoria's sitting room.

"Could use another set of hands," he called, wiping sweat from his brow.

Holmes appeared, coatless, sleeves rolled. "I'm here to further the investigation, not the interior design. But I'll lend a hand if it means you'll return your attention to Stamford's case."

With both men working, the last of the furniture was soon arranged.

A knock came at the door.

Victoria opened it to find Lawson, hat in hand. "Good afternoon, Miss Watson."

She ushered him in. "Mr. Lawson, may I introduce my father, Dr. John Watson, and his friend, Mr. Sherlock Holmes."

Watson offered a firm handshake. Holmes simply gave a slight bow of the head, eyes already scanning the man's boots, hands, and jacket.

"You've been working on brick restoration recently," Holmes said. "Chipped mortar under your nails, right hand calloused more than the left. And you favor your left knee—an old injury."

Lawson blinked. "That's accurate."

Watson cleared his throat. "Mr. Lawson, Miss Watson tells me you've overseen theatrical restorations before."

Lawson grinned. "Yes, sir. Three in total. Managed crews of up to twenty. I can provide references."

"You've worked in restoration," Holmes said. "Tell me—if you had a dry rot problem in a subflooring beam, what's your approach?"

Lawson didn't miss a beat. "Depends on the span, but generally, we'd sister a new beam beside the damaged one, seal the area to prevent further spread, and reinforce with angle iron brackets. Unless the infestation's deep, then you strip and replace."

Holmes looked him over. "Acceptable."

Watson chuckled. "High praise, Mr. Lawson."

"And what's your expected wage?" Victoria asked.

Lawson shrugged. "Less than most. I like the idea of this project. It rebuilds a legacy."

Holmes's eyes narrowed, watching Lawson as he spoke. When the man's gaze lingered on Victoria, Holmes's jaw tightened slightly.

After a round of further questions, Watson finally said, "You have my blessing, Victoria. This gentleman seems like a sound choice."

Victoria turned to Lawson. "Then welcome aboard, Mr. Lawson. We've a great deal of work ahead."

Lawson smiled. "Looking forward to it, Miss Watson."

He took his leave, and the three remained behind.

"Well," she said with a smile, brushing a curl back from her forehead, "thank you both. For the furniture, and the assistance with Mr. Lawson. I don't know what I'd do without you."

Watson rolled his shoulders and offered a warm grin. "It was my pleasure, my girl. And I daresay you've made a sensible choice. Lawson seems a capable sort."

Holmes remained by the window, glancing down at the street. "Capable, yes. But I advise caution."

Victoria's smile faltered slightly. "You didn't like him."

Holmes turned back to face her, folding his arms. "He is affable, observant, and knowledgeable. Precisely the sort of man one wants in such a role. But his ease struck me as calculated."

Watson raised a brow. "You think he's deceiving us?"

"Not necessarily. But he's playing a part—perhaps only to impress, but I trust impressions less than facts. We shall see in time."

Victoria's gaze sharpened slightly, though her tone remained light. "Are you always this suspicious, Mr. Holmes?"

"Habitually," he replied. "It's what keeps my acquaintances from ending up poisoned, blackmailed, or otherwise inconvenienced."

Watson chuckled, "He means well, dear. And he's not wrong to be wary. Still, I think Lawson bears watching, not dismissal."

Victoria replied thoughtfully. "Fair enough. I'll keep my eyes open."

"And I'll keep mine sharper," Holmes murmured under his breath.

She stepped forward and touched her father's arm. "I'll have Mrs. Hudson bring up tea in a bit, after I see to the last of the unpacking. Thank you again."

Watson kissed her cheek. "Always, my girl."

Holmes and Watson moved toward the hallway and into 221B. The familiar scent of pipe tobacco and old leather filled the air as they returned to Holmes's sitting room. Holmes immediately began sorting through the correspondence on his desk, though he paused when Watson spoke.

"You know," Watson said, easing into his usual chair, "there was a time when I never thought I'd be having afternoon tea with my daughter and my dearest friend in the same hour. I rather enjoy it."

Holmes, halfway to the sideboard, looked over his shoulder. "As do I," he said, almost too lightly—then added, "Though I would never say so where Mrs. Hudson could hear it. She'd have me hosting teas by the dozen."

Watson smiled, recognizing the rare crack in Holmes's usual formality.

There was a knock at the door, and Mrs. Hudson appeared with a tray. She smiled warmly as she set down a pot of tea, cups, and a small plate of currant scones.

"Miss Watson will be in shortly," she said. "She's just retying her hair."

"Thank you, Mrs. Hudson," Watson said, offering her a grateful smile.

When she left, Holmes turned contemplative, pouring the tea with surprising care. "The letters, the faulty typebar, the phrasing, and the weight of the paper. I was certain they were Trask's work. I also feel sure that Anne Godfrey, the maid at the dinner, was influenced by him as well."

"You think he's manipulating her?" Watson asked, stirring his tea.

"He manipulates everyone. That is his pattern," Holmes replied. "I'll pay her a visit. There's more to her story than Lestrade could draw out. Lestrade believes Anne Godfrey is the key witness. I believe she is the hinge."

"Hinge?" Watson asked, intrigued.

"A hinge opens or closes a door, depending on which way the pressure falls," Holmes said. "If she is genuine, Stamford may be guilty. But if she is acting, someone is using her to close the case too quickly."

"Sounds like a thoroughly unpleasant fellow," Watson thought out loud.

"There's something else," Holmes said. "I've been mapping the timeline again. The dinner, the poisoning, the letters, and I keep returning to one name that wasn't mentioned in any official report—Chambers."

Watson's eye opened wider. "The valet?"

"Yes. Stamford's personal valet. He vanished after the night of the poisoning and not on holiday, or sick. Simply gone."

"And you think that matters?"

Holmes sat in his armchair opposite Watson. "Trask is a manipulator. He uses people. If he planted the idea in Anne's head, who's to say he didn't do the same with Chambers?"

"Then we need to find him."

Holmes handed Watson a small slip of paper. "He boarded a train from King's Cross two days after the incident. I want you to check the lodging houses near York Station."

Holmes continued, "The letters were not simply timed for political damage, they were timed for emotional ruin. I believe he wanted Stamford to feel hunted, not merely accused. You'll go after the valet, Chambers. I've traced his travel to the York area. I suspect he was removed from the scene deliberately. If he saw something, or was in someone's way..."

"He may be in danger," Watson finished.

Holmes quietly pondered for a moment. "Or he may hold the missing piece. In either case, we must find him."

The door opened again, and Victoria entered, cheeks slightly flushed, her curls retied neatly. She smiled at the sight of them with their tea.

"Still talking about the case?" she asked, settling between them.

"Always," Watson said. "But you are the far more pleasant distraction."

Holmes merely offered her a cup of tea without a word. Their fingers brushed as she took it, and she glanced at him quickly, but he was already turning back to the table.

As they sipped and conversed, the weight of their various burdens lifted just slightly. There would be mysteries to chase soon enough, but for the moment, there was tea, and company, and perhaps, for Holmes, something quietly comforting he could never quite admit aloud.

The streets of Southwark held the scent of damp stone and coal smoke as Holmes stepped lightly across a puddle-slicked alleyway and up the cracked stoop of Number 8 Gilder Street. The building was a modest tenement with peeling paint and iron railings that had once been ornamental, now rusted into a lattice of neglect. He rapped twice on the faded door.

It opened after a pause, revealing a young woman in her early twenties, slight and pale, her light brown hair pulled tightly back beneath a simple house cap. Her hands were red from scrubbing, her eyes wary but not unkind.

"Yes?"

"Miss Anne Godfrey?"

"I am."

"My name is Sherlock Holmes." He gave a small, respectful bow. "I hoped you might permit me a few minutes of conversation."

She glanced over her shoulder, hesitating. "Are you with the police?"

"No," he said smoothly. "Though they and I frequently exchange information. I'm here because I'm concerned with the truth. Nothing more."

A nervous flutter crossed her features. "I've already told them what I saw."

"And I've read their reports. But I have found that truth often has layers. May I come in?"

Still unsure, she stepped aside. "I live with my cousin. He's out just now. But you can sit, if you like."

The flat was small but neat, a front room with a coal grate, a tiny kitchen visible through a curtain, and two worn chairs by the window. A chipped vase of lavender sat on the sill. Holmes removed his hat and gloves, settling gently across from her.

"You were present," he began, "on the night Dr. Stamford dined with members of the House of Commons?"

"I served the table, yes."

"You testified that you saw him introduce something into the wine glass before the toasts?"

Anne folded her hands in her lap. "Yes, sir. I saw him unscrew something and tip it into the poor man's wine glass when he thought no one was watching."

"From where were you observing?"

She blinked. "Just outside the dining room, sir. The door was ajar."

"Curious," Holmes murmured. "Was it not customary for household staff to remain behind the servants' door during formal toasts?"

"Well… yes, usually."

He leaned forward, his tone still gentle. "And was the dining room not candlelit? The lamps in that house are gas, but the overhead fixture had failed the week before, according to the repair record."

She blinked again. "I—I suppose it was dim."

"So, from a dim hallway, at a partial angle, through an open door—"

"It was open wide," she interrupted.

"Ah. And what exactly did you see?"

She hesitated. "He reached into his coat, took out a small vial, unscrewed it and poured something into the wine glass."

Holmes was silent a moment.

"You are certain of each of those steps?" he asked.

She looked at him slowly and quietly said, "Yes."

"You described the vial to the police?"

"Yes. It was clear glass with a cork."

"But you just said it had a screw top."

She paled. "Did I?"

"You did," Holmes said softly. "Twice, in fact."

The room grew still.

"I only want to help," he added. "There are lives at stake. If you saw what you say, then your details will stand. But if someone put those images into your mind, perhaps through repetition, or suggestion, then I must know that as well."

"I... I'm not lying," she whispered, but tears glistened at the corners of her eyes.

Holmes stood. "I believe you are frightened. I believe someone has made you feel you must say these things. But belief is not proof."

She rose as well, wringing her hands. "I don't know anything more."

He gave a slight bow. "Then thank you for your time, Miss Godfrey."

As she led him to the door, he noticed a cluttered writing desk against the wall—its drawers neatly closed, save for one. Inside was a small bundle of letters, each tied with twine. On the outermost envelope, in an unfamiliar but tidy hand, the return address read:

W. E. Trask

Holmes raised a brow, nodding toward them. "Your correspondence?"

She followed his gaze and quickly shut the drawer. "No. My cousin's. He gets letters sometimes for jobs and such."

"From Mr. Trask?"

"I don't know who that is."

Her tone was too quick now and brittle.

Holmes offered a cordial smile. "And your cousin is…?"

"Edward. He's out looking for work." She paused. "He used to work at a factory in East London. They let him go months ago. But he's been trying to get back on his feet."

"Do you recall the name of the factory?"

She shrugged. "Someplace called Easton Works, I think. Something with machinery or pipes. I don't really know."

Holmes's eyes didn't leave hers. "Of course."

He stepped out into the chill gray of the afternoon, letting the door click shut behind him. Once he reached the street corner, he took out his notebook and wrote two lines:

Anne's testimony — coached.
Letters to cousin from Trask — Easton Works = connection.

He tapped the pencil against his palm. Trask met Anne through her cousin, Edward. Trask had placed Anne at the dinner for a reason. Whether she knew it or not, she had been manipulated.

And Holmes intended to learn the truth.

The train pulled into York station with a long, metallic groan. Watson disembarked with purpose, his coat collar turned up against the chilly northern wind. It was colder here than in London, and quieter—no clamor of carriage wheels, no rising spire of smog. Just the muted bustle of travelers and the echo of announcements shouted down long brick corridors.

He paused on the platform, reviewing the note Holmes had given him: *"Chambers boarded here two days before the incident. Check lodging houses near the station. May be using an alias."*

Watson took a deep breath and set off.

Three boarding houses later, he found his first real lead.

At a modest rowhouse with a crooked sign reading *Let by the Day or Week,* a middle-aged woman with a generous waistline and sharp eyes greeted him.

"I'm looking for someone," Watson explained. "He may be using the name Charles Kent. He's in his mid-thirties, is polite and reserved. He's a former valet."

The landlady narrowed her eyes and folded her arms. "You a doctor?"

"Yes. Dr. John Watson."

"Hmph. Thought as much. You've the look of one. And a decent sort, I'll wager. All right, then, yes, I had such a man. He stayed two nights and paid in full, quiet as a church mouse. Said he needed rest. I didn't think he gave his real name, and he was careful – nervous. Watched the door more than once. Left early this morning with a small bag."

"Did he say where he was going?"

"Said he might try the mission hall on Ashton Lane, or maybe the little church nearby. He looked worn. Not ill—just worried. The kind of worry that lives deep in the bones."

Watson thanked her and made his way toward Ashton Lane.

The church was a small stone building tucked behind a row of hedges, its bell tower barely rising above the rooftops. Inside, it was quiet and cool, with dusty shafts of light falling through narrow stained-glass windows. A young vicar gave a polite nod from the altar steps but didn't approach.

Watson spotted the man in the far pew—alone, hunched, his hands clasped tightly in front of him. He wore a threadbare coat and kept his head low, as though praying, or hiding.

Watson walked slowly down the aisle and sat beside him.

"I'm not here to harm you, Mr. Chambers."

The man stiffened.

"Do you remember me?" Watson continued gently. "My name is Dr. John Watson. I'm a friend of Dr. Stamford and Sherlock Holmes."

At that, Chambers turned slightly, revealing a pale, thin face with hollow cheeks and eyes that had seen too many sleepless nights.

"Holmes?" he whispered. "I thought—surely they'd have sent the police."

"Holmes believes you may have seen something important. He asked me to find you."

"I shouldn't have left," Chambers muttered. "But I couldn't stay. I was afraid."

"Of being blamed?"

Chambers nodded, his hands starting to twitch slightly. "They would've pinned it on me. I was in the room, wasn't I? Serving. Always watching. Always nearby."

Watson let the silence settle before asking, "What exactly did you see?"

The valet swallowed hard, staring straight ahead. "I saw a figure the table near the lord's chair. I thought he was adjusting the place setting and glasses. Just a shadow, really. I didn't see the face. But the movement was wrong—too stiff. Not familiar."

"Not one of the house staff?"

"I thought it might've been one of the new kitchen lads, but we didn't have anyone new. That's what unnerved me. And just as I stepped toward it, one of the footmen came in and said I was needed in the kitchen. I left and then the toasts began."

"And you didn't return?"

"I wasn't supposed to be in the dining room again until dessert. But by then, it was too late. Lord Mornay from Parliament was already pale and collapsed shortly after."

Watson's brow furrowed. "Did you tell the police?"

"I—" Chambers shook his head. "They barely questioned me. They just asked where I was when the toasts happened. I told them. That was all. I kept my mouth shut after that. Didn't want to be caught in something. The police… they don't look kindly on valets who speak too freely. I've seen it before."

Watson considered him carefully. "Do you think Stamford did it?"

Chambers looked at him. "I don't know. But I know what I saw—or almost saw. Someone moved near that wine glass. Someone who shouldn't have been there. And it wasn't Dr. Stamford."

"Then you must come back with me," Watson said firmly. "Holmes can protect you. And if there's something in your story that proves Stamford's innocence—or guilt—we must have it."

Chambers looked down at his folded hands. "It's just… I've got nothing now. No position. No home. If I go back, they'll question me. If they think I'm lying…"

"Then Holmes will stand for you. And so will I," Watson said. "You're not alone in this."

The man breathed in, held it, and let it out slowly. "All right. I'll come."

Watson stood and offered him a steadying hand. "You won't regret it."

As they stepped into the afternoon light outside the church, Watson paused briefly on the steps and reached into his coat for a small notepad and pencil.

He scribbled a quick message and handed it off to a passing boy with a halfpenny and instructions to send it from the telegraph station immediately.

Found him. He knows something. —W.

The London Majestic was no longer quiet.

Eight weeks into renovations, the theater buzzed with life. Sunlight filtered through the grime-streaked windows, illuminating scaffolding along the balcony and tools spread in careful clusters. The scent of sawdust mingled with paint primer and the warm sting of oil rubbed into wood paneling. Where silence and dust had once ruled, hammers now tapped, voices echoed, and purpose filled the air.

Victoria stepped through the side entrance, clipboard in hand, boots scuffed from her morning walk. She paused for a moment at the back of the main house, just beneath the mezzanine, and breathed it all in— the sound, the motion, the hope.

Daisy appeared beside her, hair pinned in her usual no-nonsense twist, eyes bright.

"It's really coming together, isn't it?" she said, grinning.

Victoria smiled, surveying the progress. "Faster than I expected. It's almost unnerving."

As if summoned, Samuel Lawson emerged from behind a velvet curtain near the proscenium arch, sleeves rolled, holding a set of rolled blueprints. A pencil was tucked behind his ear, and a streak of dust darkened one cheek.

"Morning, Miss Watson," he called. "I've just finished checking the subfloor in the wings. Rotten in places, as expected, but it's not beyond saving. That will save us considerable time."

Victoria joined him, accepting the plans as he offered them. "You're certain we can keep the original structure?"

"With reinforcement, yes. We'll brace it along these joists—" he pointed to a penciled mark on the sketch "—and run a new support beam along the downstage edge. That'll keep the movement sound and the resonance intact. Old timber, when treated right, still sings."

She smiled at that. "You really do care about these old theaters, don't you?"

Lawson's eyes softened. "They've been good to me, Miss Watson. My earliest memories of my sister are on a stage like this. Seems only fair I give something back."

She studied him for a moment longer, then returned her gaze to the blueprints. "I like your suggestions here," she said, tapping a margin where someone, presumably Lawson, had made neat, annotated notes. "That is not just practical, but considerate of the aesthetic. I'm grateful."

He gave a modest shrug. "We've got a solid crew. And you've been clear about your vision. That makes my job easier."

As he moved off to speak with a plasterer, Daisy leaned in, lowering her voice. "I'm starting to like him."

"You said that already."

"I know, but now I *really* mean it. He's got charm, brains, and he gets things done. You've seen the way the new hires follow his lead?"

Victoria looked around. The woodworkers respected him, the painters laughed with him, and even the gruff stoneworker tipped his hat when Lawson passed.

She felt herself relax—a tension in her shoulders she hadn't realized was there beginning to fade.

Back in her office, which was just a converted dressing room with a desk and stacks of paperwork, Victoria sat down to review the morning's notes. A stack of invoices awaited her signature. Beneath them lay a copy of the week's layout sketches. She thumbed through them absently until one sheet stopped her.

It was familiar, her own ledger, from earlier in the week. Tucked inside was something new.

A folded slip of paper. Small, cream-colored, the edges neatly cut.

She unfolded it slowly.

"He is not what he seems. Be careful who you trust. —A Well-Wisher"

She stared at the words, blood draining just slightly from her face. It was not handwritten – it was typed.

She read it again.

Then once more.

Daisy entered a moment later, arms full of costume fabric samples she'd been sorting. She dropped them onto a side table and looked up.

"You look like you've seen a ghost."

Victoria blinked and quickly folded the note, slipping it into the front pocket of her ledger. "I'm just tired."

Daisy narrowed her eyes. "Tired doesn't usually come with a thousand-yard stare."

Victoria forced a small smile. "Have you ever received a note from an anonymous admirer?"

Daisy grinned. "Only once. It turned out to be the fishmonger's boy. He wrote me terrible poetry about trout."

"That explains a lot."

"Are you saying you've got an admirer?"

Victoria shrugged, adjusting the papers on her desk. "Something like that. It's more like a strange note. It's not worth worrying over."

But as Daisy returned to sorting fabrics, humming quietly to herself, Victoria's fingers brushed the hidden message in her pocket.

She didn't believe in coincidence.

And if someone thought she needed to be warned about someone, that meant someone was watching.

She glanced out the window, eyes narrowing slightly as the crew worked below.

The work was progressing beautifully.

Too beautifully.

Victoria Watson was not easily rattled, but she knew when to listen to her instincts.

And something in that theater—whether in the beams, the shadows, or behind the easy smile of Samuel Lawson—was starting to hum the wrong tune.

The parlor of 221B Baker Street was warm with late-afternoon light filtering through the window, its golden hue casting long shadows across the Persian rug. A teapot sat untouched on the sideboard, and Holmes stood at the hearth, restless as ever, hands clasped behind his back.

Watson entered with a quiet knock, ushering in a man with pale skin, a tidy coat two sizes too large, and eyes that flicked toward every shadow in the room. His every movement betrayed nerves.

"Mr. Sherlock Holmes," Watson said gently, "allow me to reintroduce Mr. Edward Chambers, former valet to Dr. Stamford."

Holmes turned and studied the man in one sweeping glance. "You've lost weight. Half a stone, perhaps more. No hat. Scuffed boots. A missing button. You left in a hurry."

Chambers offered a feeble smile. "I—I didn't want to be found."

"Yet here you are," Holmes replied. "Please, sit. You've nothing to fear from us."

Chambers sat stiffly, his back straight and his hands on his knees.

Holmes wasted no time. "Tell me what happened the evening of the dinner. Be precise."

Chambers swallowed. "I was in the front hall, waiting to serve when the gentlemen were ready. But just before the wine was poured, I was told to step out and that I was needed in the kitchen."

"By whom were you employed?" Holmes asked.

"Dr. Stamford offered my services, but most of the household staff was hired through Lord Mornay's connections. But the housekeeper, Mrs. Dorran—she was unfamiliar to me. I'd only met her once, days before the event. She gave orders as if she'd been there for years."

Holmes's eyes narrowed. "And you followed her instruction?"

"I did. I went to the back, but no one there needed me. When I returned, the wine glass had already been moved out of place."

"Were there guests in the dining room yet?"

"They were just starting to filter in from the smoking room. I saw nothing amiss, only that Anne Godfrey was not where she was assigned to be."

Holmes paused. "You knew her?"

"Barely. She came on quite suddenly. Said she was filling in from an agency."

Holmes paced a slow, deliberate line in front of the hearth. "And what did she say to you that evening?"

"Nothing directly. But—" Chambers hesitated. "Earlier that day, I saw her behind the house. She was speaking with a man I didn't recognize. Tall, black overcoat and wearing a bowler hat with a dent on the back. He handed her something, but I couldn't see what it was."

"Did you hear anything?" Holmes asked.

"No. But when I stepped outside, she jumped. He left without a word. She claimed it was someone asking for directions. She returned into the kitchen immediately."

"Unlikely," Holmes murmured. "Did this man have any distinguishing features?"

"I only saw his back. His hat had the same dent in the back, which is how I knew it was the same man who had been with Anne earlier. I saw him again later lingering near Lord Mornay's place setting, I would not know him if I saw him again."

"How is it that you alone saw this mysterious man?" Holmes asked, looking away from Chambers.

"I'd left the kitchen and was standing in the back doorway when a crash was heard from the kitchen. Everyone turned their heads to look. From my position the dining table was in my line of vision."

"What caused the crash?" Holmes asked.

Chambers paused and said, "Anne had dropped a tray of plates."

Holmes stilled. "Did Stamford know of any of this?"

"No. I didn't tell him. I wasn't sure what to think. But after the incident, and when they questioned me, I panicked. I thought someone would try to frame me next."

Watson leaned forward. "You weren't wrong to be afraid."

Chambers glanced between them, still hunched as if bracing for blowback. "Do you believe me?"

Holmes stopped pacing, his voice quiet but firm. "I believe you saw something important, Mr. Chambers. And I believe someone intended to remove you from the room before anything suspicious occurred."

Chambers gazed at him, as though relieved that someone believed him. "It felt that way."

Holmes folded his arms. "You're fortunate to have avoided a worse fate. But your presence now is essential. We may yet untangle this knot—but only with truth, not fear."

Chambers looked to Watson, who gave a quiet nod of encouragement. "You're safe now, and Holmes is right. We need you."

Holmes turned to the window, his fingers steepled beneath his chin.

"Anne Godfrey's testimony was too polished," he said at last. "And now we learn she met with a man prior to the poisoning. A man we may very well know under another name."

He turned back. "Trask is no longer merely a bitter former chemist. He's a saboteur. He orchestrated the letters. He manipulated Anne. And he ensured the one person who might contradict her, Chambers, was nowhere near the wine."

Watson frowned. "And if he's capable of all that..."

"He won't stop now," Holmes finished. "Not until Stamford is ruined—or worse."

Chambers stared at them both. "What should I do?"

Holmes replied without hesitation. "Stay close. Watson will arrange a room nearby. Until we decide on our next move, you're not to speak to anyone—not even police—without me present."

Chambers rose; grateful the tension was finally beginning to ease in his shoulders.

Holmes turned again to the window, his gaze sharp and distant.

"I thought we were chasing a man's reputation," he murmured. "But we're chasing his ghost."

The gaslight cast a mellow glow across the sitting room of 221B as Victoria Watson stepped quietly through the open door. She carried a small slip of paper in her gloved hand and wore a composed expression, though Holmes could detect the guarded tension in her.

Holmes stood near the hearth, pipe in hand but unlit. "Good evening, Miss Watson."

"Mr. Holmes," she replied, her tone pleasant but reserved. "Am I interrupting?"

"Not at all," he said, motioning toward the chair opposite his own. "Dr. Watson has returned home. You have me to yourself."

Victoria took the seat, smoothing her skirt as she sat. "Actually, that's rather convenient. I came to speak with you privately. I do not wish to alarm Father needlessly."

Holmes raised an eyebrow and waited.

She reached into her coat and produced the note, unfolding it with care. "I found this tucked into my ledger at the theater this morning. I've no idea who put it there."

Holmes took the slip from her fingers and held it between his own, tilting it toward the lamplight.

The message, typed in blocky, uneven letters, read:

"He is not what he seems. Be careful who you trust. —A Well-Wisher"

Holmes said nothing for a moment. His eyes scanned the paper, not just reading the words but measuring them—the spacing, the ink saturation, the slight skew in the final line.

"This doesn't appear to be theater gossip," he said.

Victoria shook her head. "No. It struck me as specific. And timely."

Holmes turned the paper over, but it was blank on the reverse. He set his pipe aside and retrieved a glass from the nearby desk. With it, he examined the letters again, brow furrowing slightly.

"There," he murmured.

"There?" Victoria echoed.

He tapped gently on the word '*seems*'. "That 's' is slightly raised above the baseline of the other letters. I've seen it before, along with this spacing anomaly."

"In the letters about Stamford?" she guessed.

Holmes offered only a brief glance—enough to confirm her suspicion without admitting too much.

"You believe the person who left this note may be connected to the same typewriter?" she asked carefully.

"I believe," Holmes said, "that someone who has gone to great lengths to hide his identity is now either losing control of the narrative, or deliberately changing tactics."

Victoria leaned back slightly, visibly digesting the implication. "You think this was written by the man behind the letters?"

"Perhaps. Or someone under his influence." He folded the slip and asked, "May I keep this?"

"Of course," she replied, sensing his uneasiness.

"Has anything unusual happened at the theater besides this?"

She hesitated. "No. Although Daisy and I both remarked how quickly things are progressing. Mr. Lawson is very efficient and organized. The crew seems to respect him already."

Holmes gave a soft hum but said nothing.

Victoria studied his expression. "You don't trust him."

Holmes's gaze flicked to her face. "I make it a habit not to trust easily."

"That isn't an answer."

"No," he agreed. "But it is a warning."

They were silent for a moment. The sounds of the street filtered faintly through the window—hoofbeats, the distant call of a street vendor. Holmes rose and walked to the fireplace, adjusting the poker though no fire burned.

Victoria watched him, her voice softer now. "You know something you're not saying."

Holmes did not turn. "I know only what I observe. But observation, when paired with instinct, can be remarkably revealing."

"I'll be vigilant and keep a sharp watch." Victoria promised.

"Good," he said, finally facing her again. "Your father would never forgive me otherwise."

Victoria stood, followed by a pause between them—not awkward, exactly, but weighted. Something unsaid lingered like the scent of tobacco in the air.

"Mr. Holmes," she said gently, "if you do discover something— something serious—I want to be told."

His expression softened just slightly. "You will be."

She gave a small nod, then moved toward the door.

"Miss Watson," Holmes said suddenly, his voice quieter, almost reflective.

She turned, one hand on the knob.

"You've come to mean a great deal to the people in this house in the months you've been here," he said. "Take care."

For a moment, her guarded composure wavered. She offered a smile—real and unguarded. "And you, Mr. Holmes, are a hard man to read. But not impossible."

She left, the door clicking softly behind her.

Holmes stood in silence for a while, then returned to his desk and retrieved the small envelope where he'd kept his copies of the anonymous letters. He laid them beside the note and compared the raised letters on the pages again.

The flaw was identical.

He leaned back, steepling his fingers beneath his chin.

"So," he murmured to the quiet room, "you've brought the machine into her theater."

He did not like the implications of that. Not at all.

Holmes stood at the window long after Victoria's footsteps faded down the hall. For a man who claimed emotion was a distraction from logic, he was unusually still, his thoughts deeper than usual, and not entirely analytical.

At last, he turned away, crossed to his desk, and cleared a space among the organized chaos. The slip of paper from Victoria's visitor, the so-called "Well-Wisher," rested beside the letters from the Stamford affair. He laid them all out, anchoring corners with his magnifier, a penknife, and his teacup.

With deliberate movements, Holmes reached for a fresh sheet of paper and began to map what he knew.

At the top, he wrote: *THE CASE AGAINST STAMFORD.*

Beneath it, he listed the known components in crisp, orderly script:

First, the three anonymous letters, each one typed and condemning Stamford's ethics in calculated language.

Second, the faulty 's' that appeared consistently across all of them, also found in the so-called *Well-Wisher* note and the messages delivered to the Home Office.

Third, the shadow of William Enoch Trask, a former colleague dismissed with cause and long suspected of retaliating through printed attacks under assumed names.

Fourth, the missing typewriter—presumed relocated, perhaps deliberately hidden.

Fifth, Anne Godfrey's testimony that she had seen Stamford lean over Lord Mornay's wineglass just moments before the poisoning.

Sixth, the account of Mr. Chambers, who had been asked to leave the room shortly before the wine was poured. He later reported seeing Anne Godfrey conversing with a strange man behind the house earlier that same day and seeing him near the dining table.

And finally, the poisoned wine itself. The victim had taken ill rapidly, while no other guests reported symptoms.

He drew a long horizontal line across the page, sketching the shape of a timeline. Along it, he marked key events in swift, efficient script: the date of Trask's dismissal; the first appearance of anonymous letters; the dinner party arranged by Mornay; Anne Godfrey's employment; Chambers' sudden dismissal from the room; the poisoning itself; and, lastly, Stamford's arrest.

He paused. Then added a question in bold lettering beneath the timeline:

Who was in the kitchen at the moment the wine glass was unattended?

Below that, he continued:

Who placed Anne in the household?

Why was Chambers sent away?

He tapped the pen lightly against the page. The answers weren't there yet—but the pattern was forming. Each piece fit Trask's known behavior. He used others and stayed hidden while controlling narratives through silence and implication.

Holmes sat back, eyes narrowing.

He wrote a single word underlined in black – *MOTIVE*.

Below it, another – *CONTROL*.

The entire sequence reeked not of rage, but of orchestration. A man like Trask wouldn't merely seek revenge. He'd construct it like a thesis. And now, he'd embedded himself somewhere new.

Holmes added a final note:

Victoria's theater = opportunity.

He underlined it.

The typewriter was no longer in hiding. It had moved with its owner into the very heart of Victoria's project—an old building with few eyes, transient workers, and easy places to disappear.

Holmes stood again, the page of deductions fluttering slightly as he moved. He picked up the letter from the Well-Wisher one last time, ran his thumb along the edge, and whispered:

"Control the setting, control the players."

His gaze flicked toward the door Victoria had passed through minutes earlier.

And now, she was part of the stage.

The scent of dust and varnish still clung faintly to Victoria's coat as she stepped into Holmes's sitting room, a bundle of papers tucked beneath her arm. Sunlight sliced across the floor in golden stripes, illuminating particles in the air and the usual clutter of experiments and correspondence on every available surface.

Holmes was seated cross-legged on the settee, a sheaf of papers in one hand, his breakfast largely untouched on the nearby tray. Watson had arrived earlier, eager to learn of any new clues for the case.

"You're early," Holmes said without looking up. "I assume that means something interesting has happened."

"I've brought something I think you'll want to see," Victoria replied, closing the door behind her.

Watson turned, eyebrows raised. "Trouble at the theater?"

"Not exactly trouble," she said, settling into the chair opposite Holmes. "But something I found puzzling, and given recent developments, I thought you both should have a look."

Holmes set aside his reading and extended a hand. Victoria passed him a folder containing several typed pages, neatly organized, each listing a task completed that week at the theater, along with the initials *S.L.* typed at the bottom.

"Mr. Lawson prepared these," she explained. "I've asked him to keep detailed logs of our progress for budgeting and oversight. He brought these to me this morning."

Holmes examined the pages in silence. The lines were crisply formatted with each bullet point organized with almost obsessive precision.

But his eyes paused at the third line of the second page. A small tilt in the "s."

He leaned forward, glass in hand, and scanned the same word again on the fourth page. Then the fifth. And there it was—slight, consistent, unmistakable.

Watson noticed his shift in posture. "What is it?"

"The same imperfections," Holmes said slowly. "This 's'—here, and here—it rises ever so slightly above the baseline. The exact same flaw we've observed in the letters received by the medical journals and in the note Victoria received."

He laid the paper gently on the table, as though it had suddenly grown heavier.

Victoria stared at the pages. "But surely that can't mean—these are routine task lists. Who would bother tampering with them?"

Holmes didn't answer at once. Instead, he leaned back, eyes narrowing as the implications arranged themselves in his mind like chess pieces.

Watson folded his arms. "You're not suggesting Lawson—"

"I'm suggesting that the typewriter responsible for the anonymous letters is now in use inside your theater," Holmes replied, his voice clipped with certainty.

Victoria drew in a sharp breath. "You think Lawson is the one who wrote them?"

"I think," Holmes said carefully, "that the same machine was used. And given what we know of Trask—his attention to detail, his tendency to use others as instruments—it is no great leap to suppose that he might use a different name in each setting."

Watson stepped forward, taking the pages from the table and reviewing them with a physician's trained eye for patterns. "He's inserted himself into her world."

Holmes's eyes met Watson's. "That theater is the perfect environment for someone like him. Constant motion. Dozens of workers. A chain of command just loose enough for someone to hide in plain sight."

Victoria drew her coat closer around her. "He's right in front of us."

"And you're his employer," Holmes said grimly.

A long silence followed. The tick of the mantel clock sounded unusually loud.

Watson finally broke it. "We can't act too soon. But if he is Trask and if we confront him now, we lose the chance to find the typewriter. And any evidence tying him to the letters."

Holmes looked at Victoria. "Have you noticed any changes in his behavior? Has he asked for access to storage areas? Changed how he reports to you?"

"No," she said. "He's been steady. Almost disarmingly so. He seems completely in control."

Holmes gave a humorless smile. "That's precisely what worries me."

"Out of all the places he could hide, why the London Majestic?" Victoria asked as she folded her arms.

"You are Dr. Watson's daughter," Holmes said lightly. "If he knows that I am on the Stamford case, which I'm sure he must, you and your theater renovation would be a perfect place for him to cause a distraction to my investigation. My fondness for your father is no secret."

A knock came at the door, followed by the soft shuffle of Mrs. Hudson's footsteps. She entered a moment later with a tray and a sunny smile. "Tea, as promised. And I've brought a bit of scone. You've all been looking far too serious this morning."

"Thank you, Mrs. Hudson," Victoria said, her voice a touch more strained than usual.

Once she'd left, Holmes poured tea for each of them and stirred his with practiced absentmindedness. "We'll need to move carefully. The game is underway, but we don't yet know all the players."

Victoria looked down at the typed list, her own handwriting scrawled in the margins—quick calculations, adjustments, budget notes.

"He's making himself indispensable," she said softly. "And I welcomed it. I was so pleased to see it all coming together."

"Don't blame yourself," Watson said gently. "You weren't meant to suspect anything. That's the brilliance of it."

Holmes rose and began pacing, one hand behind his back, the other toying with a pencil. "Until we gather more proof, we continue as we are. Victoria, you must keep acting as though nothing is amiss. Allow him to keep revealing himself."

She swallowed hard. "You're asking me to work alongside him. To pretend everything is normal."

Holmes looked at her, his expression unflinching. "Only until we can prove who he truly is. And ensure he can't slip away again."

Watson reached for her hand. "You won't face this alone."

Her gaze softened, "I know."

As tea was sipped in silence, Holmes stood once more by the window, his eyes distant.

"Let's hope he underestimates us," he murmured. "Because I do not intend to underestimate him again."

The low murmur of constables and the sharp clatter of typewriter keys filled the air as Sherlock Holmes stepped through the double doors of New Scotland Yard. Though the building was newly opened, the atmosphere already seemed familiar: the faint scent of damp wool and ink was clinging to every surface. Holmes navigated the corridors with long, purposeful strides.

Inspector Lestrade was seated at his desk, a half-eaten meat pie balanced on a stack of reports, spectacles perched low on his nose. He glanced up and groaned theatrically.

"If it isn't the great Sherlock Holmes. Come to tell me I've missed something obvious, have you?"

Holmes offered a cool smile. "Not at all, Lestrade. I'm here to comb through the details you've already collected. I find that what is labeled redundant often proves otherwise."

Lestrade grunted, "You're here about the Stamford case, I take it."

"I am," Holmes confirmed. "I'd like to see any documentation not previously reviewed with urgency. Background material. Peripheral statements. Addenda. Anything you dismissed as irrelevant at the time."

Lestrade gave him a long look. "You mean the rubbish."

"Precisely."

The inspector sighed, rising from his chair with an exaggerated stretch. "You'll be the death of me, Mr. Holmes. Come on, then."

He led Holmes to a back room lined with filing cabinets, the air mustier than the main offices. After some rifling, Lestrade drew out a slim brown folder and handed it over.

"That's all we've got marked 'miscellaneous' under Stamford. A few statements that trickled in late, and some correspondence. I'm not sure you'll find much."

Holmes accepted the file and moved to a table by the window, flipping it open with practiced fingers. For a few moments, silence reigned, punctuated only by Lestrade's grumbling as he returned to his desk and resumed his lunch.

Several pages in, Holmes paused. His eyes narrowed.

A single sheet of typing paper, folded twice, had been inserted between a witness summary and a dated memorandum. The sheet bore no official heading—just a brief statement in blocky type:

To whom it may concern:
I, Anne Godfrey, wish to clarify my memory of the events of the evening in question.
I distinctly recall Dr. Stamford reaching into his inner pocket and producing a small vial.
He uncorked it and tipped the contents into the wine glass of the Honourable Lord Mornay.
The act was subtle, but I am certain of what I saw.
I was standing in the hallway, and the dining room door was fully open at the time.
I regret that I cannot speak of this further in person. The experience has been most distressing.

The signature line simply read:
Anne Godfrey (written statement)

Holmes tilted the page toward the light.

There it was.

The same telltale irregularities—the slightly elevated "s," the faint skewing of the last line. Even the spacing between certain letters echoed the anonymous letters he'd already cataloged. Holmes let out a slow breath.

Gathering the file, he hurried down the hall to the office. "Lestrade, who submitted this?"

The inspector peered over the file from across the room. "That one? It was dropped off at the front desk a few days after our formal interviews. Came in an envelope with her name on it and a note from someone saying she'd written it at home and didn't want to appear again."

"Who delivered it?"

"No name was left. The clerk said it was a man in a bowler hat and said it was from the maid, and she hoped it would help 'resolve things.'"

Holmes closed the folder gently.

"She didn't write this," he said.

Lestrade raised an eyebrow. "What makes you so sure?"

"Because I've seen the same typeface in four different documents, including one that turned up in my flat yesterday. The odds of that being coincidence are infinitesimal."

He rose, the paper still in hand. "This was not a clarification of memory. It was reinforcement. An effort to anchor her faulty testimony more deeply in your case file."

Lestrade scratched his head. "You think someone's rewriting the facts?"

"No," Holmes said. "I think someone is scripting the narrative. One piece at a time."

He handed the paper back to Lestrade. "Keep this safe. I'll want to cross-reference it with the rest shortly."

"Mr. Holmes," Lestrade said as the detective moved towards the door, "if someone's planting statements in a case like this, it means they want Stamford gone badly enough to risk interfering with police records."

Holmes paused. "Yes," he said quietly. "And we've only just begun to understand how far they're willing to go."

Holmes sat in his armchair with the pages of the new theater task list spread across his lap like a forensic puzzle. His fingers moved lightly over the typewritten text—not reading, but scanning, interpreting, and measuring. The room was quiet save for the faint tick of the mantel clock and the scratch of Watson's pen, as he took down a few notes beside Victoria on the settee.

"You're certain this came from your manager?" Holmes asked, still not looking up.

Her voice low, Victoria said, "He left it in my office this morning. It was paperclipped to a work order. I didn't think anything of it at the time."

Holmes hummed thoughtfully, lifting the sheet toward the light.

Watson peered over. "It looks like an ordinary list to me."

"To the untrained eye, yes," Holmes said. "But observe the third line from the bottom. See how the 's' in 'inspections' is slightly elevated? And again here— 'supplies,' fourth item down. Do you see the similarities to the anonymous letters?"

Victoria's fingers clenched together in her lap. "You're saying the same machine was used?"

"Yes," Holmes replied simply. "The same machine—or at least the same broken element. The odds of that flaw appearing by chance in multiple typewriters, and all within this case, are astronomical."

She leaned forward, her eyes searching his face. "Could it be coincidence? Mr. Lawson used a secondhand typewriter with the same defect?"

He paused, carefully folding the list. "It's possible. But unlikely."

Watson leaned back, arms crossed. "What are we saying then—that Lawson is Trask in disguise?"

Holmes didn't answer immediately. He placed the paper on the table, then opened a leather folio from beneath his chair. From it he withdrew two other sheets—one from the Stamford letters, the other the warning note Victoria had received.

He laid them side by side with the task list.

They all shared the same spacing, the same faint tilt in the "e" and the same raised "s."

Victoria's face had gone pale. "I can't believe I've been working beside him every day. Speaking with him and trusting him."

Holmes finally looked at her. "Then we must consider all possibilities. Three, in fact."

He raised one finger. "First – Lawson is Trask. He has altered his appearance or concealed his identity just enough to operate unnoticed. His goal is long-term access, both to you and to the theater."

A second finger. "Second – Lawson is a real person but unknowingly working under Trask's influence. Perhaps someone else on the crew passes these lists through him, forging his name."

"Or third," Holmes finally said, "Lawson is innocent, and this is a calculated ruse—a false lead meant to divide our attention and make us question the wrong man."

Watson took a deep breath. "That last one seems far-fetched. Too many matching details."

"True," Holmes said, "but we must remain open to the improbable as long as it remains unproven. Certainty has derailed many an investigation."

Victoria stood, walking slowly toward the hearth. Her voice was barely above a whisper. "You warned me once not to trust too easily. I didn't listen."

Holmes stood as well, his tone gentler. "You had no reason to doubt him. No one would have."

"But you did," she said, turning to face him.

He hesitated. "Let's say I was… watchful. That is my profession, after all."

Victoria turned from the fire with her eyes still fixed on the papers Holmes had laid out. "But I still don't understand something."

Holmes looked at her, waiting.

"Why me?" she asked, voice edged with frustration and confusion. "Why would Trask target *me*? I've nothing to do with the Stamford case. I didn't even know it existed until you and Father brought it up. What could he possibly want from me?"

Holmes was silent for a beat. Even Watson, who had been pacing lightly, stilled.

Holmes moved back toward the table, resting one hand lightly on the edge of it. "That," he said quietly, "is precisely what I've been asking myself."

Victoria seemed slightly disappointed. "So, you *don't* know."

"I have theories," Holmes allowed, his tone measured.

Watson watched him closely now. "Let's hear them."

Holmes didn't answer immediately. He turned his attention to Victoria, as though weighing how much truth she could—or should—hear.

"Miss Watson," he said at last, "your involvement may be incidental, or it may be by design. You are visible. Intelligent. Resourceful. A woman restoring a prominent theater draws notice. Especially when her name is attached to mine, albeit through her father."

"You think this is about *you?*" she asked, startled.

"I think Trask is a man who values control above all," Holmes replied. "Control of narrative. Control of evidence. Control of space. And if he believes I have reason to be attached to your success, or your safety—"

Victoria's eyes widened. "Then he's using me."

Holmes inclined his head. "To distract. To unsettle. Perhaps even to punish."

Watson's jaw tightened. "That's a dangerous assumption."

"It's not an assumption," Holmes said softly. "It's a risk."

Victoria turned slowly back to the hearth, the light dancing across her face. "So, I'm a pawn."

Holmes moved closer. "No. You're a player on the board, and he miscalculated. He sees your theater as a structure to infiltrate. What he does *not* see—yet—is that you are not easily manipulated."

A faint smile tugged at her lips. "Flattery, Mr. Holmes?"

"Strategy," he said with a glint of something unreadable.

She quietly laughed. "I'm an actress, I'll act the part until we know more."

Watson looked between them, his concern still etched deep. "But if he's embedded already, if he's watching, you'll both be in danger."

Holmes gave a faint shrug. "So be it. None of us has ever been promised safety."

Victoria looked down at the three typed pages once more—the letters, the warning, the task lists. Her fingers hovered over them, not touching, as though they might burn her skin.

"I'll play along," she said at last. "But I won't be blind again."

Holmes watched her for a moment—this young woman standing at the edge of something vast and dangerous.

"Good," he said, "because the curtain is rising."

Holmes stood by the front window of 221B Baker Street, arms folded behind his back, eyes fixed on the street below. Victoria's silhouette had long since vanished into the bustle of London, yet he remained motionless, as though still tracking her with some invisible thread. A chill draft crept through the sash, ruffling the curtain's edge. He didn't flinch.

Watson sat nearby, the ledger he'd been updating now closed in his lap, eyes studying his friend. Holmes had said little since Victoria left, but Watson recognized the tension behind that stillness. There was the coiling energy of a mind turning over something large and complex.

A pause hung between them before Watson broke it gently.

"Do you truly believe she's in danger?"

Holmes didn't speak at once. His eyes narrowed as a passing hansom cab clattered over the cobblestones below. "Yes," he said at last, quiet and certain.

Watson leaned forward slightly. "Then perhaps she should be told. More directly, I mean."

Holmes turned from the window, his expression unreadable. "Not yet. If she believes she is simply helping us observe a suspicious employee, she will remain composed and her behavior unaltered. People don't stumble into traps when they believe they're on solid ground."

"And she's not being hunted?" Watson asked.

"She's being watched," Holmes corrected. "But not without her own sentinels."

Watson's brow lifted. "You've placed her under protection?"

A hint of a smile touched Holmes' lips. "Of a sort. The theater and the street between her flat and the work site are under the quiet observation of my Irregulars."

"The Baker Street Irregulars?" Watson's tone held both surprise and approval. "That's rather brilliant, Holmes. Trask might see them and never think a thing of it."

"They are easily forgotten," Holmes said, almost fondly. "Bootblacks, match-sellers, newsboys, and chimney sweeps. Street children who move through the city like ghosts—unseen, but never blind. They're my eyes where Scotland Yard cannot go."

Watson exhaled with relieved. "So, you set this in motion before we even knew how serious things had become."

"I had my suspicions the moment Trask's name surfaced. Once Victoria took over the theater, it seemed prudent to ensure someone was watching him… and her."

Watson glanced toward the desk, where three pieces of paper lay side by side—two anonymous letters and the task lists from Lawson.

"He's weaving quite the play," Watson murmured, then added with a frown, "But if Trask didn't want to raise suspicion, why use the same typewriter to send Victoria the warning? That flaw in the 's' could be traced."

Holmes moved toward the desk with the evidence in view.

"He needed her to believe the warning. And by making the letter match the others—whether consciously or not—he created a subconscious link. A sense of credibility. She wouldn't notice the flaw. But I would."

Watson huffed softly. "So, it wasn't sloppy. It was calculated."

"As always." Holmes murmured. "Now we enter Act Two."

Holmes reached for a folded sheet from the corner of his desk—one he'd scrawled on days earlier. Across the top it read: *Sequence of Influence.*

He smoothed the page, eyes scanning the familiar list: Trask dismissed. Anonymous letters begin. Dinner arranged. Anne inserted into the household. Chambers removed. Poison administered. Stamford accused.

But now, with new information pressing against the margins, he uncapped his pen and began to draw.

Arrows arced from Trask's name to Anne and Chambers. A sharp black line sliced from Easton Works to Anne's cousin. Another curved— almost reluctantly—toward the theater. Toward Victoria.

He paused, studying the web he'd created. The pattern was emerging, not in the events alone, but in the people Trask had touched... and the ones he intended to use.

"She isn't a loose end," Holmes said, more to himself than Watson. "She's a lever. Something Trask believes he can manipulate to move the rest of us."

Watson studied the diagram with deepening concern. "Her name in the papers. Her proximity to you. Her reputation as a woman of sense and principle. All of that makes her an ideal target."

"And because he thinks I care for her," Holmes said softly, "he believes she is a way to get to me."

Watson looked up sharply. "He's not wrong."

Holmes didn't answer. His gaze remained fixed on the paper.

Watson changed the subject gently. "You're planning to visit Easton Works?"

"There are still traces of him there, I'm sure. If nothing else, someone may remember a quiet man with a chemist's precision and a talent for managing systems. It would explain how Trask built such authority at the theater if he applied the same order and discipline he once used in the laboratory and his former position."

"I'll start digging into the agency that placed Anne Godfrey," Watson offered. "There's no chance she ended up in that household by coincidence."

Holmes gave an approving nod. "Good. But we must assume he's listening now. We communicate only here—or by cipher. No messengers. No wires."

Watson agreed with a solemn, "Understood."

Holmes folded the letters and tucked them into a leather folder, his movements slow and deliberate. He ran a hand through his hair.

"It's growing more difficult to remain objective," he admitted.

"You don't have to be a machine," Watson said gently. "She's not just a client. She's my daughter and is very special. And perhaps to you, as well."

Holmes said nothing, but the silence was not disagreement.

As Watson helped gather up the notes, he moved towards the window, intending to latch it against the evening chill. He paused.

Across the street he noticed a flicker of movement. A shape too still for coincidence was lingering near a lamppost and then gone, vanishing behind the edge of a newspaper stand.

Watson stiffened. "Holmes—"

"I saw him," Holmes said, without looking.

"We're being watched."

Holmes's reply was calm. "Let him watch. It means we're close."

The sun had dipped low behind the slate rooftops of London, casting elongated shadows across the floorboards of the old theater. Gaslights flickered to life along the walls as Victoria opened her office door, their amber glow made the dust motes dance like restless spirits.

She had returned alone, hoping to finish some paperwork before the next day's construction review. The air inside still smelled faintly of plaster and varnish—a mix of progress and decay. This should have been one of the happiest times in her life. Progress was being made so rapidly that soon she would be able to move her focus from repairs to rehearsals. But her joy was overshadowed by something darker.

As she entered the tidy room, her eyes were immediately drawn to something resting atop the blotter on her desk—a sheet of paper. Not tucked discreetly into her ledger this time. This one had been left deliberately, almost brazenly, centered in plain sight.

She closed the door behind her and crossed the room. The note was typed.

"He's in the walls.
Wearing a mask.
Do not let him inside your life."

Victoria stared at the message, her breath catching.

This wasn't a vague warning like the first. It was theatrical, almost poetic, but chilling in its clarity. Someone had not only invaded her workspace, but had done so again, after feeling ignored the first time.

Behind her, a soft knock on the inner office door startled her. She turned quickly, instinctively shielding the note behind a folder.

Daisy peeked her head in, cheeks pink from the cool night air. "You're still here? I thought you went home hours ago."

"I needed to finish some scheduling," Victoria said smoothly, sliding the warning note into her bag. "What about you?"

"Just came to fetch my gloves. I left them near the stage. Mr. Lawson is taking me to dinner tomorrow night." She grinned, unbothered by Victoria's startled expression. "He's quite the gentleman, isn't he?"

Victoria felt a flicker of cold bloom beneath her ribs. Her stomach tightened, though she kept her voice even. "Is he now? I didn't realize you two were spending time together."

Daisy shrugged with a playful smile. "He asked a few days ago, but we had to wait until he wasn't needed here late. He said we might try that little bistro near the Strand."

Victoria managed a nod. "That sounds lovely."

She masked her concern, but her mind was already racing. Of course, Lawson would charm Daisy. She was warm, trusting, and cheerfully talkative. If he wanted to get close—to observe, to infiltrate—there were few better entry points than a loyal assistant.

"Can I bring you anything? A cocoa or something?" Daisy asked.

"No, thank you. I'll just be a few more minutes."

Daisy hesitated, tilting her head. "Are you sure you're all right? You look pale."

"Fine," Victoria said with a smile that didn't reach her eyes. "I'm just tired."

"All right. Don't stay too late."

As the door shut again, Victoria's composure cracked. She turned back to her desk and let out a slow breath, her fingers trembling slightly as she pulled open her organizer to look for any sign of tampering.

Instead, she found something else.

A single sheet, neatly typed, resting atop a folder labeled *Scheduled Tasks*.

It was a task list.

Lawson's handwriting, she now realized, had never appeared on anything. The notes always came typed and this one was no exception.

Secure scaffolding for proscenium arch. Re-check basement clearance. Coordinate timber delivery for the mezzanine frame. Order fresh fittings for the balcony braces.

At first glance, it looked perfectly ordinary, methodical, and professional.

But Holmes' words echoed in her mind: *"The 's' in 'supplies'; it rises slightly above the line. See it?"*

Victoria blinked. Her eyes drifted to the final line of the list: *Tidy paint supplies near west wall.*

There it was. A high "s." Just slightly off-kilter.

The flaw she hadn't known to look for before but now couldn't unsee.

Her pulse quickened.

Was it really possible? That the same man who had been so kind, so efficient and knowledgeable was the same one sending her these warnings? Or worse, orchestrating everything Holmes feared?

She ran her fingers along the page barely touching it, as if expecting it to burn her. And perhaps it had, just not the skin. Her trust. Her instincts.

Quietly, deliberately, she folded the list and placed it inside her satchel alongside the ominous note. Then she took one last look around the office, checked the lock on her desk drawers, and slipped out of the theater.

She did not take a carriage.

She walked, coat pulled tight against the wind, the city lights shimmering along the wet pavement. She needed to think, but her destination was clear.

There were too many questions now—and only one man in London who might hold the answers.

The clink of keys and the metallic grind of the cell door sliding open echoed through the narrow corridor of the prison. The air was thick with the scent of damp stone and stale straw. Dr. John Watson followed the constable silently, his cane tapping lightly along the uneven floor. It had been years since he'd walked this path in any capacity other than as a physician. Today, however, he came as a friend, though one with more questions than reassurances.

The guard gestured toward a cell halfway down the row. "He's in there, sir. Be brief."

Watson thanked him, adjusting his collar as he stepped forward.

Stamford sat on the edge of the cot, shoulders hunched, elbows on knees, and hands clasped as though in prayer. His once-neat hair hung in disarray over tired eyes, and his face, always so composed, was now pale and drawn.

"John," he said hoarsely, rising to his feet. "I wasn't expecting—well, I suppose no one expects visitors under these circumstances."

Watson offered a sad smile. "You look like hell."

"I feel worse." Stamford managed a dry chuckle, then gestured to the narrow bench attached to the wall. "Please."

Watson sat, the two men eyeing each other in silence for a beat.

"Inspector Lestrade thinks he has enough to convict me," Stamford said flatly. "Testimony, statements, a chain of events that all seem to lead straight to me. But it's all wrong, John. I didn't poison anyone."

"I believe you," Watson said gently. "Holmes does, too."

Stamford gave a faint snort. "Well, that's something."

Watson folded his hands. "We've uncovered quite a bit since your arrest. Trask's name surfaced again linked to several events surrounding the dinner and the anonymous letters sent to the medical journals. Holmes believes Trask orchestrated it all from the shadows. He's already proven the letters were typed on the same machine—one now connected to a manager at Victoria's theater."

Stamford's eyes narrowed. "He's still at large?"

"For now," Watson said. "But the noose is tightening."

Stamford leaned back against the wall, eyes distant. "Trask. Yes, a quiet fellow. Meticulous. Smart. Odd habits. He washed his hands constantly, even when they were clean. He worked in the dispensary for a time."

"You dismissed him?"

"In a way. He resented oversight—especially mine. His involvement in some architectural planning proved possibly dangerous, and I made the fact known. He left without incident, but..." Stamford's brow furrowed. "He said something, just before he went."

Watson leaned in slightly. "What was it?"

Stamford spoke slowly, as if unearthing the words from memory. "He said, 'You've taken something from me. One day, I'll return the favor. Not with a knife or a vial, but by ruining what you treasure.'"

Watson's jaw tensed. "Did you feel that it was a true threat?"

"I thought it was nonsense," Stamford admitted. "Melodrama. I barely remembered it until I was arrested. Now I'm thinking of all the people I care about—Chambers. You. Holmes. And now... your daughter."

Watson's expression darkened.

"I'm so sorry she's been drawn into this, John," Stamford went on. "I know she wasn't at the dinner, but that hardly matters. If she's been pulled into this web, I can't help but wonder if it's because of her connection to you and Holmes."

"Holmes thinks she's being used as leverage," Watson said. "We're watching her closely. But it's getting more complicated."

Stamford sat forward again, his voice lower. "Then let me help. I'll speak with Holmes. Tell him everything I can remember about Trask—his habits, his tendencies. Anything that might be useful."

"Would you be willing to testify?" Watson asked. "Publicly, if it comes to that?"

Stamford hesitated only a moment. "If it protects my loved ones and yours? Yes, without question."

Watson stood, his expression softening. "Thank you, Stamford and take heart. Holmes is doing his best."

Stamford rose as well. "Tell her I'm sorry. I didn't know this would happen. I'm horrified that she is involved." He gave a wistful smile. "She was an adorable child. I can't help but still picture her that way."

"As do I sometimes," Watson said, his voice quiet. "I'll tell her."

The constable returned to unlock the door. As it opened with a dull clang, Stamford gave a small nod.

"Tell Holmes I'm ready," he said. "If he's staging a confrontation, I want a part in it."

Watson paused at the threshold, eyes meeting his friend's one last time.

"Then prepare yourself," he said quietly. "Because the curtain's about to rise."

The fire in the Baker Street hearth crackled with low, steady warmth, casting shifting light across the sitting room's worn carpet and the shadows along the walls. Victoria sat nearest the flame, her hands clasped tightly in her lap, posture straight but unmistakably strained. She had said little, though Watson, seated across from her, had tried gently to ease the silence.

The front door creaked open below, followed by the distinct rhythm of Holmes's steps on the stairs. A moment later, he entered, his greatcoat draped in fog moisture, his hair tousled from the wind.

"You're late," Watson said mildly.

"There was much to be done," Holmes replied, unfastening his coat. His eyes moved to Victoria immediately. "Miss Watson."

She returned the quiet greeting. "Mr. Holmes."

Watson nodded grimly. "While you were away, I visited Stamford in prison. He's frayed but willing to help. Trask once made veiled threats and said he would 'ruin what you treasure.' Stamford didn't think it literal. Not until now."

Holmes absorbed this with a grim look but said nothing.

Victoria shifted slightly. "I found something too."

She reached into her bag and withdrew two pages, placing them carefully on the small table beside Holmes's armchair. "Another list and another note."

Holmes picked up the latter first and read the typed message aloud, his voice flat but grave.

He's in the walls.
Wearing a mask.
Do not let him inside your life.

Watson exhaled slowly. "He's not even pretending anymore."

Holmes examined the task list next, using his magnifying glass. "The same raised 's,'" he confirmed. "Same uneven spacing between characters. He's embedding himself not only in your workspace, Miss Watson, but in your mind. With every letter, every suggestion. It's a calculated erosion."

"Is it possible," Victoria said with her voice quieter than before, "that the warning was meant to frighten me away from you?"

She did not look at him as she asked it, pretending instead to study the fire. Watson looked over but said nothing.

Holmes considered the note again. "It's plausible. Trask is theatrical by nature. His flair for symbolism suggests a desire not merely to threaten but to manipulate. He may see your connection to me as an avenue of influence. And if he cannot drive a wedge with fear, he will try confusion, doubt, or isolation."

Victoria finally met his eyes. "It worked before."

Holmes stepped closer, voice lower now. "Then let it stop here. Doubt the source before you doubt your instincts."

Her smile was faint, touched with irony. "I can pretend not to be frightened until I figure out whether I should be."

Watson stood and moved to the mantel. "Let me walk you across the hall to your flat, my girl. I will check and make sure all is well."

She hesitated, then approved. "Yes. That's probably best."

Holmes moved to the window. Outside, the fog curled in silver spirals beneath the gas lamps, swallowing the city inch by inch.

He watched for a long moment, then spoke to himself. "He's maneuvering us into place... but the more desperate the stagecraft, the more desperate the actor behind it."

The early morning fog clung to the brick façades and narrow alleys of London's East End, muting the clang of distant trolleys and the shouts of vendors setting up their stalls. Sherlock Holmes stood before the soot-streaked gates of Easton Works, collar turned up, a leather folio tucked under one arm. A brass plaque beside the door declared *"Easton Works Industrial Supply – Established 1859."* The letters were dulled with age.

Holmes pressed the bell, adopting the quiet, self-assured bearing of a government auditor. He had forged similar roles before—ministry liaisons, fire-safety assessors, legal observers—whatever the task required. Today, he was "Mr. Gregory Whitson" of the Board of Industrial Supply and Oversight.

An older man opened the side door with shoulders hunched beneath a brown wool coat. "Yes?"

Holmes produced a small card. "I am Mr. Whitson, here to conduct a procedural audit on temporary hires and supply transitions over the last two years. Nothing disruptive; just a review of logs and staff interviews."

The man squinted at the card and grunted. "You'll want Mr. Portman. He's shift supervisor."

He led Holmes through dim hallways of chipped paint and oil-slicked floors until they reached a small office, cluttered with ledgers and a dented kettle. Portman, a balding man with ink-stained fingers, eyed Holmes suspiciously but waved him in.

"You've picked a strange time to audit us," he muttered, motioning toward the backlog of invoices. "What exactly are you looking for?"

Holmes kept his tone mild. "Temporary chemists, builders, or supply clerks hired under short contracts. One of our records flagged a gap in documentation here and suggests a brief placement we'd like to clarify. Possibly under an alias."

Portman scratched his head. "Short contracts – we've had a few. They were usually university fellows earning coin between terms. One chap— quiet, private—joined on a three-week commission about a year ago."

Holmes perked up. "Do you recall his name?"

Portman frowned. "Went by Mr. Blythe, I believe. He's a thin man with dark hair. Bit of a strange duck—kept to himself mostly, but made suggestions about reorganizing storage, mapping access routes, that sort of thing. Nothing improper, just more interest than usual."

"Did he interact much with other staff?"

"Hardly spoke to anyone—except a delivery runner."

"Do you happen to remember his name?"

"Hmm. I think it was Godfrey. Yes, Edward Godfrey. He was short contract and worked part-time hauling crates."

Holmes glanced at the book in front of him. "May I view the employment ledger for that quarter?"

Portman retrieved a cracked binder from a lower shelf and handed it over. Holmes flipped through, noting exact dates, names, job titles. At week twelve, there was a gap—a number skipped in sequence. Between two names, no entry. No initial. No salary noted. Just a blank space with an indent, as though something had been erased or never recorded.

Holmes tapped the page. "This position. Was that Mr. Blythe's?"

Portman leaned over, squinting. "Now that you say it, yes. Strange, that. It should have been filled out. Likely a clerical error."

Holmes said nothing. His mind was already moving.

The alias *Blythe*. The interest in access points. The connection with a former employee who turned out to be Anne Godfrey's cousin. Trask had used Easton Works to test systems and gather recruits. And now, his play had moved to a far more visible stage.

"Thank you," Holmes said briskly, closing the ledger. "That will be all. I won't trouble you further."

He shook Portman's hand and made his way back through the maze of corridors. Outside, the fog had thinned, and morning foot traffic bustled along the pavement.

He turned west, toward Baker Street.

But halfway down the block, he felt it—a flicker of movement behind him. A pause in the rhythm of footfalls. He glanced into a window, catching the reflection of a man in a heavy coat lingering behind a newsstand. His face was obscured by a folded paper, but the angle of his stance was wrong—too still, too focused.

Holmes did not stop. He did not look back again. But his gait quickened, and his mind sharpened. They were not just being watched. They were being studied.

The gaslights outside the modest dining hall on Berwick Street spilled their glow in trembling halos, casting long fingers of light across the cobbled pavement. Inside, the room was cozy but unremarkable with white linens, polished cutlery, and a low murmur of conversation from other tables. Daisy adjusted her shawl and offered a bright smile to the man seated across from her.

Samuel Lawson had chosen the place—"a quiet spot away from the dust and din of the theater," he'd said, and Daisy had been flattered by the invitation. She hadn't expected it, though she'd found him kind and attentive during his time managing the restoration. Still, now that they were seated and the first course was being cleared, a subtle discomfort had begun to settle in her chest.

He was charming, certainly—well-spoken and polite—but distant. He asked about her family, her hopes for the theater, even her opinions on gaslight placement in the auditorium. Yet when she gently turned the conversation towards him—his former projects, where he'd trained, even where he had grown up—his answers became vague.

"Have you always worked in London?" she asked, stirring her tea absentmindedly.

Lawson smiled faintly. "Here and there. I follow the work. Buildings needing a touch of discipline, you might say."

"But you seem so familiar with this neighborhood. The side streets, even the history of the theater. Did you ever live nearby?"

His pause was just a second too long. "I've always had an interest in historical properties."

Daisy acted interested, trying to smooth the awkwardness with a sip of her tea. Still, the prickling sensation at the back of her neck remained.

He leaned forward slightly. "You spend a good deal of time with Miss Watson, don't you?"

The shift in topic startled her. "Well, yes, I suppose. I assist her. We're friends."

"She's quite capable," he said with a neutral tone, though his eyes gleamed with interest. "A remarkable woman. And her ties to Mr. Holmes must make life... eventful."

Daisy tilted her head, watching him carefully now. "I don't recall how you came to be recommended for the position. Did someone refer you?"

"Recommendations can be manufactured," he said with a chuckle. "What matters is whether I'm doing the job well, wouldn't you agree?"

It was meant to be disarming. But to Daisy, it felt like a deflection. She tucked her hands into her lap and offered a pleasant enough smile, though the meal had lost its flavor.

When the waiter returned with the bill, Lawson reached for it promptly. Turning to Daisy he said, "You've been very helpful during the transition."

Daisy's smile dimmed. Helpful. Not lovely. Not interesting. Just helpful.

As they stepped back into the cold night, Lawson offered his hand to help her into the carriage.

"Thank you for dinner," she said with a manufactured smile. "I think I'll walk."

He glanced sideways. "Are you sure? I can see you home."

"No, truly. It's not far."

He hesitated, only briefly, then tipped his hat. "Very well. Goodnight, Miss Dawn."

She turned and walked briskly into the night, her heart beating just a touch faster.

Behind her, the street was empty.

But she didn't look back

The fire in Holmes's sitting room had burned low, casting long shadows that flickered across the cluttered shelves and framed newspaper clippings on the wall. Victoria sat in Holmes's armchair, a blanket across her knees and a half-finished cup of tea in her hands. Her mind had calmed, and she planned to go to her flat as soon as she finished her tea. Holmes, stood by the window as usual, peering into the fog thinking.

A sudden knock at the downstairs door startled them both. Moments later, hurried footsteps echoed on the stairs. Mrs. Hudson's voice called up, "Miss Watson, Miss Daisy is here. She insists it's urgent!"

Before Victoria could rise, Daisy burst into the room, breathless, cheeks flushed with cold and something else—fear.

"Daisy!" Victoria stood quickly, setting her cup aside. "What is it?"

Daisy shut the door behind her and leaned against it for a moment before finding her voice. "It's Mr. Lawson. I—I had dinner with him tonight, and I haven't been able to stop thinking about it."

Victoria's brow furrowed. "What happened?"

"At first, he was charming, polite, even funny." Daisy walked to the fire, rubbing her gloved hands together. "But when I asked about where he worked before coming to London, or where he'd trained, he dodged every question. Changed the subject, gave vague answers. And he kept talking about you, Victoria. Over and over again. Asking how well you knew Mr. Holmes. If the two of you were close."

Victoria cast a quick glance at Holmes. His posture had subtly shifted. Alert. Listening.

Daisy shook her head. "It just felt... wrong. He's too interested in things that don't concern a theater manager. I know it sounds foolish, but—"

"It doesn't," Victoria said gently. "Come sit down."

Daisy hesitated, then took the settee beside Victoria. Her shoulders were tense, her mouth tight with worry. Holmes remained silent, his gaze fixed on them both.

Victoria placed her hand over Daisy's. "There's something you need to know. Something I should have told you sooner."

Daisy's eyes widened, but she didn't pull away.

"She deserves to know," Victoria continued, looking directly at Holmes. "She's loyal and she's already involved, whether we like it or not."

Holmes inclined his head, his expression unreadable. "Agreed."

He moved closer, his voice quiet but precise. "The man calling himself Lawson is in truth someone else entirely—a man named Trask. He's operating under a false identity and has a history of deceit and revenge. We believe he's responsible for framing someone close to us for a serious crime."

Daisy's lips parted slightly, stunned.

Holmes went on, "He's manipulated others through forged letters, falsified records, and planted documents. Recently, he's embedded himself in Victoria's theater under the guise of assisting with renovations. But in truth, he's executing a scheme—one that may very well center on Miss Watson herself."

"But why?" Daisy asked, breath catching. "Victoria hasn't done anything to him."

"Precisely," Holmes said. "Which is why her involvement is so dangerous. She may be a pawn… or the lever he intends to use to move larger pieces."

For a moment, silence stretched between them.

Then Daisy straightened her shoulders. "If someone's threatening you," she said to Victoria, "I want to help stop him."

Victoria gave a sad smile. "You always did have more courage than sense."

Daisy shook her head. "No, just enough of both."

Holmes studied her, weighing something in his mind. "We need information. Quietly gathered. If Lawson speaks again of your dinner—if he asks more questions, changes his habits, becomes careless—we need to know. But he cannot suspect that you know who he truly is."

"I understand," Daisy said. "I'll be careful."

"You'll do more than that," Victoria said firmly. "You'll stay with me tonight. No arguments."

Daisy looked grateful. "Good. I didn't want to go home alone."

She stood and pulled Victoria into a fierce hug. "Don't you dare try to keep me out of this now."

Then she turned to Holmes, eyes glistening. "And don't you dare let anything happen to her."

Holmes looked surprised by her intensity but bowed his head slightly. "I have no intention of allowing harm to come to Miss Watson," he said. "She has become an important part of... this case."

His eyes met Victoria's briefly. Something unspoken passed between them—acknowledgment, perhaps, or gratitude left unsaid.

With that, Victoria gathered her things, and the two young women exited together, their footsteps light in the hallway as they crossed into the flat opposite.

Holmes remained at the window, watching the gas lamps flicker through the fog.

He murmured to himself, "Courage comes in many forms. Victoria chose her friend well. Daisy may prove invaluable."

The air outside was damp and heavy with fog as Holmes and Victoria approached the theater's rear entrance and the late afternoon sun cast thin halos in the mist. A faint rattle of chains and the groan of a distant wagon filled the air. Holmes held a book closely to himself.

"Are you certain about this?" Victoria asked in a low voice, her gloved hands folded tightly before her.

"If he's hiding something beneath the stage, it's best we find it before he has a chance to remove or destroy it," Holmes replied. "Your invitation for me to inspect the site was perfectly natural. Just remain near me."

They entered through the side door, greeted by "Lawson."

"Mr. Holmes, Miss Watson. I wasn't expecting you."

"I've had a great interest in this restoration," Holmes said easily. "I thought I might take a closer look at the foundation work before the next phase begins."

"Of course," Lawson replied, barely concealing a flicker of unease. "You'll find it's progressing quite efficiently."

He led them down the dim, narrow stairwell into the bowels of the theater. The walls were unfinished, the brick exposed, and the corridor smelled faintly of sawdust and old mildew. Lantern light danced across shadowy stacks of timber and coiled wire.

"This lower area was neglected for years," Lawson said over his shoulder. "We've had to reinforce more than expected. Some of the older walls were bricked over decades ago."

Holmes responded with vague interest, but his eyes never stopped scanning.

"Over here," Lawson continued, unlocking a heavy iron gate. "Substage proper. You'll want to watch your step."

Before they could proceed farther, a voice called from above.

"Mr. Lawson? I need you upstairs—it's urgent!"

All three turned toward the stairwell. Daisy leaned over the rail, her face flushed. "There's a leak—one of the boiler pipes is hissing badly!"

Lawson cursed softly. "Excuse me," he said to Holmes and Victoria. "I'll be right back. Please don't touch anything."

They watched him retreat. The moment his footsteps vanished Victoria turned to Holmes.

"He didn't question it."

"He didn't dare," Holmes murmured, already moving toward the far wall.

Holmes knelt near an unusually smooth section of paneling. "New plaster. Poorly feathered. Too eager to hide."

He tapped twice.

Hollow.

Victoria held the lantern higher as Holmes slid a thin blade between the seams. The panel gave way with a faint pop.

Inside was a small, hidden workspace. Cramped and windowless, it contained a long coat and dust-caked boots, blueprints of the building, and a small chest of labeled vials and gloves.

"A workshop. A nerve center," Holmes murmured.

Victoria swallowed. "He's been working beneath our feet this whole time."

"He's perfected a narrative. One he can control from both above and below."

Holmes quickly photographed the contents. The book he had been carrying was a disguised camera. He replaced everything with clinical care.

The panel slid back into place just as footsteps began echoing from the stairwell.

Trask, smiling once more, descended the steps. "False alarm," he said tightly. "A bit of air in the pipe. All resolved."

Holmes turned with a faint, amused look. "Old buildings are always full of surprises."

"I'll take you towards the north corridor," Trask offered. "We've reinforced the load-bearing beams there. Shall we?"

Holmes inclined his head. "Lead on."

But as they followed him, Victoria cast one last glance behind at the wall. Her heart pounded, not with fear alone, but with the knowledge that they now understood.

Trask believed he had written the script.

But today, the audience had peeked backstage.

Once back above ground, Holmes waited until Trask, still wearing the mask of Samuel Lawson, had departed the premises on the pretense of handling a delivery detail. Only after the door shut behind him did Holmes lead Victoria and Daisy back towards the far side of the stage, away from the workers and well out of earshot.

They stopped beside the orchestra pit, where the sounds of the city beyond the walls were muffled to a hush.

"Thank you," Holmes said simply to Daisy. "That bought us just enough time."

Daisy nodded asking, "Did you find anything?"

Holmes didn't answer at once. His gaze dropped to the stage beneath their feet, tracing invisible lines as if seeing through the wooden planks into the hollow beneath.

Then, low and deliberate: "He's not simply hiding. He's inhabiting."

Victoria furrowed her brow. "What do you mean?"

"He's weaving illusion into structure. Stagecraft isn't just metaphorical anymore—it's architectural." Holmes turned to her. "Trask has built himself a lair beneath your theater. Not merely a hiding place—a nerve center. A concealed workspace designed to monitor, manipulate, and execute control. He's turned your building into a stage, and a trap."

Daisy froze mid-breath. "You mean... he lives down there?"

"Not constantly, I imagine," Holmes said. "But frequently. And likely with more access routes than we've discovered yet. The blueprint, the tools, the compartment behind the wall—all suggest deliberate preparation."

Victoria's arms crossed over her chest as if to stave off a sudden chill. "The second note said, 'He's in the walls.' At the time, I assumed it was meant to frighten me. But why would he warn me about himself?"

Holmes's eyes narrowed. "It's a maneuver. Trask doesn't just deal in sabotage. He specializes in psychological warfare. The note wasn't a warning. It was a demonstration. Proof that he could reach you and leave you uncertain whether to fear him or to mistrust everyone around you."

He paused. "You'll notice, he didn't tell you to leave the theater. Or contact the police. He wants you frightened, but still inside the game."

Victoria's teeth clenched. "Because if I walk away, he loses whatever advantage he's building."

"Precisely. And he's escalated. Which means we're close enough to force a mistake."

He turned to Daisy now, his tone sharpening. "He's methodical. Every timber touched, every document planted—it's all part of his construction. And now that we've seen the scope, we know this was never improvised. It was built."

Holmes's voice dropped lower. "Victoria, you must not return here alone again until this matter is resolved."

She looked as if she might argue, but he lifted a hand.

"This is not a suggestion. It is a necessity. Trask is not only dangerous, but he is also territorial. This place is no longer just a project to him. It's a domain."

Victoria exhaled slowly and gave a reluctant nod. "Then what do we do?"

"We close the distance," Holmes said. "We stop reacting and start pressing."

Daisy stepped forward. "You'll need to know the full work schedule— deliveries, crew movements, which areas are supposed to be restricted and when."

Holmes turned to her, his eyebrows raised in mild surprise.

"I've been keeping a detailed calendar," Daisy said. "Not just what 'Lawson' hands out, but my own. I've got notes on every vendor and worker, and I'm the one who confirms the supply drop-offs."

Holmes gave an approving nod. "Then I want to see it. Quietly. Look for anything out of sequence—substitutions, overlaps, names that appear or vanish without cause. If someone were replaced or reassigned, I want the when and the how."

"I can do that," Daisy said. "I'll bring the copy I keep at home."

Victoria placed a firm hand on her friend's arm. "Only if you are sure. I won't have your safety put at risk."

Daisy's smile was faint, but fierce. "Trask has left me no choice. it. I'd rather be involved and useful than unprepared and afraid."

Holmes admiring her spirit directed her. "No direct action. Quiet observation only. Trask cannot suspect you know anything."

Victoria turned toward Holmes. "What about you? What's your next move?"

Instead of responding immediately, Holmes adjusted his cuffs and looked toward the rafters.

"I'll examine the theater's supply manifests and construction permits," he said. "Every shipment, every subcontractor—particularly any not reviewed or signed off by Daisy or yourself. If he's built passageways or false walls, he needed materials, and those materials came from somewhere."

He glanced back at them both. "Trask is meticulous. But deception is laborious. And labor leaves traces."

Victoria's voice had grown steady again. "Then let's trace him until he's cornered."

Holmes looked at her with the ghost of a smile. "Exactly."

They turned to leave, but Holmes lingered a moment longer. The ghost light glowed dimly center stage, flickering in the gathering gloom like a sentinel between scenes.

Holmes studied it in silence.

"He thinks he's directing this play," he murmured. "But the final act belongs to us."

The evening darkness pressed like a damp blanket against the windows of 221B Baker Street as Holmes stood hunched over the drafting table near the far wall. A large parchment of the theater's architectural plans was spread before him, pinned at each corner. His fingers traced the substage level for the fourth time, as if willing it to reveal some unseen truth.

Watson, seated in the armchair, watched him with arms folded.

"You've been staring at that blueprint like it insulted your lineage."

Holmes didn't look up. "It is offering a confession. I am simply waiting for it to finish."

Watson snorted lightly. "And here I thought I was the melodramatic one."

Holmes traced one of the corridor lines with a fingertip, frowning slightly.

"See here—the hesitation in this pen stroke," he murmured. "The architect was left-handed, likely in his mid-fifties. Pressure here indicates some arthritis or stiffness in the knuckles. And these crowded margins—note how the lettering crowds toward the right edge. A sign of someone under stress or facing a deadline."

He glanced up. "This was not a man at ease. Which tells me the falsification was done hastily."

Holmes straightened and turned to face him, a rare flicker of tension tightening the set of his jaw. "There's a design beneath the design.

Hidden chambers. Overlapping access points that serve no practical construction purpose. We're not looking at poor planning, Watson—we're looking at deliberate misdirection."

"Like a stage magician's prop?" Watson asked.

"Precisely," Holmes said, tapping the basement plan with the end of a ruler. "He's layered misdirection into the very bones of the building. The way a magician uses curtains and trapdoors. But here, the stage is real—and so is the danger."

He began to sketch on the edge of the blueprint, using dotted lines. "These three storage alcoves… none are accessible from above. But their placement matches the spaces where Daisy noted echoes or odd draft patterns. He's built himself hidden corridors. Observation nests. Perhaps even storage for chemical agents or documents."

Watson stood, peering over Holmes's shoulder. "And he's living down there?"

Holmes gave a dry laugh. "Living? No. Thriving. Directing."

He crossed to the window, folding his arms and staring into the night. "The thing that haunts me is not just that he's been clever, but that he's been *patient*. Every element—the forged papers, the inserted lists, the warnings—it's all part of a structure. A psychological scaffold. He's not lashing out in rage. He's composing."

Watson moved towards the fire. "And what part do we play? The audience?"

"No," Holmes said. "We're the intended conclusion. The final collapse of the structure he's engineered. If we do not act soon, he'll bring the house down on all of us—and call it theater."

There was a knock, followed by the familiar creak of the door. Victoria stepped in just arriving home, cheeks pink from the cold. She carried a slim parcel in one gloved hand.

Holmes turned, his expression shifting at once. "Miss Watson."

"I had a memory," she said, "It's something I thought you'd want to know."

Holmes gestured to the seat beside the fire and leaned forward.

Victoria's voice softened. "I remember early on that Lawson was charming and attentive. But something happened that I brushed off. We were reviewing renovation priorities, and he mentioned the basement level. Specifically, the north wall."

"What did he say?" Holmes asked.

Victoria's frustration was building. "He said, 'If there's a heart in this old building, it's buried under that wall. Some structures need to be hollowed out before they can live again.' I thought it was poetic nonsense."

Watson let out a low whistle. "That sounds very much like Trask."

Holmes leaned his head back in his chair and looked towards the ceiling. "He was testing the language. Seeing how much symbolism he could lace into reality before someone noticed. Hollowed-out structures indeed."

Victoria added, "And he lingered in the wings during board meetings. I thought it odd, but I assumed he was simply observing. Now I think he was taking mental notes."

Holmes placed the blueprint aside. "This confirms it. He's been inside the frame of this plan since the beginning. You were not merely his employer, Miss Watson. You were his centerpiece."

She didn't flinch. "Then I suppose it's time we reclaim the stage."

Holmes rose from his armchair and crossed the room in three strides. From a narrow drawer in his desk, he withdrew a stack of index cards, each bearing observations in his meticulous handwriting. Victoria watched in silence as he laid them out across the table—rows and columns forming a kind of mental map.

"Observe this," he said, tapping one column. "Every incident associated with the theater—delivery delays, electrical faults, misplaced tools—occurred on a Tuesday or a Thursday. Alternating weeks, and always in the early afternoon."

Victoria leaned closer. "You're saying he created a pattern?"

"More than that." Holmes held up the most recent forged vendor invoice. "The address for the supplier is valid, but the routing code in the lower margin, this six-digit stamp, contains a transposition of numerals that is only made when items are rerouted through a contractor subcontracting depot in Lambeth. That depot is used almost exclusively by one firm we know."

"Easton Works," Victoria said softly.

"Exactly. He forged work orders, but they lacked the authentic grease smudges or folded corners of real blueprints. And this…" Holmes picked up one of the forged maintenance reports, holding it at an angle beneath the lamplight. "The paper fibers are consistent with a specific manufacturer. Only four warehouses in London stock it. I had Wiggins confirm that deliveries from one of them were signed out under the alias 'H. Blythe.'"

Watson sat up. "That's one of Trask's aliases."

Victoria's breath caught. "So, it's him."

"Yes." Holmes said. "Not only him, but a system. A mechanism by which he embedded himself so deeply into your theater's infrastructure that you could not have removed him without tearing out the floorboards themselves."

He stepped back from the table, fingers pressed together in thought. "This man's genius lies not only in architecture, but in psychological occupation. He builds rooms that become prisons not through locks and doors, but through influence and fear."

Victoria looked at the stack of papers with new understanding.

"You don't just see the facts," she said. "You see how they breathe."

Holmes gave a faint smile. "Facts do breathe, Miss Watson. And sometimes, they whisper."

A knock sounded on the outer door just after the clock had chimed the half-hour. Holmes, still standing near the window, turned slightly as Mrs. Hudson bustled up the stairs with her usual quiet efficiency.

"It's Miss Daisy," she called. "Says she's here to see Miss Watson about tomorrow's vendor schedule."

Victoria rose. "Let her in, please."

A moment later, Daisy entered, a small notebook clutched in her hand. "Sorry to barge in, but I wanted to check on the final time for the timber delivery. The foreman rescheduled again."

Victoria rolled her eyes and groaned, grabbing her own notepad. "Come on, we'll go over it in my flat. There are too many stray teacups and documents in here."

She gave Holmes a brief look, more gratitude than goodbye, then led Daisy out and across the hall. The door to 221C clicked softly shut behind them.

For a moment, silence reigned.

Watson sat back, watching Holmes without speaking. The detective moved to the fireplace, stirring the coals with more force than strictly necessary.

"She's becoming integral to this case," Watson said at last.

Holmes did not look up. "So, it would seem."

"She's also in very real danger," Watson said.

Holmes finally turned, his eyes shadowed but alert. "Do you suppose I'm unaware of that?"

Watson raised his hands mildly. "I'm saying it aloud because you haven't. Not really. Not to me."

Holmes dropped into the armchair opposite, fingertips steepled, jaw tight. "This case is…untidy."

Watson chuckled dryly. "You, Holmes, detest two things: emotional complications and imprecise data. This case is full of both."

Holmes was silent a long time before speaking. "There is a part of me that wants to treat her as merely another subject. An element in the equation. But I cannot. I find myself recalculating. Frequently."

Watson softened. "She's not just another client."

"No," Holmes admitted, very quietly. "And that troubles me more than Trask's maze of lies."

Watson stood and walked to the window, watching the lights of passing carriages blur in the fog. "You once told me emotion clouds the mind."

"It does," Holmes murmured. "But sometimes it also sharpens the purpose."

He looked toward the door across the hallway, where soft laughter could now be heard, muffled through the walls.

Watson turned back toward him. "Just don't let her become your blind spot."

Holmes smiled faintly, but there was no warmth in it. "On the contrary, Watson. She may be the only point of clarity I have left."

Watson shook his head and began gathering his hat and coat. "I'll see you tomorrow. And Holmes—get some sleep, if you can."

Seeing Watson to the door, Holmes stood looking toward the door of 221C. It was ajar just slightly, the warm glow of lamplight spilling into the corridor.

From within came the low murmur of Victoria and Daisy's voices— soft, serious, punctuated by the occasional quiet laugh. Not joy exactly, but a borrowed moment of normalcy.

Holmes didn't eavesdrop. He simply listened to the rhythm of their conversation, the way Victoria's voice steadied when speaking to someone she trusted. The same voice that had trembled only hours ago at the mention of a masked man in the walls.

He stepped back without a sound and closed his door behind him.

Then, to no one at all, he said quietly, "Let it end soon. And let her come through it unchanged."

The rain fell in a fine, cold mist as Holmes and Watson approached the gates of Wandsworth Prison. The old stone structure loomed grey against the colorless sky, its narrow windows blackened with grime and years of secrets. Even Holmes, who usually walked with brisk certainty, seemed more subdued as they stepped into the drab interior.

"I never thought we'd visit Stamford in a place like this," Watson murmured, glancing sideways at his old friend.

Holmes didn't respond, but his eyes swept the barred windows, the impassive faces of the guards, and the corridors that seemed to swallow sound.

The guard, a stooped man with ink-stained cuffs and breath that smelled of stale tobacco, led them through a metal door that groaned open with theatrical reluctance.

"You'll have ten minutes," he said before disappearing into shadow.

Inside the visitation room, Stamford was already seated. He looked thinner than either of them remembered, his face drawn and pale under the flickering overhead light. His uniform coat hung loosely from his shoulders, and his fingers twitched on the table until he saw them enter.

"Watson, Holmes," he said softly, with something like relief.

Watson stepped forward and clasped his hand warmly. "Stamford."

Holmes remained standing at the end of the table, observing the man with quiet intensity. Stamford returned his gaze, then looked away, clearly unsettled.

"I didn't poison anyone," Stamford said quickly. "You have to know that."

"We believe you," Watson replied.

Holmes's tone was calm but direct. "But you withheld something."

Stamford blinked. "What?"

Holmes's gaze didn't waver. "Not facts, perhaps, but doubts. Suspicions of Trask long before the poisoning at the dinner. A sense of something wrong. You were manipulated—and whether from pride or fear, you said nothing when it might have made a difference."

"I—" Stamford hesitated. "You're right. But what could I have said? There was no evidence. Only the feeling that I was being unwound. You don't know what it's like to have your professional reputation sliced away piece by piece. Trask—he didn't just frame me. He dismantled me."

Holmes leaned forward, softer now. "Then help us reassemble by catching the man who did it."

Stamford's gaze lifted, eyes bloodshot but steadier. "He was careful. So careful. But there were slips."

"Tell me," Holmes said.

"Once, in the hospital lounge, I was showing a photograph of my niece. He looked at it and said, 'Everyone has a weakness. I prefer to break what men treasure.' I laughed at the time. Thought it was just gallows humor. But now…"

Holmes's jaw tightened.

Stamford went on. "He had access everywhere. Knew the staff schedule better than the administrators. He had a way of asking questions that didn't feel like questions. Once, I found a cabinet in my office slightly ajar. He claimed he was looking for a patient file. I let it go."

"Did he ever use another name?" Holmes asked.

Stamford thought hard. "I think so. When he first came to us, he presented a reference letter from a Mr. Blythe. Talked about the man like an old friend. Now… I think he wrote the letter himself. Trask was both applicant and referee."

Holmes made a quick note in his pocket journal. "And medically?" he asked, his voice even. "Did he carry or use anything out of the ordinary—compounds, devices, instruments?"

Stamford recalled. "Yes. He always kept a small vial in his coat. Said it helped him sleep. I remember once asking what it was out of idle curiosity, and he said it was a compound of bromide and laudanum. Odd mix. He claimed it was something from his days abroad—a personal formulation."

Holmes's eyes narrowed. "Bromide and laudanum. That combination could cause confusion, sluggishness—"

"Or hallucinations," Watson added grimly. "Especially in small, repeated doses."

Holmes glanced at him. "Anne Godfrey."

Watson turned toward Holmes. "Her behavior during her testimony. The strange inconsistencies. What if she wasn't merely lying—but compromised? Drugged?"

Stamford's face paled. "I didn't realize. You think he used it on her?"

"We think it's likely," Holmes said quietly. "And if so, it means his reach extended farther than you knew and more precisely than we feared."

Holmes stood slowly. "You've told us more than you realize—the alias, the compound, his psychological patterns. Each is another brick in the structure. And the more detailed the profile, the smaller his shadow becomes."

Stamford looked up. "Please believe how sorry I am about Miss Watson. That she's become involved in this."

Holmes was quiet for a long moment. "I believe you. But that doesn't undo the harm. You couldn't have foreseen her involvement, but you might have helped stop him sooner. That is what you must reckon with."

Stamford looked down, guilt etched into the lines of his face.

Watson stepped forward, voice gentler. "She doesn't blame you. But she's cautious now—more careful about trust. She's being protected. That much I promise you."

There was a knock at the frame.

"Time's up," the guard said.

Holmes gave a final nod and turned. Watson paused, gave Stamford's shoulder a reassuring squeeze, and followed.

As they passed through the corridor once more, the damp echo of their footsteps filled the space between them.

Watson finally asked, "Do you believe him?"

"Yes," Holmes replied. "But belief is secondary. What matters is what we can act upon—and how swiftly."

"And if we can't act quickly enough?"

Holmes didn't answer, but his pace quickened.

Later that day, after leaving Stamford, Holmes and Watson made their way to Scotland Yard and shared what Stamford had told them with

Lestrade. Lestrade, uncharacteristically cooperative, had arranged for access to the internal memos and documents Holmes had requested.

In the dim back office, Holmes stood by the window with a stack of documents in hand. The lamp on the inspector's desk flickered unevenly, casting warped shadows across the papers. Lestrade, his arms crossed, and brows furrowed, watched as Holmes turned page after page of the forged statements that had led to Stamford's arrest.

"They appear authentic enough," Lestrade said. "Typed, signed, properly formatted—"

"—And riddled with clumsy inconsistencies," Holmes interrupted, holding up a page. "This one, for example, contains a false date: It references a meeting on a Tuesday the fourteenth, when in fact the fourteenth that month fell on a Friday. And this typed signature—look closely." He passed it to Lestrade. "The ink is from a different ribbon than the body text. Either the typist swapped ribbons midway through a document, which no clerk in his right mind would do, or it was completed later."

Lestrade leaned in, examining it more closely.

Holmes pulled another sheet forward. "And here, a remarkable oversight—see the word 'suspicious'? The 's' at the end of the word is misaligned, slightly raised. The same flaw appears in five other statements."

Lestrade was forced to conclude, "The same typewriter?"

"Exactly. And not one registered to Stamford's department. I checked the Yard's own requisition logs an hour ago." He tossed the paper back onto the stack. "There's also the curious matter of phrase repetition. This 'report' uses the phrase 'cause for disciplinary escalation' verbatim in three separate memos, supposedly written by three different administrators. No variation. No personal cadence."

Holmes paced once around the desk, hands behind his back.

"Someone went to a great deal of trouble to fake these. But not enough to avoid detection by someone trained to see patterns in dust." He turned back to Lestrade. "Stamford has enemies, yes—but this? This is orchestration. The question is no longer whether he was implicated by design, but who had both the motive and access."

Lestrade looked troubled, "Trask?"

Holmes was troubled. "And whoever he had helping him inside the system. This was not the work of one man alone."

He turned back to the window, hints of gray light breaking through the London mist.

Watson, silent until now, finally spoke. "Holmes, do you think Stamford knew how deep it went?"

"No," Holmes said quietly. "But I believe he suspected. And it's time we show him how right he was to ask for our help."

With that, Holmes folded the forged memos neatly and tucked them under his arm. "Come, Watson. Let us bring the truth to light."

The clock on the mantel struck a low, sonorous eight as Victoria spread the final chart across the small table in her flat. A steaming pot of tea sat untouched between her and Daisy, who were deep in concentration as she flipped through her thick, dog-eared notebook.

Victoria exhaled slowly. "All right. We'll go line by line. If there's a ghost in this machine, we'll flush him out."

Daisy gave a determined nod. "These," she said, pointing to her own handwritten entries, "are the records I've kept from the beginning.

Some are things I jotted down on the fly—delivery times, changes Lawson made that he didn't log officially."

"And these are the lists Mr. Holmes compiled," Victoria said, gesturing to the pile beside her. "He cross-referenced the names of those who've interacted with the basement areas, the substage, and the walls."

They began comparing notes. The silence between them was steady, broken only by the occasional scrape of parchment or the soft whisper of pages turning.

"This is odd," Daisy muttered after a while. She tapped a name halfway down one of her lists. "Victor Carey. Scheduled for stonework on May 12th, but no one ever came that day. I was there all morning. Lawson said he'd rescheduled because of supply delays."

Victoria's eyes narrowed. "He never updated the calendar and just left the name."

They checked again. No other record of Victor Carey existed.

Minutes later, Daisy leaned back, eyes wide. "There's another—look at this. Charles Finch. Supposedly worked on flooring reinforcement for a single day in June. Only… I remember doing that walkthrough. And there was no one named Finch. Just that wiry man from Crosswell Joinery."

Victoria flipped through her own meeting notes. "No invoice for Finch either. No sign-off, no delivery log."

The pile of unaccounted-for names grew.

Then Victoria spotted it.

"Here," she said slowly, laying one sheet beside another. "Henry Blythe. Stonemason. He's listed in May, June, and again last week—all tied to interior wall access."

Daisy squinted. "That name's not familiar to me. And I've met everyone doing interior stonework."

Victoria's fingers tapped the page. "No notes. No receipts. No eyewitnesses. But three appearances in high-access zones, all places connected to Trask's hidden spaces."

They exchanged a look.

"You think Blythe might be Trask?" Daisy asked.

"Father and Mr. Holmes told me the name was one of Trask's aliases." Victoria replied.

Daisy reached for her pencil. "I'll cross-check Blythe against the vendor rosters. If he doesn't show up in their logs…"

"Then we have our next mask," Victoria said.

She reached for an older stack of documents, leafing through original records from the theater before it had shuttered years earlier. Her finger paused on a familiar heading— "Management Staff, The London Majestic Theatre."

A name jumped out: *William Rodney*, the former theater manager.

Victoria thought for a moment. "Daisy, have you seen this name in any of Trask's summaries? Or even your notes?"

Daisy leaned over, eyes scanning the page. "No. Not once."

Victoria tapped the paper. "He'd have known every passageway. Every maintenance tunnel. If he's still in London, he could be invaluable. And once this is over, if he proves trustworthy, he might even be someone we ask back. But first we need to find him."

Daisy agreed, excited to pursue this new information trail. "I'll research everything I can and see if he's listed anywhere—business registries, news clippings, anything."

A long moment passed. The room, lit only by two gas sconces and the faint flicker of the hearth, seemed to hold its breath.

"Let's keep going," Victoria said at last, sitting straighter. "There may be more names like his—more cracks in the plaster."

"And if there are?" Daisy asked.

Victoria glanced toward the hallway—toward the closed door across from hers.

"Then Mr. Holmes will know where to look next."

Mere days after their previous visit, Holmes and Watson, joined by Victoria, arrived at Wandsworth Prison early in the morning under the weight of the situation. A formal request had been granted for the three to meet simultaneously with Stamford, and the warden, still uneasy about the press surrounding the case, allowed it under close observation.

The visiting chamber was stark, dimly lit, and separated by a long wooden table. A guard stood discreetly by the door. Stamford, thinner and more hollow-eyed than before, entered with cautious steps. When he saw Victoria beside Holmes and Watson, his expression faltered into something softer.

"Miss Watson," he said, nodding politely, "I hadn't expected—"

"I wanted to come, Dr. Stamford," Victoria replied. "To put faces and names together. And to ask a few questions, if you're willing."

Stamford looked to Holmes, who gestured to the bench opposite them. "We believe your knowledge of Trask, as you once knew him, may help us bridge a critical gap."

Stamford sat slowly. "He was in medicine once. A researcher. Brilliant but impatient. He despised oversight, especially from people he considered less intelligent. And I suppose that included me."

"You mentioned once that he threatened you," Watson said. "Can you recall the nature of that threat?"

Stamford gave a small, bitter smile. "He said I was standing in the way of something greater. That one day, he would build something permanent, and I'd be buried beneath it—metaphorically or otherwise. I took it as rhetorical. I shouldn't have."

Holmes leaned forward. "We've discovered that Trask eventually left the medical field and reappeared under a different name—Lawson—as a builder and architect."

"He had a fascination with architecture," Stamford said. "So, it fits. He always believed the body was just another structure to be rebuilt. The idea that he would move from one kind of construction to another is ghastly but not shocking. It was his plans for renovating a hospital wing that resulted in his dismissal. It was dangerous and I had no choice but to object to it."

Victoria finally spoke. "The man I know as Samuel Lawson helped oversee my theater's renovation. He was reserved, precise, oddly formal. But charming—when he wanted to be."

Stamford studied her. "That was his gift. Not charm, but calculation."

Holmes looked deeply at Stamford. "Did he have any physical characteristics or mannerisms you recall? Something distinctive."

Stamford furrowed his brow. "Yes, he had a tendency to tap the edge of his thumbnail against his teeth when thinking—like a rhythmic tic. And he limped slightly on cold mornings."

Victoria's eyes widened as she nodded her head in agreement. "Yes! Lawson does that."

Victoria added, "Lawson was meticulous with his gloves. He always wore them—even indoors. And his handwriting was unusually angular, almost architectural in its style. Once, I caught him murmuring aloud while walking the corridors—mapping something, I think, in his head."

Stamford nodded in accord.

Holmes's expression sharpened. "That confirms it. Same man, two identities."

"We're working to undo what he's built," Holmes said. "But I needed to confirm something. Did Trask ever speak to you of a place called the London Majestic?"

Stamford blinked. "Only once. He said it was 'a fitting stage for a final curtain.' I assumed he meant it figuratively."

Victoria shivered.

Holmes stood. "Thank you. You've helped more than you know."

As the guard returned to escort Stamford away, the prisoner looked back at Victoria.

"I pray you reclaim what he tried to steal. Not just your theater. Your peace."

Victoria said with conviction. "I intend to."

Evening had deepened into night by the time Holmes stepped into the dim stillness of his sitting room. Rain had left the streets glistening, and the lamplight outside cast long reflections in the puddled gutters. The rooms upstairs were dark and silent save for the fire Mrs. Hudson had lit for him.

He had barely removed his coat when the door to the flat across the hall opened. Victoria appeared in the threshold with her arms wrapped around a folio of papers.

"I heard you come in," she said. "We've made progress."

Without waiting for an invitation, she stepped inside and moved toward the small table, where she began laying out charts and notes with quiet precision. Holmes followed, his brow furrowing with interest.

"Daisy's just gone home," Victoria said softly as she arranged the papers. "I told her to rest, but she insisted on finishing her vendor cross-checks first."

Holmes removed his coat fully, hung it on the stand, and stepped to the table. His eyes scanned the pages she spread before him. "And what did we learn?"

"A dozen questionable entries," Victoria replied, tapping a marked column. "Three names tied to substage work don't match any face Daisy's ever seen. Several vendor swaps with no paper trail. But this one—" she slid forward a page "—is our most persistent."

Holmes leaned in. "Henry Blythe."

"He's listed as a stonemason," Victoria said. "Three separate appearances. All tied to structural access near hidden panels or the false wall."

Holmes read silently for a moment, then murmured, "No invoice. No firsthand sightings. A phantom bricklayer."

"You think Trask used the name?" she asked.

"Or gave it to an accomplice," Holmes replied. "But the pattern suggests Trask himself. These entries align with key milestones—just before the false wall was installed, before the second anonymous note, and just before we discovered his workshop. Blythe appears when the script needs him. A shadow in the wings."

Victoria's brow creased. "It's not just a disguise. It's authorship. He's writing the staff lists like they're stage directions."

"Precisely," Holmes said. "Each name creates the illusion of legitimacy. Each task assignment a curtain to hide the trapdoor. Trask hasn't merely infiltrated your project—he's written himself into its bones."

Victoria hesitated, then added, "There's something else. When Daisy and I were going through the older documentation, I found a name. William Rodney. He was the theater manager before it closed. He would've known every bolt and beam before renovations began."

Holmes's gaze lifted. "And?"

"I haven't seen his name in any of Lawson's notes," she said. "He should've been consulted or at least mentioned. It's as if he vanished with the building's history."

"Or was erased," Holmes said.

"I've asked Daisy to try to track him down," Victoria added. "Quietly."

Holmes nodded. "Tell her to be discreet. And let your father assist her. He knows how to navigate inquiries without raising alarms. I suspect Mr. Rodney's location will not remain hidden long."

Victoria turned her eyes to the open blueprint spread between them. "Do you think Rodney will help us?"

"If he's not in Trask's pocket," Holmes said, "he may be our best chance at mapping the theater as it was. Before it was... rewritten."

Silence followed. The fire, now freshly stoked, crackled quietly behind them. Victoria leaned back, her shoulders visibly tense.

"I should have seen it," she said suddenly, the words clipped. "I thought I was being careful. I vetted the staff. Watched the budget. Read every proposal. And still, he got in. Built a hiding place. Typed threats under my roof."

Holmes said nothing, allowing the confession to land in its own gravity.

"I was so determined to bring that place back to life," she went on. "To create something worth preserving. Something that mattered."

Holmes stepped closer, voice low and steady. "It does matter. That's why he tried to steal it."

She looked over at him, eyes shaded with emotion. "What I built—was it worth saving?"

"Yes," he said, without hesitation. "And he knew it. That's why he latched onto it. Parasites don't cling to dust—they seek out what's vital."

Holmes looked away from her for a moment before speaking again, "Trask sees your theater as an opportunity to complete his revenge against Stamford and distract me by putting you at risk."

She held his gaze for a long moment, then looked down. A flicker of a smile touched her lips. "I'm grateful for your comfort… and for all you're doing."

Holmes's voice softened. "I may not be skilled in reassurance, but I recognize the weight of a worthy cause. Trask chose his mark carefully. That alone tells us everything."

Victoria gathered a few pages, preparing to leave. "Trask is dangerous. We must clear Dr. Stamford and remove this menace from our community. I'm in a chess game I never asked for."

"Then play it as yourself," Holmes said. "Not as bait. Not as victim. As builder. As daughter of a soldier and a storyteller. That's what he didn't account for."

She paused at the door, one hand on the frame. "Thank you, Mr. Holmes."

He inclined his head. "Good night, Miss Watson."

When the door closed behind her, Holmes stood for a long moment in the quiet. Then he returned to the table, rolled back the blueprint to reveal the substage layers, and picked up his pen.

In the margin, he wrote:

William Rodney

He tapped the name with the end of the pen once, twice.

Then murmured, "Let's see what he can offer us."

A knock at the door startled Holmes from his reading. He put the documents he'd been scouring related to the case in a folder as he rose, moving with brisk steps across the room.

When he opened the door, Daisy stood there, rubbing her hands together for warmth. Beside her stood Dr. Watson, and just behind them, a man in his fifties—broad-shouldered, with silvery hair, deep-set eyes, and the quiet attentiveness of a man long practiced in reading a room.

"Mr. Holmes," Daisy said with pride in her voice, "this is Mr. William Rodney."

Rodney extended a hand. "Pleasure to meet you, sir. Dr. Watson said you might be able to make sense of a few things."

Holmes gave a small, approving nod and stepped aside. "Come in."

The flat was warm and softly lit, the faint crackle of the hearth casting golden light against the bookcases. Rodney's gaze swept the sitting room with the practiced awareness of a man used to backstage scrutiny, noting exits, shadows, details.

"Please, sit," Holmes said, gesturing toward the chairs. "Watson, Miss Dawn, you, too."

Rodney settled into the armchair with quiet grace. "I didn't expect to be summoned to Baker Street, I'll admit."

Daisy glanced at Watson. "We found him, just like we hoped. It wasn't easy. Mr. Rodney left no forwarding address when he left the theater."

Holmes raised a brow. "And how did you manage it?"

"I visited the Royal Theatrical Guild," Daisy said. "I told them I was doing research on the Majestic's restoration and that I'd heard Mr. Rodney had once been involved. They were kind enough to share his current address. Dr. Watson followed up, and here we are."

Rodney gave a modest shrug. "It seemed a worthy cause."

Holmes steepled his fingers. "You were the last stage manager of the London Majestic before it closed its doors. That makes you one of the few men alive who knows the building as it was."

Rodney, his eyes catching the firelight, said "She was a beauty in her time. Not grand like the Savoy or Haymarket, but she had bones. A performer's house. I worked there fifteen years. Knew every trapdoor, every fly line, every bolt backstage."

"And yet you sought no role in the theater's restoration," Holmes said, his tone just shy of accusing.

Rodney looked aside as he spoke. "I tried to. When I heard it was being purchased, I wrote to the architectural firm—then again once I heard it was Miss Watson behind the project. I offered my services. Never received a reply. Then I went in-person and one of the foremen—man named Lawson—told me the stage manager position had already been filled. Said the design team had different plans."

Victoria, who had quietly entered from across the hall when she heard Rodney's name, stepped forward. "I never saw your letter, Mr. Rodney. If I had, I would've invited you in an instant."

Rodney stood and bowed slightly. "Then I believe there was interference."

Holmes exchanged a glance with Watson. "You were kept away deliberately," he said. "We believe the man you knew as 'Lawson' is not who he claimed to be."

Rodney didn't try to hide his surprise, "Well, son of a…oh, pardon me, Ladies."

Holmes gestured toward the hallway. "Miss Watson, Dr. Watson—please remain a moment. Miss Dawn, would you mind taking Mr. Rodney across the hall? Miss Watson's sitting room may offer a more comfortable place to review the original blueprints. I'd like to speak privately with Victoria and her father before we reconvene."

Daisy, flashing Victoria a quick wink tapped his shoulder. "Come, Mr. Rodney. I'll put the kettle on."

As the two exited, the flat fell quiet again.

Holmes turned to the window, hands clasped behind his back. "Miss Watson, you were kept from a valuable ally."

Watson's voice was grim. "It wasn't chance."

"No," Holmes agreed. "It was design. Trask engineered his entrance by eliminating those who might recognize the misalignment."

He turned, eyes distant but focused. "But Mr. Rodney remembers. And memory, in a place where walls conceal secrets, is power."

The sitting room had grown quieter, though its energy had not diminished. With Daisy and Rodney now seated comfortably near the hearth, the room had taken on the air of a war council—papers spread across the table, blueprints unrolled and anchored by teacups and books. Holmes, standing by the mantelpiece, watched as Rodney's calloused fingers traced a line across the aging vellum.

"There," Rodney murmured, pointing to a section beneath the stage. "This crawlspace here—that was originally used for prop storage and maintenance materials. Narrow as a coffin, but it connected all the way to the back of house."

Holmes leaned in, eyes sharpening. "It's not in the new schematics."

Rodney snorted. "It wouldn't be. The firm contracted to survey the foundations didn't know it was there. It had no visible entrance once the old trap was covered. The only way to find it was to feel the warp in the boards."

Holmes looked at Victoria. "This is the kind of passage Trask would exploit. Out of sight, out of mind—until it isn't."

Victoria took a moment to take the information in and then turned to Rodney. "Did anyone else know about it?"

Rodney hesitated, then shrugged. "Maybe old George, our lighting man. But he passed three years ago. I used to call that space 'the rabbit's run.' Could crawl through it faster than most men walk upright."

Daisy, seated beside him with a notebook balanced on her knees, smiled faintly. "You sound like you loved that place."

Rodney's face softened, lines easing around his eyes. "I did. I spent years there. Once, during a matinee, the pulley for the house curtain snapped mid-scene. I was under the stage when it happened—heard the commotion, dashed through that crawlspace, and yanked the manual drop in time to save the scene. The actors never broke character. Whole audience thought it was part of the act."

Victoria's laugh was warm but tinged with melancholy. "I wish I'd seen it in those days."

Rodney looked at her kindly. "You've given her a second life, Miss Watson. I saw what you were doing. Even from a distance, it was clear you weren't trying to modernize her into something she wasn't. You respected her bones."

"She does more than that," Holmes said softly, "which is precisely why Trask tried to undermine it."

Rodney understood the meaning of that statement. "That man Lawson—is his real name Trask?"

Holmes folded his arms. "W.E. Trask. Former pharmaceutical chemist turned amateur architect. Disgraced, disappeared from official record years ago. He uses aliases, creates false paper trails, and builds physical fictions to hide in plain sight. We have reason to believe that he tried to murder a high-ranking government official and blame an innocent man for the crime. He's using the alias Lawson and the theater to hide and disrupt my investigation."

Watson added, "And to plan whatever other ghastly things he has in mind by using my daughter. He's not only hiding. He's manipulating the environment, architecture, schedules, and perceptions."

Rodney looked grim. "Outrageous! He's embedded himself, then. You'll need more than lockpicks and good intentions to dig him out."

"We need memory," Holmes said, meeting his eyes. "And you, Mr. Rodney, are our map."

Rodney seemed surprised but not displeased. "Then I'll do what I can. I've still got the old fire in me."

Daisy leaned forward, tapping the blueprint. "Could you walk us through what used to be here? This wall wasn't always in this place, was it?"

Rodney chuckled. "No. That was added to make space for a failing manager's office. Never did sit right—there's a void behind it. Not structural, just dead space. If your Trask needed a hiding place, that'd be a fine one."

Holmes immediately began marking the spot with quick, decisive strokes of his pencil.

"And here," Rodney continued, pointing to the western corridor. "That's where the pulley control lines ran. If he's clever, and from what you've said, he is, he could've rerouted those into a false wall. Rig it to signal him when someone enters."

Victoria stared at the blueprint. "He's turned it into his own stage."

"And like any good stage," Holmes said, "the trapdoors are disguised."

Watson looked at him. "Where does that leave us?"

Holmes stood a moment in thoughtful silence, his eyes on the blueprints as if reading music only he could hear.

"Mr. Rodney," he said at last, "you've given us the skeleton. What we need now is precision—routes, voids, sound ways, spaces built to deceive or forgotten by time. Can you mark every undocumented feature you recall?"

Rodney leaned forward again, already reaching for the pencil Holmes handed him. "I'll do what I can. Memory's a stubborn thing—slow to come when called, quick when ignored."

Daisy offered a fresh sheet of tracing paper. "Use this overlay. Mr. Holmes has been tracking changes layer by layer."

Rodney thanked her and began sketching quickly but methodically, murmuring notes as he worked. "There's an old dumbwaiter shaft, sealed at the top, but not the bottom. And here—the trap to the orchestra pit. They widened it during one of the remodels but left the crawlspace unreinforced."

Holmes, meanwhile, moved to the window and stared out into the fog-thick night. His hands were clasped behind his back, his mind whirring audibly in the silence.

"Trask builds illusions into physical form," he said finally. "But illusion has a flaw: it requires ignorance to function. The moment someone sees it for what it is, the effect dissolves."

Watson folded his arms. "So, we expose the illusion."

"Not just expose it," Holmes said, turning back. "We must force him to abandon it. Make it unstable. Unsafe."

Victoria, with a determined look said. "You mean to flush him out?"

"Yes," Holmes said. "But carefully. If we make a move too soon, he will retreat—vanish into another alias, another venue. We must make him believe the illusion is crumbling under its own weight. That his control is slipping."

Rodney paused his drawing. "You intend to sabotage him?"

Holmes raised an eyebrow. "Let's call it theatrical correction."

Daisy looked intrigued. "And how do we do that?"

"First," Holmes said, tapping the overlay Rodney had begun. "We finalize the true map. Then we use it to stage our own fiction. One that draws him out. Plant misleading information, perhaps a falsified report. Something that suggests his hidden room has been found or tampered with."

Victoria tented her fingers to her lips. "We leak just enough detail to make him feel exposed."

Holmes gave a faint smile. "Precisely. Actors are always watching the audience. He'll be watching us."

Watson leaned on the mantel. "And while he watches…"

"…we move," Holmes finished. "We set the stage for confrontation. But on our terms."

He returned to the table, picking up a pencil and marking three points on the blueprints. "These are the locations where Henry Blythe, the so-called stonemason, was recorded. If Trask operated under that name, then these spots form his axis. Rodney, can you confirm—are these points structurally connected?"

Rodney squinted. "Yes. That line runs under the proscenium arch. If he had access there, he could reach nearly everything backstage without being seen."

Holmes turned to Victoria. "Then that's where we begin. We establish a false inspection. Create activity he cannot ignore. We draw him toward his own creation while we map it in full."

Victoria's voice was steady. "And if he panics?"

Holmes looked directly at her. "Then he will make mistakes. That's where we win."

Silence fell for a moment. The kind of silence that gathers before a final act begins.

Then Holmes straightened. "Mr. Rodney, continue mapping every detail you remember. Miss Dawn, I'll need you to pass along the revised construction schedule tomorrow quietly, as if you're simply doing your job. Watson, prepare to assist her with inquiries into the workers still unaccounted for."

He looked at Victoria last. "And you, Miss Watson, must prepare yourself. Trask believes he's writing the final scene. We're going to rewrite the ending."

Victoria met his gaze. "Let's give him a closing night he'll never forget."

The group had fallen into a thoughtful silence, the only sounds the faint scratch of Rodney's pencil and the occasional creak of the settling flat. Holmes stood once more at the window, his silhouette framed by the flickering lamplight. Watson busied himself with a list of construction contacts, while Daisy began carefully transcribing Rodney's notations onto a fresh overlay.

Victoria stepped away from the table and crossed slowly to the hearth, the glow of the fire dancing across her features. She stood there for a long moment, one hand resting lightly on the mantel, as if steadying herself.

When she finally spoke, her voice was low but clear.

"When I first bought the Majestic," she said, "I imagined something grand, but not extravagant. I wasn't trying to rival the great houses or steal acclaim. I wanted to resurrect something beautiful. A place where light could live again. Music, story, laughter… I wanted to give this city a little corner of magic it could call its own. Just like it was for our family when I was a young girl."

Her eyes looked to Holmes, then back to the flames.

"But I've come to realize—it's not just the building he invaded. He hijacked the vision. The joy. He's using something meant for good as a hiding place for malice. And I cannot—I *will not*—stand aside and let that remain."

Rodney looked up from his sketches, his expression thoughtful.

Victoria continued, more fiercely now. "What he's done to Dr. Stamford is disgraceful. What he's doing with the theater is evil. He's turning art into camouflage. Creativity into cover. And the people who trusted me—who are giving their time, who believed in the promise of that stage—they deserve the truth. They deserve to know that the dream is still intact. That the *intention* was never compromised."

Holmes watched her, his face unreadable, but his eyes shone with a quiet intensity.

Watson stepped nearer, his voice gentle. "You've not failed them, my dear."

"I know," she said, "but I *must* make it right. For them. For Dr. Stamford. For myself. For all of us." She turned back to the others. "This city needs places like the Majestic. Places where beauty pushes back against cynicism. Where wonder has a stage. And I'll be damned if I let some clever madman twist that into a stage for manipulation."

Rodney set down his pencil and gave her a long, assessing look. Then he stood.

"You remind me of the founder," he said, his voice touched with admiration. "An idealist, but stubborn as winter frost. She once told me that a theater doesn't survive on applause—it survives on heart, passion, and will. And from what I can see, Miss Watson, you've got all three."

He held out his hand to her. "You can count on me for as long as you need. We'll take back every inch of that stage."

Victoria shook his hand, her grip firm.

"Thank you, Mr. Rodney."

153

He smiled. "Call me Will, if you like. I reckon we'll be in this production together for a while."

Holmes cleared his throat softly. "Then let's ensure the second act opens stronger than the first."

Victoria looked around the room, at the assembled allies—the old friend and loyal assistant, her steadfast father, the veteran stage manager, and the detective who never stopped chasing the truth.

For the first time in days, she felt *ready*.

She turned back to Holmes. "Then let's write an ending that's worthy of the stage."

Holmes gave a single nod.

"And of justice."

The London Majestic was nearly whole again.

Sunlight streamed through the freshly cleaned dome windows, throwing golden rays across the velvet seats below. Dust motes spun like dancers in the air, stirred by the movement of painters touching up trim and carpenters hammering final details into place. The scent of plaster, sawdust, and new paint filled the space—a perfume of rebirth.

Victoria stood center stage, her arms folded and her eyes scanning the proscenium arch as if searching for a hidden note in a musical score. She was dressed plainly today in a charcoal skirt, linen blouse, and practical boots while conveying calm and control. She had practiced the look in the mirror that morning: relaxed posture, polite interest, just enough concern to appear unaware of the shadows coiling beneath her stage.

They were in the planning phase now. No rehearsals yet, but it was time to prepare the company's debut production. She had not announced the title. Not even to Daisy. The less known, the better.

"Miss Watson?" a voice called from the edge of the house.

She turned. Samuel Lawson—Trask—stood below, clipboard in hand, posture easy but eyes sharp.

"Everything is proceeding on schedule," he said. "The flooring repairs backstage have been reinforced, as requested. Shall I update the vendor log?"

Victoria smiled lightly. "Yes, thank you. Once that's done, let's finalize the extra seating layout. And I want to begin measuring for curtain draping by Friday."

"Of course," he said, with a slight bow. "I'll check with the fabric supplier this afternoon."

She watched him retreat, his steps slow and deliberate. He no longer hovered over every detail—he watched. That made him more dangerous. He was trying to read her.

Good, she thought. Read this.

She crossed toward the side of the stage where Daisy was crouched, pretending to sort through a box of paint swatches. Victoria knelt beside her.

"Stage left," Daisy muttered under her breath, not looking up. "Lawson's watching again."

"Let him," Victoria said softly. Then, raising her voice just enough, she said, "I'll need those plans moved to my office. The inspector may want to see them when he comes."

Daisy didn't miss a beat. "The city inspector?"

"That's the one. We had a telegram this morning. Something about a foundation discrepancy in the blueprints." She said it loud enough to carry. "It's probably nothing, but we'll need to give him access to the substage."

There was a pause in the air. She could feel it more than hear it—Lawson's movement stopping for a fraction of a second.

"Would you like me to tidy the area before he arrives?" Daisy asked smoothly.

"Yes, if you have time. He may be here as early as Wednesday."

Victoria straightened and brushed imaginary dust from her skirt. "I'll need to leave early today," she announced, projecting again subtly.

"There's an errand I must see to—some paperwork at the licensing board."

Lawson had returned to his clipboard, but she noted the flick of his eyes in her direction.

"Carry on, everyone," Victoria said with a practiced smile. "We're nearly there."

As she walked offstage, she heard Daisy humming faintly—an old lullaby they'd both used before to signal a shared understanding. The plan was in motion.

Out in the alley behind the theater, Victoria allowed herself a long exhale. She adjusted her hat and pulled on her gloves, her fingers steady despite the cold.

The trap was set. Now it was only a matter of whether Trask would take the bait.

The gaslight flickered against the blueprints spread across Holmes's desk, casting long shadows of structural lines and sketched stairwells. Rodney stood with his sleeves rolled and spectacles perched low on his nose, a carpenter's pencil resting behind one ear. He had brought with him the final draft—a master layout of the London Majestic as it once was, before Trask's hands had ever touched her walls.

Holmes hovered nearby, eyes narrowed, fingertips pressed together in thought. "So, this section here, beneath the southern wing, this is original?"

Rodney tapped the page. "Yes, but the trapdoor system above it was repurposed in for an aerial rigging show, but this chamber remained sealed. At least, it was sealed when I left."

"And now?"

Rodney eyebrows were knitted, showing his concern. "Can't say. That's what's worrying me. If Trask is using it, he likely found a way in through the dumbwaiter or one of the crawlspaces."

Holmes leaned closer. "Which are...?"

Rodney drew a firm X across one corner. "There. The south corridor's pantry once connected by shaft to the mezzanine kitchen. If he's using it for movement or observation, it might explain how he appears and disappears so easily."

Holmes's gaze sharpened. "Could we test the passage without entering it directly?"

Rodney nodded. "Drop something light, dusted with chalk—string, a feather, a coin. If it moves or vanishes someone's in there."

A soft knock at the door interrupted them.

"Enter," Holmes called.

The door creaked open to reveal a lanky boy in a wool cap and threadbare coat. It was Wiggins, the eldest of Holmes's Irregulars, cheeks red from the cold and one boot muddy.

Holmes gave him a brief nod. "You've news?"

"Yes, sir," Wiggins said, brushing his sleeve across his nose. "The theater. Last night, 'round two o'clock. Saw a tall gent slip in the side alley—had a key. Long coat, heavy on the shoulders. Didn't see his face, but the walk looked familiar."

Holmes's voice was low. "How long did he stay?"

"Near two hours. No lantern. No companion. Came out with the same care he went in. He didn't look back, neither."

Holmes looked to Rodney, who had gone very still.

"That's him," Rodney muttered. "That's Trask. It must be."

Holmes turned back to Wiggins. "Good work. Get a hot meal from Mrs. Hudson and return to your post by ten. Keep watch in rotating shifts. You know the signs—if he leaves, or if he's followed."

Wiggins gave a short nod and slipped out.

Rodney exhaled slowly. "He's nesting in there. Using the structure like a second skin."

"He's begun to think of it as his," Holmes said grimly. "But the moment he fears exposure, he'll act—rashly, or violently."

Rodney's jaw tightened. "Miss Watson is in danger."

Holmes's silence confirmed the truth more than words might have.

"I've taken precautions," he said at last. "She's watched on her way home. Irregulars monitor her building. But I'm no longer convinced those measures are sufficient."

Rodney moved toward the fire, the light catching the silver at his temples. "I've seen performers forget themselves in a role. But this man is rewriting the entire stage around himself."

Holmes joined him, his eyes distant. "Then it's time we write him into the final act."

A hush had settled over Victoria's flat, broken only by the faint tick of the clock on the mantel and the soft clink of teacups as Watson poured them each a measure. The windows were drawn against the night, lamplight casting golden halos across the papers and sketches strewn across her table.

Watson leaned back in his chair, cradling his teacup. He watched his daughter carefully—the slight tremble in her fingers as she straightened a stack of notes, the set of her jaw, the fatigue that clung just behind her eyes.

"I saw Holmes this evening," he said gently. "He tells me things are escalating."

Victoria let out a sigh, not looking up. "They are."

"Victoria," He hesitated. "Are you certain you want to keep going with this?"

She raised her gaze then, steady and clear. "It's not just about the theater anymore, Father, or Dr. Stamford."

He waited.

"It's about not letting fear dictate what I do. About refusing to let someone like Trask manipulate the truth and shape my future in secret." She paused, her voice quieter. "This was supposed to be a restoration. A new beginning. And instead, he's tried to twist it into something ugly."

Watson set his cup down with care. "I know. And I understand what's driving you—I do. But I've seen what men like Trask are capable of. This isn't just cleverness or deceit. It's obsession. And obsession is dangerous."

Victoria's voice softened, but her spine remained straight. "You taught me to fight for what matters. To speak when it would've been safer to stay silent. Dr. Stamford deserves the truth to come out. The people involved deserve to be safe. And I—," she paused, emotion tightening her throat, "I deserve to take back what's mine."

Watson reached across the table and took her hand. "You're braver than I ever was."

She gave him a tired smile. "You fought wars."

"Yes," he said. "But you're fighting something more insidious. A man who hides in shadows and rewrites the truth while the world applauds the performance. And you're meeting him in his own arena."

Victoria looked down for a moment, then stood and crossed to a drawer near her writing desk. She pulled out a slim, leather-bound volume and handed it to him.

"What's this?"

"My theater journal," she said. "I started it when the renovation began. I thought it might help me organize the chaos. But now, there are entries in here that might help Mr. Holmes. Notes about timing, people, comments that seemed odd, but I dismissed at the time."

Watson turned the journal in his hands, visibly moved. "You've always had your mother's sense for detail."

Victoria gave a wistful laugh. "She would've loved this place."

"I think she would've loved you more, for bringing it back."

A silence passed between them—warm, fragile, full of things neither needed to be said aloud.

Victoria glanced toward the hallway, then back to her father. "Do you think Mr. Holmes is still up?"

Watson offered a soft smile. "Even if he isn't, he won't mind being disturbed."

He stood and tapped the cover of the journal. "This may prove more useful than you know."

Victoria returned to her seat, her hands now still. "I hope it's enough."

Watson shook his head. "The fact that you're still standing here, still fighting, tells me it already is."

The lamps outside flickered with the wind. Inside, Holmes stood at his desk, examining files with Rodney.

Victoria and Watson knocked and then entered together, the leather-bound journal in her hands. She held it close, as though reluctant to part with it.

"I thought this might be useful," she said simply, offering it to Holmes. "It contains my notes throughout the renovation—every oddity, every comment that seemed harmless at the time."

Holmes accepted the journal with a quiet nod, his eyes flicking toward her with appreciation. "Excellent. Your timing is fortuitous. We were just discussing a plan to safely examine the theater without risk of Trask's presence."

Rodney scratched his head. "If we had a few uninterrupted hours, it could help us. The trick is ensuring no one's watching."

Victoria stepped forward, her expression thoughtful. "I may have an idea."

All eyes turned to her.

"I've been planning a thank-you dinner for the crew—nothing extravagant. Just a private room and a meal to celebrate the end of renovations. Lawson is invited. Daisy can help. If we seat him at the far end of the table and keep him socially engaged, you'd have the entire building to yourselves for a few hours."

Holmes blinked, visibly impressed. "An elegant solution. Simple, natural, and with plausible motive. Precisely the kind of distraction he wouldn't suspect."

Rodney chuckled. "Clever girl."

Victoria's lips curled into a brief, satisfied smile. "I'll let Daisy handle the finer points of the seating arrangement. No one corrals a dinner guest quite like she does."

Holmes clasped his hands. "Then we'll coordinate our timing with the dinner. Watson, Rodney, and I will examine the theater."

Rodney replied resolutely. "Then we're agreed. We set the stage and see what emerges from behind the curtain."

Rodney paused, then turned back toward the others. "I see the value of getting Lawson, Trask, out of the building long enough to search uninterrupted. But forgive me, I don't yet understand how this helps clear Dr. Stamford's name."

Holmes's gaze sharpened. "Because we believe Trask used this theater as a hiding place for the falsehoods that condemned Stamford."

Watson leaned forward, his expression grim. "Anne Godfrey's statement was typed with the same flawed machine Trask uses now. We believe he drugged her, manipulated her memories, and planted evidence to make Stamford appear negligent or worse."

Rodney nodded slowly. "And you think the proof of what he did and how he did it might be hidden in the Majestic?"

Holmes spoke evenly. "He's a man who believes in the permanence of his schemes. He leaves trails for himself, not others. Our hope is that somewhere in his secret domain, his nest, he's kept a record, a note or draft, or a trophy. Something he never thought anyone would find."

Victoria's voice was soft but firm. "And if we find it, Dr. Stamford's story changes. The world hears the truth."

Rodney straightened, his eyes now fully alight with understanding. "Then let's find it."

The flat had grown still again. The voices had faded, the door had closed behind the last of them, and Holmes stood in the silence. Outside, the city hummed faintly with distant carriages and lamplighters finishing their routes.

Holmes crossed to the side table where Victoria's journal lay waiting. He took a moment, fingertips resting against the leather cover, before drawing the chair nearer to the hearth and settling in.

The first entries were precisely what he expected—pages of measurements, vendor comparisons, lists of delivery dates and material shortages. She had annotated the earliest ones with hesitant strokes, as if unsure of their value, but as the journal continued, her voice grew steadier, more purposeful. There were sketches, floorplans, snippets of overheard conversations, all interspersed with the occasional reflective paragraph.

One entry spoke of the first time she had stood in the unfinished gallery and imagined an audience rising to its feet. Another, penned in a tighter hand, described her fear when she realized things were going wrong— how she didn't know who to trust, but refused to be driven out.

Holmes paused over a brief note about Daisy's unwavering support: *"There is courage in kindness, and I see it every day in her."*

He turned another page—and stopped.

This section was different. Shorter paragraphs written in the margin beside a half-filled ledger of renovation tasks. It had clearly been added later, and the ink was a shade darker.

"Mr. Holmes has surprised me."

Holmes blinked.

"I thought I understood his mind—precise, logical, driven by results. But there's more. A kind of quiet loyalty that refuses to be named. I've seen it in the way he listens when Father speaks, in the silences he leaves when I'm struggling to find words. I never expected to find such comfort in a man so formidable."

Holmes leaned back slightly, as if the weight of the words had shifted the room.

"I don't know if he thinks of me as anything beyond a curious addition to this case, but I've come to trust him more than I ever intended. Perhaps that's foolish. But it's real. And sometimes, even the foolish things deserve a place."

He stared at the page for a long time, one finger resting beside the final sentence. The fire popped gently, but he didn't move.

Affection, trust... perhaps even something warmer. A passage she clearly hadn't meant for him to see.

For a moment, the great detective of Baker Street said nothing. Then, carefully, he closed the journal and set it beside the chair.

His eyes returned to the flames. Not analyzing. Not deducing.

Only feeling.

After a time, he spoke aloud, though no one was there to hear.

"Even the foolish things."

And he smiled.

But only briefly.

The smile faded, and Holmes leaned forward again, taking the journal back into his hands. He forced his thoughts into more familiar channels. There was work to be done.

He flipped several pages forward, scanning briskly until something made him pause. He read it again aloud:

"Interior wall materials ordered from Monksfield & Sons arrived early. Lawson insisted we keep it in the substage hallway for a week before installation. He said it needed to adjust to humidity."

Holmes took a long, deep breath.

"Monksfield... Monksfield," he murmured. "No record of that vendor in the company invoices. Wall materials don't 'adjust' to humidity. He was buying time or hiding something."

His fingers moved faster now, rifling toward an earlier section. He found it—an earlier note in the margin from weeks prior:

"Odd request from Lawson: He asked that I change the material supplier on a wall buildout due to 'fireproofing concerns.' He said his acquaintance at Monksfield had a better option."

Holmes stood abruptly, journal in hand. "There was no acquaintance. No concern for fireproofing. It was the delivery itself. It must have been the moment he moved materials inside."

He crossed to his desk and pulled out the latest theater blueprint. He whispered as he moved a ruler across the page.

"He redirected the delivery to the substage. Not for staging. For construction. *New* construction behind the Blythe wall."

Holmes looked again at the journal.

"If he built something using Monksfield material, and it never appears on any official order, then it's his final blind spot. A compartment. A

166

vault, maybe. And no one but Trask—or someone watching this closely—would know."

Without hesitation, he grabbed his coat and strode to the door. Victoria's flat was only steps across the hall, but the urgency demanded movement.

A quiet knock echoed.

After a pause, Victoria opened the door in her dressing robe, hair slightly tousled, expression alarmed. "Mr. Holmes?"

He held up the journal. "You wrote something I believe you've forgotten."

Her eyes widened. "What?"

"The wall materials delivery from Monksfield & Sons. Kept in the substage corridor. That wasn't storage—it was concealment."

He saw the dawning understanding on her face.

"If I'm correct," he said, voice low and intense, "you may have unknowingly documented the moment Trask built his hiding place. And tomorrow, we'll begin the process of uncovering it."

The brass bell above the office door gave a half-hearted jingle as Holmes pushed it open. Victoria followed, adjusting her gloves as she stepped into the cramped front room of Monksfield & Sons, a building tucked neatly between a shuttered pawnbroker and a tobacconist.

The room smelled faintly of old wood and linseed oil. Rolled blueprints leaned like sleepy sentinels against the walls, and dust hung in beams of sunlight that filtered through half-cleaned windows. Behind a tall desk, a clerk looked up, startled.

Holmes offered a polite nod. "Good morning. Mr. Monksfield, if he's available."

The clerk blinked. "And whom shall I say is calling?"

"Sherlock Holmes and Miss Victoria Watson."

At the sound of her name, a voice called from the back: "Send them in, Henry."

They were ushered through a narrow hallway to a small office where Thomas Monksfield, balding and bespectacled, stood beside a drafting table cluttered with measuring tools and worn leather-bound ledgers. He wiped his hands on a handkerchief and stepped forward with cautious warmth.

"Miss Watson," he said. "I recognize your name from the renovation contracts, though I have never had the pleasure of meeting you directly. And Mr. Holmes—well, you're known to anyone with a newspaper."

"I should hope not all of them," Holmes replied with dry precision. "We appreciate your time. Our visit concerns a question of access and authorship."

"Go on," Monksfield said, waving them to the small chairs across from his desk.

Holmes motioned to Victoria. She opened her satchel and produced a folded blueprint, carefully spreading it on the tabletop.

"This is the draft submitted to our site foreman by a man calling himself Samuel Lawson," she said. "My concern is that he may not have received this through proper channels or that alterations were made and passed off as your work."

Monksfield adjusted his spectacles, leaning over the page with care. "This is certainly our template," he said. "But the note here, this margin about the substage ventilation, it's not in our hand."

"You're certain?" Holmes asked.

"Absolutely. Whoever wrote this did so after it left our office. The ink's different, and so is the spacing. It's subtle, but unmistakable."

Victoria exhaled slowly. "He was laying groundwork early. Modifying access routes before we even knew where the walls would land."

Holmes's gaze sharpened. "May I ask – was there any correspondence or visit from a Mr. Lawson during the early proposal stages?"

Monksfield furrowed his brow. "Lawson... the name rings a faint bell. Yes, he came once asking about damp-proofing and crawlspaces. He said he was assisting your site team. I assumed he was part of your staff."

Victoria exchanged a glance with Holmes. "He wasn't."

"Did he leave a card?" Holmes asked.

"No, and I didn't think to question it. He was pleasant enough. Inquisitive, but not suspiciously so."

Holmes tapped the corner of the blueprint. "The areas he inquired about were the same ones now under scrutiny. He was mapping vulnerabilities, then inserting himself into the repair."

Monksfield's eyes widened slightly. "I had no idea."

"Few do," Holmes said. "It's not your fault. Men like this rely on assumption. He becomes part of the landscape until the moment it matters."

"Dear me!" Monksfield murmured under his breath.

"Is it possible to see all documentation related to the theater project?" Holmes asked.

"Certainly," Monksfield eagerly replied, "You have our full cooperation."

With sleeves rolled and spectacles perched low on his nose, Monksfield led them into the back office. Stacks of ledgers, delivery receipts, and catalogues crowded the space, but everything had a place. He moved like someone who'd been navigating these shelves for decades.

"Now then," he said, drawing up a thick ledger and flipping through it with deft fingers. "We've handled many orders for the Majestic in the past year. Mostly lime plasterboard, timber battens, sacks of horsehair compound—things your renovation crew would need for proper interior work."

Holmes and Victoria exchanged a glance. Victoria stepped forward. "We're particularly interested in deliveries marked under the name Lawson—or anyone connected to interior wall access in the substage areas."

"Right." He turned several more pages, then paused. "Here we are. Mr. Lawson signed for deliveries on four occasions. Two major orders and two smaller consignments."

"May we?" Holmes asked, gesturing toward the record.

The clerk passed it over, and Holmes bent over the book, tracing a finger along the line. "September 14, October 26, and November 2."

"November 2?" Victoria gasped. "That's the day the second anonymous note appeared. The one warning me not to let him into my life."

Holmes's brow furrowed. "And one day before the phantom stonemason, Blythe, was scheduled to work."

Monksfield perked up. "Blythe? That name's familiar." He moved to a second stack of books and thumbed quickly through a smaller volume. "Yes, Henry Blythe signed for a delivery of lime plasterboard. Only once. Odd order. Just two boards and some wooden lath strips. But it wasn't delivered to the main entrance. He requested it be left by the tradesmen's alley access."

Holmes turned to Victoria. "The alley door. The one Daisy found unlatched the night we searched the substage."

Victoria nodded slowly. "That would've allowed Trask, or his accomplice, to smuggle materials in and out unseen."

Monksfield raised an eyebrow. "I assumed they were working late to patch something minor. But I'll admit—the request struck me as peculiar. Most site managers want everything delivered in full view for accountability."

Holmes closed the ledger gently. "This has been most helpful. Might we have a copy of these entries?"

"Certainly," the clerk replied, already rising to retrieve paper and ink. "Would you like them certified?"

Holmes gave a small smile. "Indeed. Please include the delivery location notes."

Victoria watched as he moved to the back room. "Well?"

Holmes's voice was low, but taut with purpose. "We have confirmation that both aliases, Lawson and Blythe, were used to sign for materials likely tied to Trask's concealment efforts. More importantly, we've just found the supply trail leading into the hidden sections of the theater."

Leaving Monksfield's offices, Victoria exhaled, her breath white in the chilly air. "Then we're not just building a case, we're digging a path straight to him."

Putting on his gloves Holmes replied, "And now, Miss Watson, we'll see how much longer the phantom bricklayer can remain behind his wall."

The clatter of hooves on wet cobblestones provided a rhythmic undercurrent as the carriage made its slow turn toward Baker Street. Inside, the chill air still clung to their coats despite the coal-heated footwarmer between them.

Holmes leaned back, gloved hands resting loosely in his lap, his gaze fixed on the mist-fogged window. Victoria sat opposite, arms wrapped around a slim leather folder—the clerk's certified copies tucked safely inside.

For a time, neither spoke.

At last, Victoria broke the silence. "I'm thinking Saturday evening for the dinner."

Holmes blinked and turned his head.

"The thank-you supper," she clarified. "For the renovation crew. Most of the major work is complete, and Daisy and I have been meaning to host something before rehearsals begin. It would be the perfect cover."

Holmes nodded slowly. "It should give us several uninterrupted hours. Once Trask is out of the building…"

"You, Father, and Mr. Rodney will have full access," she finished. "Assuming Lawson accepts the invitation."

"He will," Holmes said quietly. "He'll feel obligated to maintain appearances. If he declines, it might raise suspicions."

Victoria adjusted the edge of her coat, her thumb brushing the edge of the folder absently. "It's strange, isn't it? Planning a cheerful staff celebration knowing it's all just camouflage for a hunt."

"Stranger still," Holmes said, "is how well you've adapted to it."

She looked at him then, tired but steady. "I never wanted to become someone who thinks in strategies and traps."

"You haven't," he said. "You think in terms of protection. Of reclamation. That's a different sort of strength."

Victoria's eyes fell to her hands. Then, with a soft exhale, she offered a small smile. "I wish you could be there."

Holmes arched a brow. "At the dinner?"

"Yes. Not as a spy. As a guest." Her voice was light but sincere. "You've done as much to rebuild this place as anyone on the crew."

His lips curved, just faintly, and he leaned forward slightly in the darkening cab.

"You forget," he said, "I'm hardly festive company."

"I disagree," she replied. "You're observant, dry-witted, and unpredictable—three qualities that make for an interesting dinner companion."

Holmes regarded her for a moment. Then, without a word, he reached across the narrow space and placed one hand gently over hers.

The motion was brief. A touch without pressure. Warm through the layers of leather and wool. And then it was gone.

But Victoria didn't move. She didn't need to.

The city blurred beyond the window, the sky smudging into soft gray as the carriage rolled on.

And within that quiet space, between flickering lamplight and memory, two minds rested, for a moment, not as strategist and soldier, not as detective and witness, but as something quietly, undeniably human.

The private dining room of Maison Tournier glowed with soft amber light, its gas chandeliers catching on polished glassware and warm mahogany. The air was rich with the scent of roasted meats, crusty bread, and a faint trace of orange peel in the mulled wine that flowed freely from the decanters.

Victoria stood near the entryway, glancing toward the clock above the bar. It was just past seven. The crew had been arriving steadily since half-past six, laughing and shaking the rain from their coats as they found seats. The long table down the center of the room was already abuzz with conversation, coats draped over chairs, napkins unfurled.

She greeted each arrival with a warm smile, offering a word of thanks or a quick compliment. It wasn't difficult to mean it. These men and women had worked tirelessly through poor weather, unexpected setbacks, and late nights to help restore the theater. And though tonight's dinner was a strategic maneuver, it was also genuine.

At the far end of the table, Daisy waved her over. "We're short one corkscrew and Mr. Munsey's been threatening to use his teeth if someone doesn't open that next bottle," she said with mock severity.

Victoria laughed and signaled to the server. As she stepped away, her gaze passed over the man seated just to Daisy's left.

Lawson.

Samuel Lawson—or rather, the man known to Holmes as Trask.

He was impeccably dressed, his collar crisp and his cuffs modestly adorned. His smile was courteous but tight, as though holding something back. The lines around his mouth were deeper tonight, his eyes more guarded than gleaming. He held his wine with a practiced ease, yet Victoria noted he had already emptied two glasses.

She gently bowed her head at him. He returned the gesture with a slight raise of his glass and an unreadable smile.

"Enjoying yourself, Mr. Lawson?" she asked lightly.

"Very much," he said. "It's good to see everyone relaxing. There's been a great deal of strain these past few weeks."

"That's true," she said, her voice neutral. "But the hardest part is behind us."

Lawson tilted his head. "If only that were always the case."

Victoria moved on quickly, heart steady but alert.

At the table's midpoint, Daisy had taken it upon herself to become the evening's unofficial master of ceremonies. She introduced toasts with theatrical flair, and kept Lawson engaged in genial conversation, never too close, never too far. When he looked like he might rise to circulate, Daisy leaned in with a laugh or a question, drawing him back into place.

She was also liberally refilling his wine glass.

When the meal had been cleared and coffee began to circulate, Victoria stood. Her glass in hand, she tapped a spoon gently against its side. The room quieted.

"I won't keep you long," she said. "But I couldn't let this project near completion without pausing to thank the people who've made it happen. When I first stepped inside the Majestic, it was dust and ruin and memory. Now, because of you, it's becoming a home for stories again—a place where beauty and meaning can live side by side."

There was a murmur of approval, a few claps.

She smiled. "So tonight, please enjoy the food, the company, and the knowledge that your work has built something truly special."

Daisy stood and raised her glass. "To calluses, creativity, and carpentry!"

The toast earned laughter, cheers, and the clink of glasses.

Lawson rose a moment later, somewhat unsteadily. He adjusted his waistcoat, cleared his throat, and held up his glass.

"If I may…" His voice was even, but his gaze roved the room with an odd intensity. "Buildings remember things. They carry impressions—shadows, if you will. Not ghosts, but echoes. A hammer striking a wall… footsteps in the dark backstage… laughter spilling from the upper gallery. These things never truly leave."

The room quieted further, attention drawn in.

"I've been part of many renovations. Most forget the past as they build the future. But this one… this one respects both." He raised his glass higher. "To memory. To mystery. And to the things that hide."

He held his glass aloft a moment too long. The smile on his face remained fixed, but his eyes were far away, as if watching something only he could see.

Then, almost as an afterthought, he added, "…in plain sight."

A few scattered claps followed—tentative, unsure. The moment lingered uncomfortably before Daisy broke it with a bright laugh.

"Well, cheers to that! And to walls that know when to keep a secret!" she called, raising her own glass in mock solemnity.

Laughter rippled through the room, grateful for the release. Conversation resumed, more cautious now but flowing again like a stream that had hit a rock and found a way around it.

Lawson took his seat slowly, a small frown tugging at the corner of his mouth. He reached for his wine, but Daisy, ever helpful, leaned in and gently plucked the decanter from his side.

"Oh, let me get that for you," she said sweetly, pouring only a half-glass this time. "Pace yourself. We still have pudding coming."

He looked at her with narrowed eyes—only for a second—before the mask slipped back into place. "Quite right," he said, lifting the glass with a slight nod. "Can't toast to the end without dessert."

Victoria observed all of it from a few seats away, her own smile fixed, her heart ticking like a metronome.

Daisy was handling him brilliantly keeping him entertained, distracted, and just foggy enough to slow any sudden thoughts of departure. Every so often, Victoria caught Trask glancing toward the door, then towards her, as if recalculating a route in his head.

She made her way over to the corner of the room where two of the crew were recounting a humorous incident involving a saw, a tin of paint, and an unfortunate pair of boots. She laughed along, offered a comment, asked after one of their wives—and all the while her peripheral gaze kept drifting to the clock above the bar.

It was almost eight.

Holmes, Watson, and Rodney had been inside the theater for nearly an hour.

Victoria said a silent prayer, "Dear Lord, make him stay seated and distracted. Just a little longer."

Daisy now had Lawson deep in a conversation about curtain weights and pulley systems, a topic she knew only enough about to keep him talking. He seemed increasingly invested in explaining the exact advantage of a dual-line counterbalance system.

Victoria took the opportunity to refill her own glass. She caught the eye of the maître d', who offered her a polite nod. Everything was running smoothly—on the surface.

And beneath it, the stage was shifting.

She glanced again toward Lawson.

He was speaking animatedly, his posture more relaxed now, but there was something in his expression. Not quite contentment. Not suspicion either. Something in between. Like a man who suspects the punchline is about to arrive but hasn't quite caught the setup.

Her fingers tightened slightly on the stem of her glass.

She thought to herself, "You don't get to ruin this. You don't get to turn something meant for light into darkness. Not here. Not tonight."

Lawson laughed, too loud this time, at something Daisy said. His hand slapped the table. The sound made several heads turn.

He immediately composed himself and raised both palms in apology, looking at Daisy. "Forgive me. I do enjoy good company."

Daisy smiled, unruffled. "Then you're in the right place."

Victoria watched as he reached for his glass again, slower now.

She smiled and turned towards the crew again, accepting a compliment on the duck and laughing at an offer to redo the orchestra pit "free of charge if the wine keeps coming."

All the while, the seconds ticked by, measured not in minutes or conversation, but in every motion that kept Samuel Lawson seated at that table, and the doors of the Majestic wide open to truth.

The hush of the empty theater was different at night—heavier somehow. Not silence, exactly, but the deep inhalation of a building holding its breath. Holmes, Watson, and Rodney moved through the dim backstage hallway with care, lantern light flickering against aged brick and newly painted trim. Every sound—footsteps, the creak of a hinge—seemed magnified.

"Miss Victoria's crew dinner party must be filled with wine and laughter by now," Rodney murmured as he held the lantern higher. "Can't believe we're just down the road from it all."

Holmes stopped near the infamous "Blythe wall." He crouched, fingertips grazing the baseboard. "Which is exactly what Trask counted on. Noise and distraction above—construction and concealment below."

Rodney knelt beside him. "This portion here—see the difference in plaster tone? That wasn't part of the original plan. Whoever added this didn't use the same lime mix."

Watson unrolled a slim crowbar from a canvas satchel. "Shall we test the theory?"

Holmes gave a curt nod.

The wall yielded with surprising ease—more so than it should have. The crowbar loosened a panel that swung inward with a whisper, revealing a dark passage not on any blueprint.

They stepped inside.

The air changed immediately—damp, stale, and still. This wasn't merely a hidden alcove. It was a living space.

Holmes swept the lantern beam slowly. There was a narrow cot, made military tidy. A wooden desk held neatly stacked documents, jars of pencils, sealing wax, and a cracked teacup. Beside it, a shelf lined with books—some philosophical texts, others architectural. The air smelled faintly of oil and something chemical.

"This is more than a hideout," Watson said, voice low, "it's a headquarters."

Rodney looked stunned. "He's been living here. In the belly of the building."

Holmes was already rifling through the papers. "Schedule drafts. Observation logs. Diagrams of the theater—old and new. He's been tracking the renovations alongside Victoria's public announcements." He held up a half-finished sketch of the auditorium. "This is her dream, copied and dissected."

Watson moved toward a side table and paused. "Holmes. Here."

He held up a glass bottle, half-full of amber residue. The stopper had a faintly sweet, medicinal scent.

Holmes took it and tilted the bottle toward the lantern. His eyes narrowed. "Bromide and laudanum mixture. Just as Stamford described."

Watson exhaled slowly. "The same compound used on Anne Godfrey."

Rodney looked ill. "He meant to use it again."

Holmes set the bottle down with care. "This space... it's been engineered. Not cobbled together. Designed to be soundproof, insulated from vibration, even the air vents are redirected. He could've lived here for months. Longer, if need be."

Rodney moved toward a set of ledgers stacked at the foot of the cot. "The man's a phantom. He builds a lair beneath a stage, and no one notices."

"That was the goal," Holmes murmured. "A life within a life. He inserted himself into the fabric of the building—trusted, unnoticed. And now..."

He looked to the open panel behind them.

"…he's part of its bones."

For a long moment, no one spoke.

Then Holmes straightened, gathering the most damning documents into a satchel. "We have what we need for now. Leave the rest. He'll return, and when he does, I want him to believe nothing's been disturbed."

Watson looked at Holmes asking, "And Victoria?"

"She's nearly at the crescendo," Holmes said. "The final act is near."

The energy in the room had shifted again.

Daisy had somehow managed to get "Lawson" dancing—twice. He'd had several glasses of wine by now, and though he moved with the awkward stiffness of a man unaccustomed to levity, he seemed determined to participate in the festivities. His hand was firm at Daisy's waist, his laugh a fraction too loud, his smile sharp around the edges. Still, Daisy wore her brightest expression and played her part perfectly, keeping him just entertained enough to forget the time.

Victoria watched them from a small distance. She could feel the minutes slipping past, each one a precious second gained for Holmes and the others at the theater.

Suddenly, Trask disengaged from Daisy mid-spin and turned toward Victoria, catching her eye with a lopsided grin.

"Your turn," he declared.

Victoria's stomach fluttered—not with nerves exactly, but a sharpened awareness. She couldn't risk offending him. Not now. So, she set down her glass, forced a cordial smile, and stepped forward.

He took her hand with a kind of mock-chivalry, guiding her onto the makeshift dance floor near the center of the restaurant, where a small trio of musicians had begun another waltz.

"I must confess," he said as they began to move, "you've impressed me, Miss Watson."

"Have I?" she replied lightly, aware of every eye in the room, every second ticking by.

"Most people wouldn't have got this far," he said. "Rebuilding a ruin, turning it into… something that matters." His breath carried the scent of wine and something sharper underneath. "It's rare, these days. Vision."

Victoria offered a reserved smile, stepping neatly in time with him. "Thank you."

He glanced down at her, and for just a moment, his expression softened. "You remind me of someone I knew. A long time ago. She had your same… clarity. Purpose."

"That's kind of you to say."

He tilted his head. "It's too bad that—" He stopped. Something in his eyes flickered. She said nothing, letting the silence stretch, hoping he'd continue.

He did.

"It's too bad that time is such a stubborn thing," he muttered. "You build something beautiful, and still… it has to burn."

Victoria's heart thudded.

Trask smiled again, slow and nostalgic, as if remembering something private. "But I suppose that's the nature of theater, isn't it? Ephemeral. Illusion, rising from ash."

She gave a faint laugh, masking her unease. "I prefer restoration over destruction."

He gave a slight snort. "Of course you do. That's why I like you." Then, after a pause, he added, "But the ash always comes, Miss Watson. Always."

Before she could respond, the music began to fade. Trask gave her hand a parting squeeze, bowed in an exaggerated, theatrical gesture, and turned to reclaim his wineglass.

Victoria stood still for a moment, her pulse ticking at her throat.

"Still... it has to burn."

The words echoed in her mind like a match struck in a darkened room.

She scanned the crowd, caught Daisy's eye, and gave the faintest nod. Daisy blinked, then moved quickly to reengage "Lawson" in conversation, steering him toward another toast, another distraction.

And Victoria, her face calm and pleasant, slipped quietly toward the door, hand brushing the small timepiece pinned discreetly inside her sleeve.

"It's been two hours. Maybe more." she thought, "Mr. Holmes had better be ready."

The key turned softly in the lock as Victoria stepped into her flat. The glow from a single lamp lit the room in amber, and she sighed as she kicked off her shoes, her body aching from the effort of keeping poised under pressure. Daisy trailed behind her, still radiant from the evening but clearly exhausted.

"You were brilliant," Victoria said, offering her a tired smile as she set her reticule on the side table. "I don't know how you managed to keep him occupied for that long."

Daisy flopped onto the settee with a dramatic exhale. "Charm, quick feet, and a great deal of wine." She smirked. "Although I suspect I may never get the smell of claret out of my dress."

Victoria chuckled and poured her a glass of water. "Well, you certainly earned your place in the theatre's history tonight."

Daisy took the glass with a grateful nod, then leaned her head back against the cushions. "He was watching everyone," she murmured, "but me especially. I think he was trying to figure out if I were playing a part."

"You were," Victoria said lightly. "And you were magnificent."

After a beat, Victoria's expression sobered. "Still, I'd feel better if you stayed here tonight."

Daisy opened one eye. "Are you sure?"

"I am. I didn't like the way he looked at you after that last dance. It's probably nothing, but even 'nothing' doesn't feel safe anymore."

Daisy stood and stretched with a yawn. "The guest room it is. And I'm locking the door, just in case."

They exchanged tired smiles, and Daisy disappeared down the hallway.

Victoria was reaching to turn off the lamp when she heard it—the faint click of a latch across the corridor. A moment later, the creak of a door closing. Holmes had returned to Baker Street.

She hesitated. Then crossed the hall.

Before her fist touched the door, she heard that familiar voice say, "No need to knock."

She opened the door gently and found Holmes settling behind his desk, rolling his sleeves to the forearm, with the journal still open beside him.

He looked up as she entered, and for a moment neither spoke.

"I just couldn't wait until morning," she said.

Holmes gestured silently to the chair opposite. She took it, her hands folded in her lap.

"We kept him there the entire time," she said. "Three hours. Maybe more."

"Daisy did her part?"

"She was brilliant," Victoria said. "She kept refilling his wine glass until he was quite rumdum. He danced with her twice. Then decided he wanted to dance with me." She gave a faint, humorless laugh. "We spun awkwardly in a corner while he told me he liked me."

Holmes arched a brow but said nothing.

"He said I reminded him of someone he knew long ago. He respected me for restoring the theater. Then he started to say, 'It's too bad that...' and caught himself." She looked directly at him. "Then he said, 'It's too bad it has to burn.' Could that have simply been the wine talking?"

Holmes froze. The change in his posture was subtle but unmistakable stillness where there should have been motion, focus sharpening to a blade.

His hand moved to the margin of the open journal and made a quick note.

"He's planning something," Holmes said quietly, voice taut. "Something imminent. Fire would destroy evidence... and endanger everyone."

Victoria's face paled. "You think he actually intends to burn it down?"

"I think he was too careless tonight to lie entirely," Holmes replied. "He's begun unspooling. He knows we're circling him, and now he's preparing a final act."

She leaned forward, her voice quieter. "What did you find at the theatre tonight?"

Holmes's expression turned grim.

"The hidden room exists. Just as we suspected. It's behind the Blythe wall, completely sealed from the rest of the substage." He tapped the table. "Soundproofed. Reinforced."

Her throat tightened.

"He's been living there?"

"It appears so," Holmes confirmed. "We found bedding, journals, several disguises—and something worse."

She held still.

"A bottle with remnants of a compound. Bromide and laudanum in precise suspension. The same drug Stamford described. The one likely used on Anne Godfrey."

Victoria's hands clenched in her lap.

"It's one thing to suspect," she said softly. "It's another to know. He's been beneath us this entire time—watching, hiding, planning."

Holmes nodded. "It's a maze. He built it to contain himself until the right moment."

"And we've forced his hand," she whispered.

They sat in silence for a moment. Then Victoria looked up, eyes searching Holmes's face.

"Mr. Holmes, how much danger are we in?"

The question hung in the air, not as a challenge—but as a plea for honesty.

Holmes leaned back slightly. For once, his gaze didn't sharpen. It softened.

"I don't know," he said. "Which is why I worry."

Victoria swallowed.

"He's intelligent," Holmes continued. "But desperation makes men reckless. And he has fewer moves left with every passing day." He added quietly, "I will consider the matter tonight. We'll need to speak before you go back to the theater."

She said nothing, but he could see the strain in her shoulders, the slow rise and fall of her breath.

"I promise you this," he said finally. "We won't wait for him to strike."

Victoria whispered, her voice barely audible. "Good."

She hesitated, then asked, "Do you think it's enough now? The hidden room, the drugs, the false identities... Is it enough to go to Inspector Lestrade? Enough to arrest Trask—and clear Dr. Stamford's name?"

Holmes didn't answer immediately. He moved to the desk, fingers resting beside the journal as he weighed her words.

"Not quite," he said at last. "We have strong circumstantial connections. Enough to justify a deeper investigation, but not yet enough to hold him. Not without risking that he vanishes before we can force a confession or find more direct proof."

Victoria's shoulders sagged, but she agreed.

"And Dr. Stamford?" she asked.

Holmes's voice became gentler. "This is the closest we've come to exonerating him. Another step or two—one more undeniable link—and we'll have what we need to force Lestrade's hand."

She straightened slightly, the fight returning to her posture. "Then we'll find it."

Holmes's expression was quiet but resolute. "Yes. We will."

She stood slowly.

"I'll let you rest," she murmured. "We'll talk again in the morning."

Holmes rose with her. At the door, she paused and turned back.

"Thank you. For always telling me the truth."

"I don't know how to do otherwise," he said. Then, with a softness rarely heard, he added, "I respect you too highly."

She gave a faint, tired smile and slipped out into the hall.

Holmes stood still for a long moment before returning to the journal on his desk, the quiet of the night pressing close around him once more.

He stared down at the open pages without seeing them. His mind moved rapidly revisiting Trask's patterns, weighing escape routes, exit timelines, fire hazards. But beneath it all, something deeper stirred.

If anything were to happen to Victoria…

He gripped the edge of the desk, jaw tight.

He had never allowed himself attachments. Not like this. Yet here she was—clever, courageous, unexpected—and now directly in the path of a man who would burn a theatre to the ground without hesitation.

Holmes straightened and reached for a fresh sheet of paper. Plans would need to be drafted. Resources gathered. Surveillance increased.

He would protect her.

Not only because it was logical.

But because if she fell, if Trask succeeded, he would never forgive himself.

And neither would the man he had once believed himself to be.

The street outside was still wrapped in pale dawn when Holmes heard the knock at the door. Despite the early hour he was already dressed, the fire low in the grate and a half-drained cup of coffee growing cold on the table beside him.

"Enter," he called, even as the door opened.

Watson stepped inside, shrugging off his coat and scarf. "I hoped you'd be up."

"I rarely sleep when matters reach this stage," Holmes said. "Coffee?"

"Please," Watson replied, settling into the chair across from him. "You look like you've been turning things over all night."

"I have."

Holmes poured a second cup, handed it over, then leaned against the edge of the mantel. For a moment, he was quiet.

Then he spoke. "He made a mistake last night."

Watson glanced up. "Trask?"

Holmes said with an arched brow, "He drank too much wine, thanks to Miss Daisy. And he danced with Miss Watson. He told her she reminded him of someone he once knew. Then said it was 'too bad that—' before catching himself. Afterward, he told her, 'It's too bad it has to burn.'"

Watson froze, cup midway to his lips. "Burn?"

Holmes nodded solemnly. "I believe he was speaking of the theater, or perhaps something more symbolic. Either way, it confirms our suspicion, He's not finished."

"Is Victoria safe?"

"She's fine," Holmes said. "For now. But it was close. Too close." He folded his arms. "We must implement new protective measures. A discreet rotation and someone watching her at all hours."

Watson answered immediately, "Agreed. Whatever's needed. I will take shifts myself."

Holmes looked over sharply, then softened. "Excellent."

Watson watched him for a moment, then tilted his head. "There's more, isn't there?"

Holmes didn't answer right away.

Watson leaned forward, his voice quiet. "You care for her."

Holmes turned slightly toward the window, as if that might delay the answer. "I care for many people, Waston."

"You know that's not what I mean."

Holmes slowly moved toward the fireplace. Then, with a slight exhale, he spoke. "It is… a complication I did not anticipate."

Watson offered a small smile. "No one ever does."

Holmes finally looked at him. "She is not just a brilliant woman. She is *your* daughter. That reality carries a weight I cannot ignore."

Watson's expression remained steady. "I trust you with my life, Holmes. And with hers."

"That's what terrifies me," Holmes murmured. "If something happens to her—if I misstep, hesitate, or miscalculate—it will not only destroy me. It will destroy you."

Watson sat in thoughtful silence for a beat. Then he rose and walked to stand beside him.

"We are not alone in this," he said firmly. "You, me, Victoria, Daisy, Rodney—we're in this together. Trask has had the shadows to himself for too long. Now he's the one being watched. He's cornered."

Holmes looked at him then, genuinely—without mask or performance.

"You do not resent it?" Holmes asked. "This attachment?"

"I see it for what it is," Watson said. "A sign you're human. And perhaps, finally willing to let someone past the walls you've so carefully maintained."

Holmes's eyes dropped. "It's unfamiliar ground."

"Then consider me your guide," Watson said lightly. "I've had some practice in these matters."

That drew a dry chuckle from Holmes, though it faded quickly.

"She mustn't return to the theater alone again," Holmes said quietly.

"She won't," Watson replied. "Whatever comes next, we'll face it as a unit."

Holmes nodded once, tightly.

Watson clapped a hand on his shoulder. "We'll win this, my friend. And when we do, I suspect Victoria will be the one giving the toast."

Holmes managed a faint smile. "Let us hope it's not 'to the things that hide.'"

They shared a glance of understanding, and the day began to unfold beyond the windows.

A soft knock echoed on the sitting room door. Holmes rose, crossing the floor in three swift strides. When he opened it, Victoria stood on the threshold, with Daisy just behind her, clutching her gloves.

"Come in," Holmes said quietly.

Victoria stepped inside, and her face softened as her eyes found Watson. "Father."

Without hesitation, she crossed to him and wrapped him in a gentle embrace, pressing a kiss to his cheek. Watson smiled, his expression touched with both affection and worry.

Daisy offered a small wave, slipping in behind her.

"We didn't mean to interrupt," Victoria said, glancing between the men, "but I felt it would be best not to delay."

"Quite right," Holmes said, gesturing toward the chairs by the hearth. "Please, sit."

They gathered close. The fire offered a steady warmth, grounding the room in comfort despite the tension that hung in the air.

Holmes folded his hands. "I've been considering your return to the theatre today. It presents both an opportunity and a risk. We cannot remove you from that environment, but we can alter the conditions under which you interact with him."

Victoria straightened slightly.

"You once mentioned your plans to redesign your office," Holmes continued, his gaze fixed on her. "A full renovation. I propose you move forward with it—today."

She tilted her head. "With Lawson?"

Holmes answered. "Yes. Request that he manage the renovation personally. Provide a detailed design brief—enough to make it clear this is a high-priority project. Mention, too, that you've hired a designer to consult on the aesthetic."

"A designer?" Daisy asked.

"A Scotland Yard sergeant whom I've worked with before." Holmes replied. "He'll appear to be part of your artistic team. In reality, he'll be watching Lawson every moment."

Victoria gave a slow nod, already seeing the shape of it.

"In addition," Holmes went on, "I'll place two men among the cleaning crew scheduled to work. They'll alternate shifts, always in view, but never obvious. Off-duty officers. Experienced and loyal."

He looked at Victoria, then at Daisy.

"You'll never be left alone. Not in the hallways, not backstage, not even in the upper galleries. He will be watched, and more importantly, he will know he is watched."

Daisy exhaled. "That's a relief. Last night, I tried to laugh it off, but I didn't like the way he looked at me. Not one bit."

"He's aware that your role in the theater extends beyond programs and refreshments," Holmes said. "You unsettled him without realizing it."

Victoria reached across to squeeze Daisy's hand. "You were incredible, but I won't let you face him again without protection."

Daisy squeezed Victoria's hand back, her smile faint but real.

Watson cleared his throat softly. "It's a good plan. A bold one. The more we keep him performing, the more likely he is to slip."

Holmes turned his eyes back to Victoria, the firelight catching the darker flecks in his eyes. "He may sense the pressure increasing. If he lashes out, it will be with haste—and that is when he will make mistakes."

Victoria held his gaze a moment longer than necessary, then gave a slow, deliberate nod. "Then let him feel it."

For a moment, the group sat in quiet unity, the strategy forming between them like the structure of a stage set—wood and fabric and will, all crafted for a final act.

Daisy rose first. "I'll prepare the office for the 'designer's' visit," she said with a little smirk. "Should I pretend to care about color swatches?"

Holmes allowed a thin smile. "Only if you want to frighten him."

Laughter rippled softly through the room—brief, but welcome.

As Watson moved to refill the tea, Victoria lingered near Holmes. She spoke quietly, just for him, though the others were still within earshot.

"You remembered that I wanted to redesign the office."

"I remember everything that matters," Holmes replied just as quietly.

Her lips curved into the faintest smile. Her eyes held his for one moment more.

Then she stepped back. "Shall we begin?"

As the ladies left Daisy, pausing near the door, narrowed her eyes playfully at Holmes. "One question, Mr. Holmes."

"Yes?"

She tilted her head. "This 'designer' of yours—how exactly is a police officer going to pass for someone with an eye for crown molding and velvet drapes?"

Holmes didn't miss a beat. "He once went undercover in a Covent Garden art forgery ring. His critique of chiaroscuro nearly cost him his life."

Daisy blinked. "Oh."

Then she laughed. "Well. I suppose wallpaper will be a step down in danger."

Holmes gave the faintest incline of his head. "Though no less theatrical."

Victoria smiled, reaching for her gloves. "Then let the scene begin."

Holmes walked them to the door, then moved to the window watching closely as Victoria and Daisy disappeared into the morning light.

As the door clicked shut, he turned back towards the hearth—only to find Watson still standing by the fire, one hand tucked into his coat pocket.

"She's stronger than I imagined," Watson said softly. "But still, my heart clenched when she walked out."

Holmes groaned, "I know the feeling."

They stood in companionable silence for a moment.

Then Holmes, more quietly, added, "She's walking into a trap. But this time, the trap is ours."

Watson turned to him. "Just make sure we spring it first."

"I intend to," Holmes replied. But the look in his eyes suggested it was not only justice he was hoping to preserve.

The morning light slanted through the frosted windows of Victoria's office. Despite the calm, Victoria's heart beat a touch faster than usual. She and Daisy were early, arriving before the rest of the staff. The air still held the scent of fresh plaster and paint—familiar now, almost comforting. Almost.

A quiet knock signaled the arrival of the "designer."

She opened the door to find a well-dressed man in his mid-thirties with fair hair, soft hands, and an impeccable portfolio under his arm. "Miss Watson?" he asked, voice pleasant but clipped.

Victoria smiled warmly and extended her hand. "Mr. Elmsley. Do come in."

Daisy, arranging fabric swatches on the desk for show, cast a subtle glance toward the hall, then gave the man a once-over. "He's more convincing than I expected," she muttered just loud enough for Victoria to hear.

"I want the room to serve several purposes," Victoria said as she led him in. "Part office, part dressing room, and a quiet corner with a divan and table—somewhere I can nap between rehearsals or jot notes in peace."

Mr. Elmsley nodded toward the far wall. "Shall we begin with the lighting? I understand you have specific ideas for the tone and atmosphere of the space."

Victoria motioned him forward. "I do. I've dreamed of warm gaslight levels, nothing too stark. A place to read and plan without feeling like one is under interrogation."

As they moved deeper into the room, Holmes appeared in the doorway, carrying a small bundle of notes and looking entirely casual. "Good morning," he said to no one in particular. "I believe the creative consultations are underway?"

Victoria gave him a slight nod of acknowledgment, continuing the ruse. "We were just discussing the sconce placement."

Holmes stepped inside and shut the door gently behind him. "Mr. Elmsley, thank you for joining us. You'll be working closely with Miss Watson and her assistant." He cast a glance toward Daisy, who beamed with exaggerated excitement.

"I'm simply thrilled," Daisy said, stepping closer. "Though I'm not sure I'll be much help with the design part. I mostly just make tea and keep track of the theater cats."

"You underestimate yourself," Holmes said, tone faintly amused. Then, with a shift in tone so subtle it might have passed unnoticed to anyone else, he added softly, "Let's be mindful—assume every word is being overheard."

Sergeant Alec Grey, playing the role of Mr. Elmsley, offered a nearly imperceptible dip of the head. Just enough.

Holmes unfolded his notes. "Miss Watson, earlier you mentioned the renovations you once dreamed of for this space. That was quite some time ago. Now is your opportunity."

Victoria caught his meaning instantly. "Oh yes," she said with performative enthusiasm. "I want to bring that old sketch of mine to life. Daisy, do you remember the archway between the outer office, the dressing room, and the inner lounge? And the paneled wainscoting? The rich color, like cranberry velvet?"

Daisy giggled. "She's been describing that room since we first crossed the ocean. Honestly, I think she already designed it in her sleep."

"Marvelous," said Elmsley smoothly. "I'll need to measure both the structural width and sound carry between those rooms."

Victoria moved toward the old desk in the corner. "Then let's start here. I want this whole area reimagined. It's too cold—too formal."

From the hallway, footsteps echoed. A shadow passed outside the frosted glass before continuing down the corridor.

Victoria didn't glance toward it, but her spine stiffened imperceptibly. "He's here," she said softly.

Holmes offered no visual reaction. "Good. Let's not disappoint him."

Daisy stepped forward and whispered just loud enough for the room, "I still don't know how exactly a police officer is supposed to pose as a professional designer."

Holmes, still not looking at her, replied evenly, "He spent two years embedded with a firm that specializes in private home restorations for the gentry. He has designed guest rooms, sitting parlors, and one unfortunately ornate gazebo. His eye for proportion is, I assure you, genuine."

Grey gave a modest shrug. "The gazebo wasn't that bad."

Victoria stifled a smile. "So, this is what trust looks like in your world."

"Only when lives are at stake," Holmes replied.

Then he lowered his voice, speaking with the kind of quiet authority that made the air still around him. "The cleaners will arrive tomorrow morning—two former constables with excellent instincts and a keen eye for detail. You won't notice them, but they'll always notice you. No one will be alone again."

Victoria lowered her voice to match. "And if Trask tries to change tactics?"

Holmes met her gaze for a heartbeat as he turned to leave. "Then we'll change faster."

"Before you go," Victoria said over her shoulder, "there's someone I think you should meet."

Holmes raised a curious eyebrow. "A suspect, I presume?"

Victoria smiled. "Not quite. Someone whose profession might interest you more than you'd expect."

The backstage corridor of the London Majestic still smelled faintly of sawdust. Holmes followed Victoria past the costume room and prop cages, their footsteps echoing lightly in the dimly lit hallway. From somewhere above, faint laughter drifted from the upper dressing rooms.

She opened a narrow door labeled *Makeup & Wigs – Authorized Only* and led him into a small but impeccably organized room. The shelves were lined with tins of greasepaint, bottles of spirit gum, brushes, boxes of crepe hair, hand-rolled mustaches, and sculpting wax. In the center stood a trim man with silver-threaded hair and pince-nez glasses, arranging brushes in a jar.

"Mr. Holmes," Victoria said warmly, "this is Mr. Aldous Alcott—our theatrical makeup supplier and illusionist-in-residence."

Alcott looked up and smiled with professional enthusiasm. "An honor, Mr. Holmes. I've long admired the accounts of your cases, especially the inventive disguises Dr. Watson describes in his stories."

Holmes inclined his head. "I find a well-constructed disguise to be a useful tool."

"Indeed," Alcott said, gesturing toward a high stool. "And I've often wondered what innovations might interest a man like you. Would you allow me to demonstrate a few of my materials?"

Victoria chuckled and stepped aside as Holmes, intrigued, took the offered seat.

"You've used putty or wax to alter facial structure, yes?" Alcott asked, already lifting a small tin of molding wax. "This is beeswax-based, softens with touch but firms in the air. It can create false brows or cheekbones with less risk of melting under pressure."

Holmes studied the tin with interest. "More malleable than gutta-percha, but less likely to degrade in humidity."

"Exactly," Alcott said, pleased. "And here—hand-knotted crepe hair. Dyed, curled, and mounted on lace, should you require quick application of a false beard or sideburns. This adhesive—my own concoction—will hold through perspiration, even heat from gaslight."

Victoria leaned against the doorframe, watching the exchange with quiet amusement.

"I'm impressed." Holmes admitted.

Alcott gave a modest bow. "They are purely for the stage, of course, but I'm confident I could meet the demands of someone working, shall we say, offstage."

Holmes gave him a faint but approving smile. "You take your work seriously."

"Always. And I value discretion. Anything I prepare for you would remain private."

Alcott handed Holmes a small, wrapped package. "It would be my honor if you would accept this, Mr. Holmes. Miss Watson told me how much help you've been in the theater project. Consider it my personal thank-you."

Holmes unwrapped it just enough to reveal the corner of a finely crafted leather case, neatly compartmentalized. Inside were blending brushes, greasepaint wheels, lace hair, and small tins labeled in Alcott's tidy script.

"Lightweight enough for travel," Victoria said. "And it fits neatly inside a violin case."

Holmes gave a soft laugh. "You've thought of everything. Thank you."

Alcott bowed once more. "It's been an honor, sir."

Holmes tucked the case beneath his arm. "Miss Watson," he said quietly, "you continue to surround yourself with remarkable allies."

She arched a brow. "Only the very best."

With a final nod to Alcott, Holmes followed her back into the corridor—quietly pleased.

The Diogenes Club remained, as always, a temple to silence. Beyond the heavy oak doors, conversation was unwelcome, eye contact discouraged, and opinions filed away like cigar ash—never shared aloud. But within the narrow confines of the Stranger's Room, one voice was never reluctant to speak.

Sherlock Holmes entered without knocking.

Mycroft looked up from behind his polished desk, a cup of dark tea in hand and the faint trace of impatience already forming around his eyes.

"You're early," Mycroft said to his brother, setting his cup down with precision. "That usually means something is either very wrong or very interesting."

"I believe it is both," Sherlock replied.

Holmes removed his coat and took the seat opposite, folding his long frame into it without ceremony. His eyes moved swiftly over the room, though he'd seen it a hundred times before—maps pinned to cork, classified reports arranged like a chessboard behind glass, and that ever-present smell of ink and starch and quiet influence.

"Well?" Mycroft prompted.

Holmes placed a slim folder on the desk. "You're familiar with the Stamford poisoning case?"

"Of course," Mycroft replied without reaching for it. "Parliamentary staffer. Unfortunate scandal. Stamford, a successful, respected doctor under arrest. It was all handled very neatly. Suspiciously so."

"There's a reason for that. Stamford is innocent."

Mycroft arched an eyebrow but said nothing.

Holmes leaned forward. "The real culprit is one W.E. Trask. He was dismissed years ago by Stamford for unethical behavior, promising revenge. He's resurfaced under an alias. He's infiltrated the London Majestic Theatre renovation under the name Samuel Lawson."

That, finally, caused Mycroft to blink. "The London Majestic Theatre?" He narrowed his eyes. "Isn't that the building that—"

"Recently purchased by Dr. Watson's daughter," Holmes confirmed. "Yes."

Mycroft's brows lifted in recognition. "Ah."

"There's more," Holmes continued. "Trask initially became involved in the renovation as a means to gain proximity to me—through her. He knew she and I are neighbors, and both connected to Watson. But what began as surveillance evolved. He embedded himself fully. Created a false identity, secretly took over key decisions in the renovation, and manipulated schedules and staff placement."

202

Holmes rose and began pacing.

"He constructed a hidden room beneath the stage, soundproofed and self-contained. We found bedding, disguises, forged documents, and remnants of a drug compound—likely the same mixture he used on one of the witnesses, Anne Godfrey. Trask has been living there, watching, planning. And now he may be preparing to burn the entire structure to the ground."

Mycroft sat back slowly, his gaze sharpening.

Holmes's voice was tight. "He is not simply targeting Stamford. He chose Victoria... Miss Watson, at first to distract me from the investigation—but he underestimated her. What began as convenience became obsession. Now he sees her strength as a threat—and wants to control it... or destroy it."

Mycroft studied him for a long moment before steepling his fingers.

"So that's what this is," he said softly. "You've become emotionally compromised."

There was no derision in the statement. Merely observation. A clinical conclusion drawn from ample data.

Holmes stopped pacing and faced him. "This is not sentiment, Mycroft. Not mere concern. She is intelligent, capable—and still being hunted by a man who thinks in riddles and operates in shadows. If she were anyone else, I would be involved." He hesitated. "But she is not anyone else."

"She's Watson's daughter."

Holmes gave a single nod.

Mycroft's voice lowered. "And more than that, it seems."

Holmes said nothing.

Mycroft pushed the folder gently back toward him. "What do you require?"

"Quiet cooperation," Holmes said. "If this comes to a head, I may need your authority to keep Scotland Yard from bungling it. And if something happens to me, I want the proper narrative followed."

"The narrative being?" Mycroft asked.

"That Stamford was innocent. That the theater was targeted as a strategic point, not a coincidence. That Trask—under whatever name he dies—was never a ghost, but a man with no moral tether."

Mycroft raised one brow. "And if something happens to her?"

Holmes's gaze grew sharp. "I will not permit that."

The room fell into a moment of stillness.

Finally, Mycroft looked at his brother. "And what do you need now?"

"Time," Holmes replied. "And to know that when I call, you'll answer."

There was a long pause. Then Mycroft leaned back and exhaled.

"She has captured your affections?"

"I don't have time for that."

"I didn't ask whether you had time," Mycroft said, a ghost of a smile tugging at his mouth. "Only whether it was true."

Holmes didn't answer.

"Very well," Mycroft said at last. "You'll have your support. But do be careful, brother. You've always been brilliant, but brilliance burns out faster when fanned by emotion."

Holmes nodded and turned for the door.

"Sherlock?"

He looked back.

"She has made you braver. I didn't think that possible."

Holmes gave no reply. He simply closed the door behind him and vanished down the long corridor.

The corridor smelled faintly of sawdust and paint, the final touches of renovation still clinging to the walls. Victoria walked briskly beside "Samuel Lawson," her posture open, her tone perfectly neutral.

"I know how invested you are in the theater," she said, glancing up at him. "Which is why I'd like your help ensuring this next part goes smoothly. My office—well, it's the heart of things, really. I want it done beautifully, and I trust you to keep an eye on the work."

Lawson gave her a curious look, then smiled faintly. "Of course. I'd be honored."

She returned the smile without warmth. "The designer arrived this morning. I've asked him to begin planning the space today."

They reached the door, and Victoria opened it with a practiced gesture. Inside, Sergeant Grey—alias Mr. Elmsley—was already at work, sketching elevations on a pad and murmuring measurements to himself.

He turned as they entered, immediately standing to greet the newcomer.

"Mr. Lawson," Victoria said smoothly. "This is Mr. Elmsley, the designer I mentioned. He'll be working on the renovation of my office. I'd like the two of you to coordinate closely."

Grey extended his hand. "It is a pleasure to meet you. I understand we're creating something special."

Trask—Lawson—smiled easily, but his gaze lingered a moment too long. "So, I'm told. Miss Watson's taste is distinctive."

Victoria gave a light laugh and stepped back. "I'll leave you to it, then. Mr. Lawson, I trust you'll give him every assistance. This space means a great deal to me."

Trask inclined his head. "Naturally."

With that, she slipped from the room, allowing the door to close gently behind her.

Inside, silence stretched for a moment.

"Have you worked in theater renovation before?" Grey asked, voice casual as he resumed sketching.

"Oh yes," Trask replied, his tone soft but unreadable. "I find them fascinating. All those hidden beams and hollow spaces. So easy to forget what's behind the walls."

Grey didn't respond immediately but continued making marks on the drawing. "Yes. But walls remember."

Daisy walked by the office door on the way to the tradesmen's stairwell, a ledger in hand, pretending to tally a delivery.

From the landing above, she heard their voices—low, male. Only one was familiar.

"Everything's on track," Trask was saying. "Don't bother with the wainscoting. By next week, it won't matter what they build. She'll be gone."

Daisy slipped quickly around the corner and down a separate hall, heart pounding as she went to find Victoria.

Daisy burst into Victoria's temporary work room without knocking. Victoria, seated at a desk reviewing schedules, looked up sharply.

"He said it," Daisy whispered, breathless. "I heard him. On the tradesmen's stairwell."

"Who said what?"

"Trask. I mean—Lawson. He said, 'By next week, it won't matter what they build. She'll be gone.'"

Victoria sat back slowly. Her throat tightened.

"Are you sure?" she asked quietly.

Daisy put her face in her hands for a moment. "He said it like it was already decided."

Victoria looked toward the hallway, where the soft sounds of construction and conversation continued as if the world had not just shifted.

"Then we have less time than we thought," she said.

The small room had gone quiet in the wake of Daisy's breathless arrival. Outside the window, the late afternoon sun angled toward the rooftops. The warmth in the room didn't match the chill that settled over Victoria.

"He said it like it was nothing," Daisy murmured again, pacing now. "Like it didn't matter who was listening."

Victoria folded her hands together and pressed them against her lips, thinking. Finally, she lowered them.

"How brazen," she said quietly. "To make a remark like that to someone he just met."

"I thought he might be testing him," Daisy said. "Daring him to respond."

"If so, that's foolish. But it also means he's confident. Or desperate."

She stood and crossed to the window, staring out without seeing. "At least now there's a witness. Elmsley, Sergeant Grey, can report it. If it comes to a hearing, that remark may help establish intent."

Daisy looked up sharply. "Then we tell Mr. Holmes, right? Now?"

Victoria didn't answer right away.

They both knew what it meant to go to Holmes with this information. It meant acceleration. Escalation. The trap would be sprung sooner than planned, and if Trask sensed that, he might act even faster.

"Every instinct says yes," Victoria said at last. "But if we rush to him now, Trask may feel the net tightening and strike preemptively. He said, 'by next week.' That gives us a window. I'll discuss it with Mr. Holmes tonight at Baker Street."

Daisy swallowed. "All right."

They exchanged a long look. Friends, co-conspirators, and now something closer to soldiers.

"I'll stay close to him this evening," Daisy said. "I'll find some excuse. Maybe offer to help with finishings in the costume loft."

Victoria's gaze sharpened. "You most certainly will not! You must not put yourself at risk."

"I know," Daisy said. "But I'm not letting him make you 'gone.'"

They both managed faint smiles.

Victoria turned back to her desk and picked up a pencil.

"Then let's finish this week's supply orders," she said, as if nothing were wrong at all.

And they did.

Victoria stepped through the door to Baker Street, the scent of old wood greeting her like a familiar refrain. She closed it softly behind her, grateful for the sanctuary, however temporary, it still offered.

Upstairs, voices were already in conversation. She climbed quickly, her steps light but determined, and found Holmes and her father deep in discussion at the sitting room table. Charts and schedules were spread before them—notes on cleaner rotations, vendor arrivals, coded names written in Holmes's meticulous hand.

"Good evening," she said quietly.

Holmes looked up immediately. "Miss Watson," he said, rising halfway. Watson stood and moved to embrace her.

"Are you all right?" he asked, giving her a quick but warm hug and a kiss to the cheek.

"I am, Father," she said, then hesitated. "But something's changed."

Holmes's posture shifted at once. "Tell us."

Victoria stepped closer, lowering her voice. "Daisy overheard a conversation this afternoon on the tradesmen's stairwell. Lawson was speaking to Mr. Elmsley, that is Sergeant Grey. She said the tone was… unsettling."

Watson leaned in. "What did he say?"

Victoria drew a breath. "He said, 'By next week, it won't matter what they build. She'll be gone.'"

The effect was immediate. Holmes froze for half a second then turned to the fireplace and snatched the small calendar from its hook on the wall. He laid it flat on the table, eyes flicking across the days.

"That aligns with the next vendor delivery—timber and plaster routed through a third-party name we flagged as unfamiliar," he murmured. "The supplies are scheduled to arrive Wednesday morning. Trask is planning something around that date."

Watson's fatherly instinct raised his level of worry. "But what does it mean? Sabotage? Fire? Kidnapping?"

"Any are possible," Holmes replied. "Trask would want minimal traces. Fire creates destruction, yes, and it obscures evidence. Abduction creates confusion and fear. Either would allow him to disappear under the chaos."

Victoria sank into the chair beside Holmes. "Daisy was as pale as a sheet. She thinks 'she' means me. That he's going to make me disappear."

Her father reached over and touched her hand gently. Holmes, meanwhile, was silent for a long moment. Then he drew his notebook closer, and with a sharp motion, crossed out a block of dates.

"Then we accelerate."

Watson's eyebrows lifted. "What are you proposing?"

"A staged emergency. Something that demands the building be cleared without raising suspicion—an inspection, a structural hazard, a fire code violation. It must appear real and immediate. No time for him to pivot or alter course. We'll flush him out."

Watson looked between them, concern lining his brow. "But won't that bring more danger to Victoria and Daisy?"

Victoria shook her head. "Father, it's better than waiting to be hunted. We've been on the defensive long enough."

"She's right," Holmes said. "He expects us to be cautious. We won't be. I'll contact Mycroft. He'll arrange the inspection under official authority. Rodney can assist with the falsified findings—mention of foundational shifting, perhaps moisture damage near the panel Trask uses."

"And in the meantime?" Watson asked.

"In the meantime," Holmes looked directly at Victoria. "I will remain close. Publicly. For the sake of our supposed... deepening rapport."

Victoria blinked. "You mean we act as if—"

"Yes," Holmes said. "His intention has been to use you to distract me from Stamford. He may still see you as the key to my movements. If he believes I'm emotionally invested, he may underestimate what we're planning."

Watson gave a low chuckle. "And are you?"

Holmes offered no response, but his glance toward Victoria lingered.

Victoria gave a faint smile. "If that's our strategy, it's one I can accept."

Holmes's tone softened. "Miss Watson, Victoria, you've entrusted me with much. I will not let you be taken."

Her reply was barely above a whisper. "You already haven't."

They stood there, not touching, but somehow connected all the same.

Watson cleared his throat. "Then I'll inform Rodney. And I'll stay close to Daisy during the evacuation. If Trask tries anything he'll find I'm not as easily fooled as I look."

Holmes didn't take his eyes from Victoria. "We'll see this through."

"And she'll not be gone," Victoria added, echoing Trask's chilling words.

Holmes said with quiet sincerity. "No. You'll be exactly where you belong."

And though the room was hushed, something unspoken passed between them all—no longer fear, but determination. A storm was coming, but this time, they would not weather it—they would command it.

The London Majestic stirred early that morning, its corridors quiet but charged with purpose. Victoria arrived before the bustle of the crew, grateful for the moment of silence. Trask—*Lawson,* she reminded herself—was out on a supposed supplier visit and wouldn't return until later that afternoon. It was a small window, but Holmes had assured her it would be enough.

Rodney was already waiting near the tradesmen's entrance, a cap pulled low, and a large set of keys clipped to his belt. With him were two men dressed in plain work clothes—former constables now playing the role of post-construction cleaners. Victoria hadn't expected Rodney to be the one bringing them, but Holmes had reasons.

As if reading her thoughts, Rodney murmured, "He asked me to fetch them myself. Less attention that way—my face draws less notice among the staff than his."

Victoria gave a small nod, then turned to the men. They looked utterly ordinary, blending perfectly into the theater's background. But as Rodney introduced them as Mr. Greaves and Mr. Toller, Victoria noted their calm alertness, the kind that marked them as professionals beneath the dust and work aprons.

"These two will be in and out of earshot at all times," Rodney said quietly. "They won't hover, but they'll never be far."

Victoria forced a smile and led them through the service entrance. "Gentlemen, thank you for coming. We're hoping to tidy up before final inspections, I am so sorry about the short notice."

They tipped their caps and grunted their agreement with the practiced rhythm of men used to following orders while appearing invisible.

She glanced at the clock. Right on cue, Holmes entered through the main corridor, coat unbuttoned, satchel slung over his shoulder. He looked for all the world like a man who was simply checking in on a project—not preparing to corner a predator.

"Miss Watson," he said with a pleasant nod which she reciprocated.

"Mr. Holmes," Victoria replied, falling into step beside him. "Everything's in motion."

They moved down the corridor toward the substage area, speaking softly but casually. Rodney joined them, keeping to Holmes's left.

It was Daisy who interrupted the rhythm.

"I found something odd," she called from just outside the costume room. "I think you should look at this."

She pointed towards a section of wall at the base of the back stairwell. At first glance, it was unremarkable—painted the same as the rest, partially obscured by a stacked crate of unused equipment. But something about it seemed too seamless.

"I tripped and put up my hand to steady myself on the wall but then realized it wasn't really a wall. I've never seen this door before," Daisy said, her voice low.

Holmes stepped forward. What looked like paneling was, upon closer inspection, a narrow flush-set door. The paint was newer, the edges precise.

"A concealed entry," he murmured.

"Rodney?" Holmes stepped aside.

Rodney stepped forward, ran his fingers along the frame, then stepped back, his brow furrowed. "This wasn't in the original blueprints. Not even as a utility access. I'd have remembered."

Holmes knelt, examining the threshold. "There is recent scuffing. Someone's passed through—multiple times. This has been in regular use."

From his coat pocket, Holmes withdrew a small pick set and, with fluid precision, opened the lock. A faint groan of hinges accompanied the door as it creaked inward, revealing blackness and the faint scent of damp plaster.

Victoria shivered. "What is it?"

"A bolt hole," Holmes replied. "A private passage. An emergency escape. Or perhaps a staging area for surveillance. In his mind, it's safety."

Rodney retrieved a lamp from the prop room nearby and lit it, shielding the flame as he stepped inside. The passage sloped down slightly before opening into a crude space barely wider than a broom closet, but deeper than expected. A broken chair leaned against one wall. A pile of discarded papers lay in the corner, along with two empty bottles and what looked like a coil of wire. Scratches lined one wall where something heavy had once been dragged.

Holmes stepped in next and crouched beside the papers. He scanned them swiftly—most were blank scraps or old technical drawings, but one bore faint, water-damaged notes in a handwriting none of them recognized. Holmes pocketed it without comment.

"This connects to the sealed Blythe room," he murmured. "It's part of a loop. One he controls from the shadows."

Victoria's voice, when it came, was steel wrapped in silk. "Then we close it. Lock it. Post someone here if we must. But no more blind spots."

Holmes offered a solution. "We'll rotate the constables. No pattern. Just presence."

He stood for a moment longer, his hand resting on the cold frame of the hidden door. His jaw was tight, and Victoria could see the calculations behind his eyes. She stepped a little closer.

"What are you thinking?" she asked softly.

"I'm thinking it's not enough to watch him. We need to outmaneuver him."

He turned to Rodney. "If he tries to flee, this is where he'll go. This is where we catch him."

They exited the passage and stepped back into the corridor. Daisy was still there, her arms crossed tightly.

"If he's using these… places…, how can he keep hiding?"

Holmes didn't answer at once. He turned back, looked at the now-shut door, and pressed his palm against it.

"No more hiding," he said under his breath.

He turned to Victoria, his voice quiet but clear. "He doesn't own this place. You do."

Victoria drew a breath, grounding herself in the moment. "Then let's remind him."

Holmes allowed a brief flicker of a smile, but his eyes remained hard. The trap was nearly complete. But the final act still lay ahead and this time, it would be on *their* terms.

Holmes adjusted his coat. "Come. I want to speak with our designer."

They made their way up to Victoria's office, where Sergeant Grey, still in character as Mr. Elmsley, was reviewing sketches near the window.

"Mr. Elmsley," Victoria said smoothly, "a moment?"

The man turned, his manner deferential. But Victoria could see it in his eyes—the calm readiness of a man waiting for instructions.

Holmes closed the door behind them. "We may have our trap door. I need you to station yourself nearby this afternoon. Keep your demeanor casual, but your eyes sharp. If Trask inspects that stairwell—or vanishes for more than five minutes—I want to know."

Grey nodded once. "Understood."

Holmes added quietly, "And if he runs—we'll be the ones waiting."

The final traces of daylight had melted into lamplight as the London Majestic quieted for the evening. Crew members filed out in twos and threes, murmuring their goodnights as they disappeared into the street. Most of the renovation crew had long since gone, and only a few lanterns remained lit behind upper windows.

Holmes offered Victoria his arm as they stepped through the front entrance of the theater. She took it—lightly, naturally—as though it were a daily habit and not part of the illusion they were crafting. His coat brushed hers as they descended the steps toward a waiting carriage.

"Do you think he's watching?" she asked under her breath.

"Most certainly," Holmes replied. "This is the narrative we've fed him. He would be a fool not to watch it unfold."

The doorman gave them a nod as he opened the carriage door. Holmes assisted Victoria inside and followed her in, shutting the door with a quiet thud behind him. The coachman tipped his hat and flicked the reins.

As the wheels began to turn and the theater slipped from view, the mood within the carriage turned still. The steady clatter of hooves and the creak of suspension filled the quiet between them.

Victoria rested her gloved hands in her lap, then clasped them more tightly. "It feels like we're standing in the wings," she murmured. "Just before the curtain rises."

Holmes glanced toward her. "A fitting simile."

"Daisy said something earlier," she added. "After you left the office." She gave a faint smile. "She asked me whether we'd be rehearsing our roles for this 'developing relationship.' Then she tried to wink but managed a blink instead. It was terribly unconvincing."

Holmes huffed a sound that might've been a laugh. "Perhaps I should be grateful we haven't enlisted her as an actress."

"Oh, she's trying," Victoria said. "And she's terrified, but she hides it well. She said today felt like being in a play with real consequences."

"In some ways," Holmes said, "it is."

They lapsed into silence again.

Victoria turned her face towards the window, watching the city drift past in blurs of gold and grey. "I keep thinking about Dr. Stamford," she said. "Locked away while the man who set all this in motion walks freely, plotting and watching. It's cruel."

Holmes's voice was low. "Cruelty often thrives where justice has grown complacent. But that tide is turning."

Victoria looked over at him. "Because of you."

"Because of you," he corrected gently. "You saw what others did not. You kept asking when others stopped. Your instincts have likely saved lives—including mine."

She blinked. "Yours?"

Holmes's gaze didn't waver. "Had I pursued Trask blindly—without understanding the depth of his reach or the stakes—he might have anticipated my moves, drawn me into a trap, and turned the case against me. Men like him thrive when their enemy underestimates the gameboard. But you saw the theater for what it was becoming. You saw *him* for what he was."

Victoria was silent, absorbing his words.

Holmes added, more quietly now, "You anchored me to the human cost. To the people in the shadows of the case, not just the facts. Without that I might have solved the puzzle but lost something far more essential."

Victoria looked down at her gloved fingers. "You've believed me when I wasn't even sure I believed myself. You've protected me without making me feel fragile. I know how rare that is."

Holmes said nothing for a moment. Then, very quietly, he said, "Trust is the one element I've never been able to manufacture. I can fake it, maneuver it, even use it to my advantage—but to give it freely." He shook his head slightly. "That's different."

She looked at him carefully. "And yet, you've given it to me."

He didn't reply. But the answer was in his expression—quiet, grave, and sincere.

"I suppose we're both in unfamiliar territory," Victoria said softly. "I don't know what any of this will look like when it's over. But I do know this—I'm not disposable. And you've never treated me as though I were. That matters."

Holmes turned his hand slightly on the seat between them, not touching hers but resting close enough that she could feel the warmth of it. "You are not disposable," he said. "You are the reason the theater still stands. And the reason Trask hasn't already vanished into smoke."

Victoria exhaled slowly. "We must win, Sherlock. Not just for Dr. Stamford, or even for me. For all the people who've been used and buried."

"We will," he said, his voice firm. "Trask will not succeed."

As the carriage turned another corner, lamplight poured briefly across their faces casting them in silver and shadow. Their hands brushed as the carriage shifted. Neither moved away.

Then the moment passed, and Victoria gave a small smile, calm and steady.

From high above, in one of the upper corridors of the London Majestic, a pair of unseen eyes followed the departing carriage.

Samuel Lawson—W.E. Trask—stood half-concealed and unmoving.

He'd seen everything.

The arm offered. The carriage entered together. The look shared through the glass as the wheels turned. He watched until the last flicker of motion disappeared into the fog.

And then, without a word, he turned from the window and stepped into the dark.

The air in Rodney's modest flat carried the scent of old varnish and tobacco, relics of his days in active service. A map of the London Majestic's lower-level lay spread across the table, weighed down by a teacup on one corner and a brick trowel on the other. Holmes and Watson stood over it, arms folded, and eyes narrowed in thought.

Before they began, Holmes paused beside Rodney, eyeing his slightly askew collar and ink-stained cuff.

"You were drafting until well past midnight," Holmes observed. "And you've skipped breakfast—your pocket still holds the half-eaten apple you intended to finish hours ago."

Rodney blinked. "That's entirely correct."

Holmes offered the briefest of smiles. "A man who prepares thoroughly is a man I can work with."

Rodney closed the ledger in front of him and looked across the table at Holmes and Watson. "The boiler room's ceiling joists are original, and a few are cracked. The drainage beneath the substage is still subpar. We can present both as pressing code violations."

Holmes looked at the ledger thoughtfully, his fingers steepled. "And the gallery stairwell?"

"Still warped and needing repair," Rodney replied. "That's our third infraction."

"Excellent," Holmes murmured. "Three visible faults, all easily exaggerated. Enough to justify an emergency inspection without raising undue suspicion."

Watson leaned over the layout Rodney had brought—an updated floor plan sketched in fine ink. "And this is where Trask's workspace connects to the access corridor near the prop loft?"

"Yes," Rodney confirmed. "The inspectors can begin there. He'll be forced to clear out while they 'assess structural safety.' We'll have an open window to search."

Holmes glanced up at Watson. "You're comfortable escorting the inspectors?"

Watson smiled faintly. "Certainly. If Lestrade's men come with me, I can control what they see—and what they overlook. Thank God you finally were able to make Lestrade see reason, Holmes."

Rodney raised a skeptical brow. "He's changed his mind?"

"He's seen the papers from Anne Godfrey, and the testimony from Chambers. The falsified documents were the final piece." Holmes folded the note crisply. "Stamford's release is now a question of timing."

"Good man," Rodney muttered. "A bit late, but good."

Rodney raised an eyebrow. "Won't Trask find it suspicious? A fire and safety inspection with police presence?"

"That's why the police presence will be subtle," Watson said. "And Holmes will be seen escorting Mycroft's 'structural consultant'—the same one who flagged irregularities last week."

Holmes nodded. "Wiggins will create a delay at the front just long enough to make Trask uncomfortable. That pressure may trigger something telling."

Rodney reached for his cap. "Then I'll make the final alterations to the stair railings and crack the floor joist in the boiler room to make it look plausible. Nothing dangerous—just real enough."

"Be mindful," Holmes said. "The illusion must hold under brief scrutiny, but not close investigation. We only need a delay—time to access Trask's den."

Watson frowned as he studied the timetable Holmes had drawn. "He's been careful. We've only had slivers of opportunity to investigate."

"Which is why," Holmes said quietly, "we must make him feel the floor shifting beneath him. Even the clever grow careless when the trap closes."

There was a short silence. Then Watson glanced toward Holmes, his tone softer.

"You believe he meant to harm Victoria personally?"

"I do." Holmes's voice was flat. "I believe he's still planning to."

Rodney's face darkened. "Then let's not miss our moment."

Holmes leaned forward, tapping the table. "The inspection will be tomorrow. Victoria will call a staff meeting this afternoon to make the announcement. You'll be with her, Watson?"

"Of course."

"Good." Holmes looked to both men. "Then let's give Trask something to worry about."

Holmes thought silently for a moment. "After the inspection is announced, Trask will accelerate. The delivery scheduled for Wednesday of plaster and timber ordered under an alias is his final play. I need that shipment watched."

"You'll use these Irregulars of yours?" Rodney asked.

Holmes elaborated. "A few of the older boys—ones who know how to keep their heads down. Toller and Greaves will assist. No uniforms. Just tools and timing."

Holmes allowed himself a breath. "Then the curtain's rising."

He gathered the map and the marked blueprints, slipping them back into his satchel. "I'll return to Baker Street and update Victoria tonight."

Rodney glanced once more at the map, then back to Holmes. "You're ready to end this, aren't you?"

Holmes's expression didn't change, but something flickered in his eyes—resolve sharpened by something quieter, more personal.

"I'm ready," he said softly. "And this time, the fire will be his undoing—not hers."

Rodney watched Holmes and Watson go without another word, the door clicking shut behind him like the final cue before the scene began.

The staff lounge was already filling with murmurs and the clatter of chairs when Victoria stepped inside. A morning fog clung stubbornly to the windows, muting the light and casting a gray hush over the room. The crew, comprised of repair workers, set builders, electricians, and decorators gathered in clusters, sipping tea and glancing curiously at the folded sheet of paper in Victoria's hand.

Daisy stood near the window, giving her a quick nod. Trask, still wearing the face of "Mr. Lawson," leaned casually against the wall near the tea cart with arms folded. He watched her, unreadable as ever, though the tension in his posture hadn't gone unnoticed by Victoria.

Holmes was absent by design; his absence as calculated as every other step in the plan.

"Thank you all for making time," Victoria said, her voice even and calm. "This won't take long, but it is important."

Chairs squeaked as people turned toward her. She held up the folded page—Holmes' forged Preliminary Inspector's Report —and unfolded it deliberately.

"We've received notice of a fire and structural inspection scheduled for tomorrow morning. This was triggered by findings from a preliminary architectural review—the same one that flagged minor water damage beneath the eastern wing. Additional concerns were raised about the stability of the substage stairwell and the condition of some original joists."

A low ripple of surprise moved through the room.

Daisy raised her hand with just the right tone of interest. "Will it affect the schedule? Or just be a walk-through?"

"Hopefully just a walk-through," Victoria replied. "But to be cautious, they've asked for full access to the main structural areas—the boiler room, substage, storage corridors, and especially the west gallery stairwell. I've promised our complete cooperation. Safety, after all, is paramount."

She let that hang in the air for a moment before folding the report and placing it on the table.

Trask shifted. "Will the inspection interfere with deliveries?"

"I've alerted the suppliers," Victoria answered smoothly. "They'll hold any nonessential shipments until clearance is granted."

"And what about private workspaces?" he asked, too casually. "Will inspectors be entering offices?"

Victoria offered a light smile. "Only those adjacent to structural access points. It's not personal—it's protocol. All of us will be temporarily displaced during the inspection window. I appreciate everyone's flexibility."

Trask gave a stiff nod. His smile was practiced, his voice mild, but Victoria caught the flicker of muscle in his jaw, the quick dart of his eyes toward Daisy and the stairwell door.

"Will someone be walking with the inspectors?" he asked.

"Yes," Victoria replied. "Dr. Watson will be accompanying them on behalf of the Board. He's reviewing the medical readiness of the space as well."

Daisy asked another question—this one about whether the theater's lighting grid would be checked—and the conversation briefly veered into technical chatter. But Victoria kept one eye on Trask, who had grown uncharacteristically silent.

When the meeting concluded, staff began drifting back to their duties. Daisy gave Victoria a quick, meaningful glance, then moved to tidy up the tea area. Trask exited without another word, disappearing down the hallway with the same feline grace he always carried—but something in his gait was faster and less fluid.

A few minutes later, Daisy caught up with Victoria outside the wardrobe storage room. She spoke low, her voice tight.

"I passed him by the stairwell. He didn't see me, but he was muttering to himself—angry. I heard him say, 'We'll have to move sooner.' That's all I caught before he rounded the corner."

Victoria felt slightly queasy, her stomach tightening. "You're sure of the words?"

"Exactly that. I'd swear to it."

Victoria took a deep breath saying, "I'll check in."

The west utility corridor behind the scenery lift was dim and unused, the perfect spot for a discreet meeting. Victoria stepped lightly over a coil of wire and turned the corner.

Holmes was already there, coat collar turned up, his expression still and focused.

She didn't speak at first. She handed him the small envelope she'd prepared, containing a summary of the morning's events and Daisy's overheard remark.

He read it quickly, then met her eyes. "He's moving up his timeline."

She thought out loud. "His reaction wasn't loud, but it was definite. He asked about private offices. Deliveries. Specifics. He's rattled."

"He should be," Holmes said softly. "It means we struck the right nerve."

"Daisy's brave," Victoria added. "But I don't like how close he's getting to her."

"We'll double the watch on her." Holmes's voice was low, controlled. "She's not alone. Neither are you."

They stood in silence for a moment, the hum of pipes and distant hammering filling the air.

Then Holmes turned slightly, angling his body so he could see her more directly. "Well done, Victoria. You delivered the performance precisely as needed."

"It wasn't a performance," she said quietly. "Not really."

Holmes didn't smile, but his eyes warmed. "Then that's all the more to your credit."

Back in the corridor near the lounge, Trask stood partly in shadow, watching the path Victoria had taken just moments before. He said nothing. But the slight turn of his head, the narrowing of his eyes, and the tension in his jaw all spoke for him.

The game was shifting—and he knew it.

The countdown had begun.

The inspection had begun in earnest, with workers and constables in plain clothes working alongside of them, moving about the London Majestic's halls in careful choreography. Victoria had handled the announcement with poise, and now, Trask—under the pretense of cooperating—had stepped aside from his usual domain. His office stood momentarily unguarded.

Holmes, Watson, and Rodney moved quickly through the hall and into the vacated space.

Rodney closed the door behind them and turned the lock.

"Ten minutes," he said. "Maybe fifteen."

Holmes gave a curt nod, his eyes already scanning the room. "We'll make use of every second."

The room was surprisingly orderly almost as if it had no occupant. A drafting table stood by the far wall, architectural sketches pinned neatly above it. A cabinet of files. A crate labeled "Stage Supports— FRAGILE." Holmes moved to it first.

Watson crossed to the desk and began sifting through a set of rolled documents while Rodney checked the floorboards along the wall paneling.

"Chemical scent," Holmes muttered, lifting a cloth from the crate. Beneath it, several glass jars were nested in straw, one still crusted with a chalky orange residue. "He was preparing something."

"Slow-burn reaction?" Rodney asked, peering over his shoulder.

"Likely," Holmes replied. "Oil of vitriol and potassium chlorate, judging by the smell. Mixed correctly, it could create delayed ignition. Perfect for fire… and confusion."

Watson discovered a thin file folder hidden under the top desk drawer. Flipping through the contents he suddenly stilled. He pulled out a set of papers—some typed, others handwritten in a jagged scrawl.

"What is it?" Holmes asked.

"Drafts," Watson replied bleakly. "Anonymous notes. All addressed to 'Whom It May Concern.'" He read aloud.

It has come to my attention that Miss Victoria Watson ignored structural deficiencies in the theater. She was warned repeatedly that exposed wiring and poor ventilation near the furnace posed a risk, yet no action was taken. I fear her negligence may cost lives.

Watson lowered the page slowly.

"He meant to frame her," he said. "If the place went up in flames, these were to surface. False evidence of her knowledge… her guilt."

Holmes took the papers and examined them closely. "Hasty. Inconsistent. He's under pressure. These were written recently, perhaps even in the last few days." He held one up to the light. "See the corrections. The retyped lines. He couldn't decide which version would be most damning."

Rodney opened a narrow drawer beneath the desk and pulled out a rolled blueprint. He uncurled it on the table. "Another forgery," he muttered. "It lists structural reinforcements that were never installed. It would look like Victoria approved unsafe work."

Holmes stepped forward, jaw tight. "This confirms his intention to both harm and discredit her. The fire would have erased his traces. The notes would've explained away the loss—and shifted blame. And with her gone she would not have been here to defend herself."

Watson leaned heavily on the desk, his expression deeply troubled. "She is my daughter. He'd have killed her, then made the world believe she was at fault."

Holmes placed a steady hand on his shoulder. "He didn't. And he won't."

There was a long pause.

Then Holmes turned to the cabinet one last time. A false panel gave way with a press of his thumb. Inside, more jars—some empty, others corked. A smell of smoke and acid lingered.

"He's close to acting," Holmes said. "But this gives us the advantage. We know his method—and we have motive, evidence, and timing."

Watson gave a sharp nod. "Then it's time we ended this."

Holmes closed the cabinet with deliberate care. "He's desperate," he said. "And that makes him dangerous."

Watson met his gaze. "But now we have proof. And soon, we'll have him."

Rodney slipped towards the door and opened it a fraction to check the hall.

"All clear."

They slipped out, one by one, the evidence secured and the trap tightening.

The clock was ticking, and Trask had just lost the element of surprise.

The sky outside Baker Street had turned the color of slate when Victoria stepped into the familiar sitting room. Holmes and Watson were already there—Holmes standing near the mantel, fingers steepled in thought, and Watson seated beside the desk with a file folder resting across his knees.

They both turned as she entered. Holmes gestured toward the fire. "Come in, Victoria. We have something to show you."

Victoria set down her gloves and crossed the room, her eyes flicking between the two men. "You found something."

Watson nodded sternly and opened the folder. "This was hidden in Trask's desk. There were several like it. This one was nearly complete."

He passed the paper to Holmes, who read aloud in a clipped tone:

"I never meant for a fire happen. I should have known the renovation was too fast, too reckless. I take full responsibility for the structural faults—"

Victoria's eyes widened as she looked at the forged note with her own signature. "He was going to set me up to take the blame for the fire."

Holmes looked up. "Yes. He drafted this false confession in your name. A letter to be discovered after the fire. It would have explained everything—with tragic finality."

Watson stood and moved beside her. "There were at least four versions. Two mention you explicitly suggesting negligence, or worse. He meant to cast you as careless, professionally incompetent, perhaps even suicidal with remorse."

230

Holmes laid the paper gently on the desk and reached for a sheet of tracing vellum. "He's been constructing this plot meticulously. First, emotional manipulation. Then public doubt. Now, a planted confession. It's not just sabotage—it's also character assassination."

Victoria spoke slowly, her voice low but steady. "And if I'd been caught in the fire, there'd be no one left to deny it."

"Exactly," Watson murmured, fists clenched. "To the world, it would have looked like guilt."

"Or" Holmes added, "like a cover-up gone wrong."

He reached for a diagram from the table and unrolled it. "The chemicals found match bromate compounds. They're reactive to heat, but delay combustion, making it appear accidental. We suspect he planned to trigger the fire with a fume discharge from the substage venting ducts."

Victoria stepped closer to study the diagram. "The Wednesday shipment – the one we flagged?"

Holmes gave a single nod. "Timber and solvent. Ordered under one of Trask's aliases. If it arrived quietly, the fire would have followed within hours. And then this letter 'found' among the debris, likely inside a fireproof strong box, would seal your disgrace."

Watson's jaw tightened. "The perfect end to his play."

Victoria turned to Holmes. "You were right. About him. About how he thinks. You saw the danger long before we understood it."

Holmes looked down. "I didn't see it soon enough."

Holmes thought out loud. "He turned his obsession inside out. The spaces he once tried to heal through design became instruments of psychological torment. The theater gave him something Stamford never intended, a perfect stage to ensure his vengeance would be complete."

Victoria stepped forward. "And by hiring him—Lawson, that is—I gave him the platform."

"You were the key to drawing Holmes into the trap," Watson added gently. "The moment you became involved, he knew Holmes would never walk away. My daughter would become the perfect distraction from the Stamford case."

Holmes said nothing, still studying the blueprint. But his voice, when it came, was steady.

"He believed himself a maestro of space, using architecture to manipulate thought and feeling. What he failed to understand," he added, eyes lifting to Victoria, "is that the human will is not so easily shaped by bricks and corridors."

Victoria met his gaze. "No. It is not."

Her gaze didn't waver. "Then let's make sure he doesn't get the finale he wrote."

Holmes allowed a breath of quiet approval. "Agreed."

He slid the forged note into a protective sleeve. "This goes to Lestrade tonight. It's more than enough to place Trask under direct suspicion."

"I'll take it," Watson said, extending his hand. "He needs to see it immediately."

Holmes met his old friend's eyes, then looked to Victoria. "We must assume Trask will act sooner. If he feels the net tightening, he'll strike before the delivery."

Victoria's voice was calm. "Then we strike first."

Holmes studied her a moment longer—recognizing not just bravery, but clarity. "Then the next time he tries to vanish into the walls," he said, folding the diagram, "we'll be there waiting."

Outside, the streetlamps of Baker Street flickered to life. Inside, the trap moved closer to its final setting—this time with the prey nearly in sight.

The scent of fresh tea and toast lingered in the warm air of the downstairs sitting room. Victoria sat in the armchair near the fireplace; her hands wrapped around a delicate china cup. She wore a trim coat and gloves, ready to depart for the theater but content to linger in the homey atmosphere while waiting for Holmes and her father. Mrs. Hudson bustled in and out from the kitchen, humming under her breath as she tidied the breakfast dishes.

"You seem lighter today," Mrs. Hudson said, pausing beside Victoria's chair. "Almost cheerful."

Victoria smiled faintly. "It's the first morning I haven't woken in dread for a very long time. I'm happy that the conclusion of this horrid business is within our grasp."

Just then, the front door opened, and Dr. Watson's familiar voice echoed down the hall. "Ladies? Are we ready to face another day?"

Victoria rose and greeted her father with a hug. "You're early for once."

"I've learned my lesson," he said with mock solemnity. "The last time I was late, Holmes commandeered my tea."

Before Victoria could respond, a knock came at the door. Mrs. Hudson's brows lifted. "Now who could that be?"

She opened it to reveal a tall, poised young woman with golden blonde hair swept into a soft updo, her green eyes sparkling beneath a smart cloche hat.

"Aunt Mary!" the young woman said warmly. "I hope I'm not intruding."

Mrs. Hudson's face lit up. "Angela, my dear!"

Dr. Watson turned toward the door and let out a surprised laugh. "Angie Hill! I'd know you anywhere."

Angela beamed and stepped inside. "Dr. Watson! It's been too long."

Victoria watched with polite interest as introductions were made. Angela removed her gloves with easy grace, revealing elegant fingers and an heirloom ring.

"She lived here for nearly two years, helping Mrs. Hudson," Watson explained to Victoria. "And she and Holmes... well, they became very good friends during that time."

Victoria raised an eyebrow. "Friends?"

Miss Hill chuckled. "Your father makes it sound far more dramatic than it was. Mr. Holmes was always kind to me. Thoughtful, in his own rather curious way."

"Curious is a good word," Mrs. Hudson added with a knowing smile.

Victoria, still smiling, offered her hand. "I'm pleased to meet you, Miss Hill."

"Oh, please, call me Angie," she said.

"And, what brings you back to Baker Street today, Angie?" Victoria inquired.

"I only came today to share a bit of happy news." She lifted her hand to show the ring. "I'm engaged. His name is David Brighten. We met through the musical society in Kensington."

"My dear!" Mrs. Hudson squealed with joy as she embraced her niece, "How wonderful! I'm so very happy for you."

"Oh, congratulations!" Victoria said warmly, and the genuine relief behind her words didn't go unnoticed.

"That's wonderful news," Watson said with a grin. "We wish you every happiness, my dear."

Angie, still hugging her aunt, smiled at them all. "I'll be in town a few more days, but I had to tell you first. This place was home to me once."

She turned toward the stairs. "Is Mr. Holmes in?"

"He's upstairs," Mrs. Hudson replied, "but likely buried in one of his diagrams."

"Then I won't disturb him," Angie said brightly. "Just tell him I called, and that I'm very happy."

As Angie left, Watson turned to Victoria, amused. "You looked a touch tense just now."

"I did not," Victoria said with a slightly defensive tone to her voice.

Mrs. Hudson raised an eyebrow. "You did a bit, dear."

Victoria crossed her arms. "I'm sure it was only the sunlight in my eyes."

Just then, footsteps sounded on the stairs. Holmes descended, coat neatly buttoned, his face set in thoughtful concentration. "Are we late already?" he asked without preamble.

"Not quite," Victoria said breezily. "We were just talking about former residents of this establishment."

Holmes glanced between them with a brow furrowed in curiosity at their expressions. "Is something amusing?"

"Only that you missed someone from your past," Watson said lightly.

Holmes gave him a long-suffering look. "I always do."

Victoria looped her arm through her father's. "Let's go or we'll be late."

Watson chuckled as they stepped into the morning sun.

The wheels of the hansom cab clattered rhythmically over the cobblestones, muffled slightly by the damp from the previous night's rain. Inside the carriage, Holmes, Watson, and Victoria sat together, their breath clouding faintly in the cool morning air.

Watson adjusted the cuffs of his gloves and looked out the small window toward the approaching silhouette of the London Majestic. "How go rehearsals?" he asked.

"Our first production," she sighed with anticipation, turning to face them both. "an original musical comedy – *The Reluctant Bride.*"

Watson smiled. "That's quite a title."

Victoria laughed. "It suits the story. It's set in New York City—modern, bustling, full of possibility. The heroine is a spirited young woman who wants to live freely, explore, dance, sing, make her own choices. Her father is an old-fashioned businessman who tries to marry her off to a wealthy suitor."

Holmes tilted his head. "And does she?"

"Mr. Holmes," Victoria said as if shocked by the question, "You know I can't give away the ending. I will tell you that she outsmarts him at every turn. She is a singer in a fancy restaurant and has a few misadventures, including one in Central Park. Eventually, she does fall in love—but I won't say with whom. And not until she's good and ready."

Watson chuckled. "Sounds like someone I know."

Holmes gave a faint, amused glance in Victoria's direction. "Indeed. The thematic resonance is impossible to ignore."

Victoria grinned. "Oh, I'm quite aware. She's a woman who wants to choose her own path. No forced matches, no convenient arrangements. Just freedom—until she finds something, or someone, worth choosing."

Holmes looked at her a moment longer than necessary before replying. "London audiences may find it bold."

"I hope so," Victoria said. "It's lively and full of wit. Dance numbers, lively melodies and ballads, strong characters. I wanted to make a statement with the first production—that the Majestic is a place where voices can rise."

Holmes smiled slightly. "Then it's a worthy beginning."

A beat of silence followed, broken only by the sounds of hoofbeats and wheels.

Watson leaned forward, clasping his gloved hands. "I must admit, I'm eager to see you on the stage. I've only enjoyed your career through clippings, you know."

Victoria smiled warmly. "I've missed that, too. Though I confess, I'm nervous. American humor doesn't always translate well."

"I suspect your delivery will help considerably," Holmes murmured, his voice quieter now.

She turned to look at him. "You plan to attend?"

"I imagine I'll be in the audience," he replied. "Likely seated beside your father, both of us wincing every time someone swings from a chandelier."

Watson laughed. "Speak for yourself. I rather enjoy a good musical romp."

Victoria studied Holmes a moment longer. "Well then, I'll try not to disappoint."

"You never have," Holmes said quietly.

Their eyes met in the dim morning light.

Outside, the London Majestic loomed ahead, grand and gleaming. The cab began to slow.

As the trio prepared to disembark, the mood had shifted—not heavy, but laden with the weight of anticipation. The show was coming. The trap was being set. And beneath it all, something more fragile was beginning to rise, like the first notes of an overture, building toward something greater.

Holmes extended a hand to help her from the cab. She took it.

The curtain was about to rise.

Lestrade met Holmes, Watson and Victoria at the theater door. They made their way toward Trask's hidden chamber, ready for the confrontation. The evidence they had collected was finally enough that an arrest could be made.

They watched Trask step into his lair from a distance. They already knew it was there, but seeing Trask enter it himself was further evidence of his connection to the secret workspace—and his guilt.

Lestrade shot Holmes a wary glance. "He led us straight into it."

"Let him think he still has the advantage," Holmes murmured. "He won't for long."

The hidden panel groaned open, and Holmes stepped through first. Watson's revolver was drawn and angled low. Victoria followed behind Lestrade, her heart pounding. She quietly slid the panel shut behind them, sealing off the corridor and any chance of retreat.

Inside the narrow room, Trask stood at his worktable with his back to them, engrossed in his work and oblivious to their presence. A candle flickered nearby, its flame blackening the corner of a document he had just touched to it. The paper curled upward like a burning tongue. A small bottle of blue-gray powder sat open beside it, along with a folded length of wire and a second intact sheet of paper—typed, unsigned.

Holmes said sharply, "Trask!"

Trask turned—and froze, but only for a second. He reached for the black-lacquered case beside the candle.

"Don't," Holmes shouted, but Trask's hand was already moving.

Holmes lunged, grabbing his wrist and slamming it down on the edge of the table. The revolver dropped from the case and skittered across the floor. Watson kicked it aside as Holmes forced Trask backward into a chair with a hard shove.

Lestrade moved forward, firmly clamping his hand on Trask's shoulder.

Trask exhaled slowly, brushing back his coat with a theatrical calm. "Impressive, Holmes. I was beginning to wonder if you'd ever stop eavesdropping and join the conversation properly."

Holmes kept his stance rigid, eyes sharp. "We've seen the forged confession, the chemical stockpile, and the falsified inspection reports. It's over, Trask."

Trask gave a small, maddening smile. "Is it? You're here. She's here. The fire didn't start, but the match has already been struck."

Victoria stood just behind Holmes, staring in disbelief. The space was too perfect—too clean. The typewriter, the paper, the tools... all arranged with obsessive care. The illusion of order hiding the machinery of destruction.

"What is this?" she asked softly. "A confession?"

"No," Trask said, turning to her with chilling ease. "It's the epilogue. Yours or mine—I suppose that depends on how clever your Mr. Holmes truly is."

Trask's calm demeanor gave way to an angry outburst. "I want to be understood!"

Holmes gave a sharp glance to Victoria, who remained silent beside him, eyes fixed on the man who had invaded her life. Holmes said nothing, so Trask continued.

"I loved this theater before you were ever born," he said, looking at Victoria. "I was a boy—nine or ten—when my father brought me to see Emily Boothe's first full production here. *Echoes in Velvet*. It is one of the rare happy memories from my childhood. I still remember the

240

curtain rising. I remember how the dust caught in the footlights, how the whole world went quiet in that breathless second before the first line was spoken."

He leaned back. "Emily Boothe wasn't just a founder—she was a visionary. She believed that theater was sacred, that it could stir nations or save a soul. She took in people like me—runaways, vagrants, overlooked boys with good ears and quiet feet. She gave me a job. I was painting flats at twelve, rigging lines at thirteen, shadowing her at fourteen. I knew every beam of this place by sixteen. I stayed withing this refuge for years."

Victoria's voice was low, but steady. "But she didn't name you as her successor."

"No," Trask said. "She died before she could. And the trustees—greedy men who didn't care about vision—sold the Majestic off piece by piece. I fought to buy it back. I offered to restore it, fund it, protect it. They laughed." His mouth curled bitterly. "They gave it to a real estate firm. Men who didn't care about what it was. What it stood for."

"And when I bought it…" Victoria said.

"You *rescued* it," Trask said with something like reverence. "I read the articles. An American heiress with a stage background and no taste for aristocracy? I thought Emily Boothe herself had returned from the grave. I even told you so, didn't I?" He smiled faintly at the memory. "'Heart. Passion. Will.' That's what she used to say."

"Then why try to burn it down?" Victoria demanded.

"Because your arrival came with *him*." Trask turned his gaze to Holmes. "The moment I learned you were taking the Stamford case, I knew it was only a matter of time. I had secrets buried deep—evidence that could undo everything I'd planned. So, I needed a distraction. Something personal."

"You chose Victoria," Holmes said coldly.

"I chose the best bait," Trask replied. "Your closest friend's daughter. Newly returned, unknown to you and vulnerable. But clever—like her father. Like Emily. She would draw your attention, your concern, your *complication*. I thought she'd slow you down, if not stop you entirely."

He looked between them. "But then… then I saw how you looked at each other."

Victoria's breath caught faintly. Holmes did not move.

"And I realized," Trask said softly, "I could kill *three* birds with one stone. Stamford—disgraced or imprisoned. Holmes—ruined or grieving. And sadly, you my dear Victoria—consumed by fire, body and reputation both. A martyr to my masterpiece."

"You mean your revenge," Victoria said.

"I mean justice," Trask snapped. "Stamford cost me everything. You think I didn't know he testified against me? That he smeared my name?" He paused, composed himself again. "So, I integrated two solutions. First, I used the theater's renovation to mask my movements. Deliveries, fake vendors, even forged staff identities—easy when you control the supply chain."

"And the second?" Holmes asked.

"Control the narrative," Trask said. "If *you* were distracted from the case by grief, if Miss Watson's death seemed accidental—or better, the result of her negligence—it would destroy all three of you. The fire would erase the evidence. The forged letters would blame her. You'd be helpless to clear her name."

"And yet here we are," Holmes said quietly. "You're the one in the dark, telling stories to people who've already turned the page."

A slow smile crept across Trask's lips. "But you're not finished, are you?" He turned to Victoria. "You don't know who helped me."

Holmes stiffened. Victoria's eyes narrowed.

"Helped you?" she repeated.

"Oh yes," Trask said. "You think I built all this alone? Some doors only open with two keys. Some lies need two tongues. I had a partner. A very… strategic one. Someone close to the board. Someone who made sure I had access."

Holmes took a step forward. "Name them."

Trask simply smiled. "I'm caught, but I'm not alone."

Victoria's fists clenched. "And what now? You still think this story ends with applause?"

"Oh no," Trask said. "It ends with truth. And truth, Miss Watson…" He met her eyes, "is rarely graceful. It's cruel. Cold. But it lasts longer than love."

Holmes turned on his heel. "We're done here."

But Trask's voice followed them as they moved to leave. "Not quite," he said. "You've stopped *me*—but not the fire." Laughter such as only comes from a madman flowed from Trask, Lestrade handcuffed him.

Holmes froze.

"I told you," Trask whispered. "I planned for every outcome."

Holmes paced in front of the hearth, fingers laced behind his back, his brow furrowed in thought. The gaslight cast restless shadows on the walls as Watson and Victoria sat nearby, watching him.

"Someone helped him," Holmes said flatly. "Someone close to the theater—close enough to bypass hiring protocols, arrange fake deliveries, and grant Trask access under his alias."

Victoria closed her eyes and sighed deeply.

Watson leaned forward. "Who among the theater board had that kind of authority?"

"Only a few," Victoria replied. "My solicitor, Mr. Worthing. Eleanor Brayford, the treasurer, and Nigel Croft. He is an architect that was appointed as a liaison when I purchased the property. The firm that handled the sale recommended him."

Holmes's head snapped up. "Croft."

"You know the name?" Victoria asked.

"I've seen it. On Trask's falsified delivery manifests. Croft approved expenses for the fake vendors."

Victoria's expression tightened. "He was so helpful in the beginning and said he admired my initiative. He even called me a 'spark of fresh air.'" She rolled her eyes in disgust.

Watson gave a low grunt. "That smells of condescension disguised as praise."

Holmes browsed through his collection of large reference books of clips and articles of public figures, pulling out the one labeled "C (P to Z)".

Turning the pages, he found what he was looking for. "Here he is – Croft. A property in Croft's name was recently leased to what is mostly likely a bogus company."

Victoria exhaled. "So, Croft gave Trask access and possibly protected him on the books."

"And may still be shielding him," Holmes added, "which means Trask's threat wasn't theatrical bluster. If Croft's preparing a fallback plan—"

"He may try to ignite the fire himself," Watson finished grimly.

Holmes sat down, fingers steepled in front of his mouth. "We must act. If Croft is still active the danger remains real."

Only Watson moved. He crossed the room, poured three cups of tea, and set one by each of them without a word. Then he spoke, low and firm.

"Croft," he said. "I don't understand it. Why would he do it? Why help Trask with this madness?"

Holmes turned from the window. "Because madness often makes persuasive sense to those with a grudge."

Watson's eyes narrowed. "Grudge?"

Victoria glanced up. "Against whom?"

Holmes gave a single nod as he again referred to the file. "Croft was once in line for a major architectural commission at Parliament—one that would've cemented his career. Stamford was appointed to the review committee. He authored a scathing critique of Croft's structural proposal, citing reckless shortcuts and disregard for safety codes. That report destroyed Croft's credibility in government circles."

"Would that be enough to make him an accomplice to attempted murder and arson?" Victoria asked.

Referencing his file Holmes said, "Croft didn't just lose a contract—he lost his firm. Investors pulled out. He was humiliated. For more than a decade, he nursed that failure. When Trask approached him with a plan for revenge against Stamford, Croft saw a path to redemption—twisted though it may be."

Victoria's voice was quiet. "What could Trask have promised him?"

"Reputation," Holmes replied. "By staging a sabotage scandal tied to poor construction oversight, Croft would 'discover' and report the flaws just in time to be the hero. His name restored. His prestige renewed."

"But with Trask captured…" Watson began.

"He must go double or quits," Holmes said grimly. "If the theater burned, and Victoria was implicated, Trask's fabricated reports, supported by Croft, would still serve their purpose. He could claim he'd tried to intervene. That he'd issued warnings no one heeded. Either way, he would come out clean."

Watson exhaled slowly. "So, Trask offered Croft a lie he could live with."

Holmes looked at Victoria. "And Croft offered Trask legitimacy—an architect's seal, a forged trail of reports, and access to restricted blueprints. Without him, Trask's plan would have been flawed. But with him—"

"It looked real," Victoria finished. "And legal."

A pause followed.

Then Watson asked the question that had been forming behind his furrowed brow.

"Holmes, if Croft is complicit, where is he now?"

Holmes crossed to a small envelope left by Wiggins that morning and opened it. Inside was a brief note.

"Gone," Holmes said. "He left town two days ago under the name 'Alan Forrester.' Took a train to Edinburgh, according to Wiggins and the Irregulars. No forwarding address."

Watson frowned. "You had Wiggins following Croft?"

246

Holmes gave a slight nod. "After discovering Trask's duplicity, I instructed the Irregulars to quietly observe anyone closely tied to the project—board members, and major suppliers. I suspected someone with access had either aided him or been used by him. Croft fit the profile. It appears he recognized the net tightening and slipped away."

Victoria interjected. "If he's left town, how would he still pose a threat here?"

"That," Holmes replied, "is the question. Because Trask's attempt at arson failed, we must assume they had a secondary plan in place—one that could be executed even with Croft at a distance."

Watson sat forward. "A device? A proxy?"

"Possibly both," Holmes said. "Croft is an architect with a grudge, but he's also meticulous. If he and Trask anticipated failure, they would have built in redundancies."

Victoria was disturbed by the revelation. "So, Trask recruited someone with a personal vendetta."

Holmes nodded. "He convinced Croft that Stamford had cost him a fortune—and that revenge would be sweet, quiet, and long overdue. Trask offered him something he longed to have."

"Trask manipulated him with a mix of resentment and reward," Holmes continued. "And now we must discover how they planned to finish what they started—if the fire in the substage failed."

"But now, with Trask in police custody, having made a full confession of his part in the scheme, what motive would Croft have to complete the planned arson?" Watson asked, scratching his head.

Holmes was silent for a moment. "Because Croft is not finished. He does not act out of loyalty to Trask—his motive was always his own. Trask gave him purpose, a stage, but the grudge Croft bears against Stamford, against the establishment—is deeply personal. He may see

Trask's confession as a betrayal. Or, more likely, as a weakness. He might also consider it an opportunity."

He stood and paced a short distance. "Imagine Croft's mindset: If the fire occurs, Trask's so-called confession appears incomplete, the ravings of a madman, or even coerced. Croft becomes the hidden hand, the unseen prophet who tried to stop it all but was ignored."

"Painting himself as a protector?" Victoria asked quietly.

"Precisely," Holmes replied. "It gives him a shield of righteousness to hide behind. The crime completes the statement, and he emerges not as a villain—but as a tragic witness who is now respected in society once again."

Victoria crossed her arms. "If he's in Edinburgh, what can he do from there?"

Holmes gave her a sidelong glance. "He can *instruct* someone else. Or worse—he could have already done so. A timed mechanism. An overlooked delivery. The trap could still be set—we simply haven't tripped it yet."

He pulled the case file and pulled out recent order invoices. Taking a fresh sheet of paper he began creating a list.

"What is that you're doing, Holmes?" Watson asked.

Holmes handed it to Watson. "This is a list of all materials Trask ordered under his name or aliases in the last six weeks that were approved by Croft. Several shipments went to a warehouse in Camden under the name 'Henry Blythe.'"

Watson opened the list and scanned it. "Solvents, wiring, lathwork, and calico sheets. There's enough here to build a theatrical façade—or set a controlled blaze."

Holmes continued, "I've already sent the fire inspectors through the theater. They found no active igniters, but that doesn't rule out embedded triggers—especially if Croft constructed a delayed mechanism."

"And surveillance?" Victoria asked.

"Two men posted outside at all times," Holmes said. "We've also supplied them with a maintenance schedule to catch any unregistered entrances. No one is entering that building without being seen."

"But if Croft knows all of Trask's secret places better than any of us," Watson said, "he may have hidden something deep—something even Rodney missed."

Holmes turned back toward the desk and spread out the theater's original plans. "That's what we must uncover. Before the next shipment. Before Croft returns—or before he triggers the final act from afar."

Victoria stepped closer, her tone quiet but firm. "Can we force him back to London?"

"I intend to," Holmes said. "Taking out a pad, he scribbled a message. Stepping into the hallway he called in a loud voice, "Billy, I need you."

"What are you doing now?" Victoria asked, trying to stop her head from spinning.

The lad raced up the stairs and stood before him. "Yes, Mr. Holmes?"

"I need you to take this to the telegraph office for me and send it." Holmes instructed. "It's most urgent."

The lad took the paper and ran off quickly on his mission.

"I'm sending a forged telegram to the Caledonian, purporting to be from a city inspector, requesting Croft's urgent presence in London for a 'follow-up on the Majestic's compliance review.' It's the most likely place Croft would stay in Edinburgh. If he takes the bait, he'll be on a train by tonight."

Watson arched a brow. "And if he doesn't?"

"Then we follow the trail from Camden. Someone is still in play here. An accomplice who is perhaps unknown to us, but essential to Croft's contingency."

Victoria touched the corner of the blueprint gently. "They planned to burn it down... twice. In case the first performance didn't go to script."

"Yes," Holmes said softly. "They wrote an encore."

He turned, facing both of them. "We must find the backup plan. Croft may be distant, but his designs are not. We must revisit the substage, the supply corridor, and the gallery floorboards—everything Trask and Croft had access to. If we miss even a single wire or latch, it could all still go up."

Watson folded the shipment list and tucked it into his coat. "Then let's begin immediately."

Holmes gave a short nod. "I'll join you at the Majestic within the hour. First, I must meet with Wiggins and review Camden's warehouse records. If there's an accomplice still in the city, he won't stay hidden long."

As he moved towards the door, Victoria called after him.

"Sherlock, what happens if Croft realizes his plan's unraveling?"

Holmes turned, his expression unreadable. "Then he'll come back. Not to rebuild it—but to bury the evidence before we find the rest."

He opened the door, pausing just a moment longer. "Let's make sure we find it first."

The London Majestic loomed in the gray afternoon light, its domed roof streaked with rain. Inside, all was hushed save for the occasional creak of boards and the distant hum of stage lights. Holmes, Watson, and Victoria stood just inside the service entry to the backstage corridor, joined by Rodney, who held a clipboard and wore a deeply focused expression.

"Any sign Croft received the telegram?" Watson asked, adjusting his coat.

Holmes shook his head. "Not yet. Wiggins and the Irregulars are watching King's Cross and local authorities the Caledonian terminal in Edinburgh. If Croft boards a train south, we'll know. But for now, we assume he's in motion—and that he'll arrive under false pretenses within the day."

Victoria crossed her arms. "Remind me how you worded it?"

"A request from the city inspector's office," Holmes replied, "for a compliance follow-up tied to recent fire code irregularities. The sort of thing Croft couldn't risk ignoring if he wishes to keep his name out of scandal."

Rodney gave a low whistle. "And you expect him to walk into the lion's den."

"I expect him to believe it's his chance to take control of the narrative," Holmes said. "But while he's en route, we must deal with the more immediate threat—whoever is still here, following his instructions."

He gestured toward the hallway that led to the substage. "We move now."

They descended into the underbelly of the theater, where the air was colder and tinged with dust and varnish. Gas lamps flickered on the walls, casting long shadows.

Rodney led them to the rear of the substage corridor. "The wiring's been checked. Vent housings show signs of tampering, just like you said."

Holmes crouched and examined a wall bracket near a vent. "This one's been adjusted within the last forty-eight hours. Not by Trask—he's in custody. Which means someone else was down here."

Watson frowned. "Croft?"

"Unlikely. He vanished days ago. Which leads us to another accomplice."

Victoria stepped forward. "So, we lay a second trap."

Holmes nodded. "We'll post a fabricated work order in the backstage area—a routine substage clearance scheduled under Croft's name. It will look like part of the inspection process tied to the telegram. Anyone still working with Croft will believe the plan is resuming... and will act accordingly."

Rodney pulled a folded sheet from his pocket. "I drafted the notice you requested. Standard phrasing. 'Inventory Reconciliation. Per architect Croft's direction.' That should do it."

"Post it," Holmes said. "And have two men nearby at all times. Not to interfere—only to observe who reads it, who reacts, and who makes contact."

Watson crossed his arms. "You're hoping the accomplice breaks cover."

"I'm counting on it," Holmes replied.

They fell silent for a moment, the hiss of the gas lamps steady above them. Then Victoria spoke, her voice thoughtful.

"Croft is aware that Trask is in custody. He'll likely want to speak to me to see how much we know."

Holmes gave a small smile. "That's why you won't be here. You'll be seen leaving mid-afternoon for a fictitious meeting in the city. Daisy will make sure word of it spreads backstage."

"And I'll come in later," Watson added, catching on. "So, no one suspects we're waiting."

"Correct," Holmes said. "Croft will assume he's arriving ahead of any serious investigation. If he contacts the accomplice to check the theater's status, we'll intercept it."

Rodney tucked the work order under his arm. "And if neither of them shows?"

"They'll show," Holmes said flatly. "Croft is vain enough to believe he can salvage this. And his partner, whoever he is, won't abandon a plan this close to its conclusion."

He turned, his voice low. "We've taken Trask off the board. Now it's Croft's move. Let's make sure he walks straight into it."

"I'm still shocked to know I likely saw Trask as a youth working at the Majestic," Rodney said, shaking his head. "Of course, I had little to do with the young helpers the Miss Emily allowed backstage. And time does change a man." Shaking his head, Rodney peeled away to post the notice.

Holmes glanced at Victoria, then Watson.

"Get some rest, both of you," he said. "I want your minds clear when we face him. The real curtain call is coming—and we'll need every actor in place."

As Holmes turned to leave Victoria put her hand on his arm. "Sherlock, please be careful."

He managed a weak smile and placing his hand over hers said, "I will."

As they ascended the steps back into the upper levels of the theater, the wind outside picked up, and with it came a tension, silent and watchful, waiting for the final piece to fall into place.

Later that night, Holmes paced the floor of his sitting room, a copy of the forged telegram in hand. Victoria sat curled in one of the armchairs, her shawl drawn tightly around her shoulders, while Watson stood near the hearth, sipping lukewarm tea.

Holmes stopped suddenly. "Croft is still in Edinburgh. Wiggins has seen no sign of movement at his London residence or office. But he'll come. He has no choice."

Watson glanced at the document. "Is that a copy of the telegram?"

Holmes held it aloft. *City Inspector's Office – Urgent Compliance Review, London District Fire Registry.* "If Croft believes there's even a chance his name could be publicly tied to fire code violations, he'll return to control the narrative. He's not the mastermind—Trask was always the architect of this revenge. But Croft gave him the tools. And now, without Trask to shield him, he's exposed."

Victoria studied the forged letter. "You think he'll walk into a trap just to protect his reputation?"

Holmes resumed pacing. "Croft's ego has always been his weak point. Trask knew this. He promised Croft redemption—restored credibility, a triumphant reentry into society. And Croft believed him. When Trask was captured, Croft ran. Not to regroup—but to vanish."

Watson folded his arms. "So, if Croft fears discovery..."

"He'll return to try to contain it," Holmes finished. "But he didn't act alone."

He stepped to his desk and opened a folder containing Victoria's renovation ledgers. "There's one name I keep returning to—quiet, consistent, unassuming. Eleanor Brayford. The theater's treasurer."

Victoria looked surprised. "She signed off on the accounts and kept the books, but she was never heavily involved in day-to-day operations."

"Precisely," Holmes said. "And yet her signature appears on multiple expense approvals—ones that should've raised flags. I cross-checked them this morning. They include supply payments routed through Croft's contacts and work orders tied to forged architectural revisions."

Watson didn't hide his surprise. "Was she working with Croft?"

Holmes's voice was thoughtful. "I suspect she was working for Trask, but aware that Croft was involved. Whether out of loyalty or something deeper, I do not yet know. But her silence and access made many of Trask's deceptions possible."

Victoria blinked. "Easton Works wasn't even on our vendor list. It was the company that dismissed Trask some time ago."

"And yet Croft reused that name in phantom invoices. The paperwork was meant to look legitimate—and Eleanor Brayford was the one person who could slip it through without scrutiny."

Holmes closed the file and reached for his coat. "We must assume the accomplice is still active. If Brayford were involved, she may still be following instructions. I'm going to verify the delivery of the telegram. If Croft is on his way back to London, he may try to contact her."

Watson set his teacup down. "And if not?"

"Then we follow the second thread," Holmes said. "Brayford."

Lestrade met them at the central stairwell in Scotland Yard with a sheaf of papers in hand, still wiping the past night's sleep from his eyes.

"The telegram reached the boarding house," he confirmed. "Delivered to Mr. Croft care of a Mr. Forrester—the alias Croft used on his travel documents. No official reply, but the clerk said the gentleman seemed 'troubled' after reading it."

Holmes was unsurprised. "Croft will come. He will assume the names were given to the fire inspectors by his accomplice. He thinks he can outmaneuver this."

"We've posted men at King's Cross and Victoria," Lestrade added.

"See that the men stay subtle," Holmes warned. "He'll vanish if he even *suspects* we're watching."

Lestrade smirked faintly. "I *have* worked with you before, Mr. Holmes."

"Good," Holmes said. "We need eyes on him the moment he steps off the train."

Ink-stained ledgers lined the counter of the telegraph office. Holmes presented his credentials, and the clerk—somewhat flustered—granted access to the most recent transmission logs. Watson hovered near the door, watching passersby in case a familiar face involved with the case should be coming their way.

Holmes scanned the entries. "There. A pattern."

He laid out a short stack of payment slips.

"Rush telegrams sent from this office and another near Covent Garden that are all filed under the Majestic's financial account. Paid by Eleanor Brayford. Three of them were addressed to the Caledonian."

Watson stepped closer. "She was funding his escape?"

"Possibly," Holmes said. "Or ensuring his silence."

He pulled one final ledger from the stack and pointed to a date. "This payment—four days ago. A courier was dispatched to deliver a sealed packet to a solicitor's office in Mayfair. No return address, but the delivery fee was charged to Brayford's personal account."

Watson arched an eyebrow. "Mayfair. That's where Trask's barrister is based, isn't it?"

Holmes smiled faintly. "Precisely. That's our next stop."

Holmes unwound his scarf as he stepped inside.

"She's paying for Trask's defense."

Victoria looked up sharply. "Eleanor Brayford?"

"She's the one funding his solicitor. I've just come from the clerk's desk at the barrister's chambers. The payments are routed through a private account in her name. But her handwriting is on the payment authorizations."

Watson exhaled. "So, she's the accomplice."

Holmes responded. "And possibly more. She wasn't merely following orders. She was investing in Trask's future. We've long assumed Trask to be cold and strategic, but even the most ruthless minds can manipulate through intimacy."

Victoria's expression darkened. "She's in love with him."

"That would explain the silence, the access, the money," Holmes said. "And now, with Croft returning to London, she may try to trigger the final act."

He spread the blueprints of the theater across the table.

"Whatever Trask planned, he entrusted Brayford to finish it. Now that Croft is on his way, we must assume he'll try to rendezvous with her. And when he does... we'll be waiting."

The clatter of teacups and rustling paper filled the parlor of Victoria's flat. Daisy perched cross-legged on the floor, surrounded by ledgers and vendor manifests. Watson sat at the writing desk near the window, outwardly calm but alert, his revolver discreetly tucked in his pocket ready for anything. Victoria leaned over the table examining the papers with deep concentration.

"It's all here," Daisy said, flipping to another page. "This is the contractor schedule Trask gave me as Lawson before his capture. The shipping dates, the orders—none of them match the payment logs from the accounts Eleanor Brayford signed."

Victoria pressed her fingers to her temples. "We know she falsified the paperwork. But the scale of it... It wasn't just one favor. She covered for Trask again and again."

"And Croft," Watson added, his tone dire. "We now have two collaborators—and likely more deception buried beneath these ledgers."

Daisy glanced up. "But why would Miss Brayford do it? She's always been polite—bland, even."

Victoria didn't smile. "She was in love with him. Or thought she was."

Watson looked up from the desk. "Holmes believes Trask manipulated her emotions the same way he manipulated Croft's ego."

Victoria turned toward the fireplace, arms crossed. "I remember her once asking me, in an offhand way, whether I found Mr. Lawson 'charming, in an unconventional sort of way.' I thought nothing of it. But now—"

Daisy made a face. "That man was about as charming as a cold cod."

A soft knock at the door interrupted them. Watson stood quickly, hand brushing his coat pocket, and crossed the room. He opened it to reveal Holmes, rain-speckled and brisk as ever, removing his gloves as he stepped inside.

"I've confirmed she's funding the barrister," Holmes said without preamble. "I traced the payments from Brayford's private account directly to Montague Hill, Queen's Counsel—one of the most expensive criminal solicitors in London."

Watson whistled. "No way Trask could afford that on his own."

Holmes raised a brow. "And yet there it is—Hill has received no fewer than three deposits, each just under the amount that would trigger financial reporting. Classic pattern of personal laundering."

"Mr. Holmes," Daisy asked, "How were you able to see Miss Brayford's personal financial documents?"

"The important thing is that I did see them," Holmes replied with a wink, "it's best you don't know how I did."

Victoria's expression tightened. "She's doing more than helping. She's preserving him. Protecting him."

"Exactly," Holmes said. "Brayford isn't just a silent partner—she's emotionally entangled. Trask promised her something – likely marriage. It's the only explanation that accounts for this level of risk."

Watson sank into the chair by the window. "So, she forged documents, funneled payments, and kept Trask's secrets all while smiling at Victoria in board meetings?"

"More than that," Holmes said. "She also arranged at least one of Croft's Edinburgh deliveries. I have a telegram receipt sent from the same Covent Garden office, addressed to 'Mr. Forrester.'"

Daisy, still sitting cross-legged, looked up sharply. "So, what now?"

"Now," Holmes said, "we watch her. Discreetly. She may attempt contact with Croft when he arrives. Wiggins is already on her trail."

"And if she doesn't?" Victoria asked.

"Then we draw her out," Holmes replied. "We'll arrange for a harmless rumor to circulate backstage—a whisper that Croft has been arrested by authorities. Daisy, I believe you could make this happen efficiently. If she believes her part in the scheme may be exposed…"

"She'll panic," Victoria finished. "And try to silence him. Or run."

Holmes's eyes flicked to Daisy. "You're always to remain close to Victoria. Do not let her attend rehearsals or meetings alone."

Daisy gave a serious nod. "Yes, sir."

"Dr. Watson will stay in his old room." Holmes added. "Victoria, I'd like you to stay close. Please sleep in my bed."

"My blushes, Mr. Holmes!" Daisy blurted out without thinking.

"Daisy!" Victoria scolded.

Ignoring the mishap Holmes put on his overcoat "I'll return before dawn."

Victoria tilted her head. "And you? Where are you going?"

"To the Majestic," he said. "There's one storeroom still unaccounted for in the original plans. If Brayford left anything behind—or if Croft planted a final surprise—I intend to find it."

He turned to go, pausing as Victoria approached him.

"Sherlock—" she said softly.

He looked at her as she gently put her hand on his arm.

"Be careful," she said.

He gave a faint smile. "I intend to be."

And then he was gone.

The London Majestic stood silent in the hush of the night, its darkened corridors echoing only with the occasional groan of settling beams and distant water pipes. Holmes moved purposefully through the backstage passageway, his coat damp from the rain and the master key Victoria had entrusted to him weighing heavily in his pocket.

He paused at a narrow door concealed between a wardrobe cabinet and a maintenance panel. The door was unremarkable—unlabeled, unnoticed—but Holmes had seen it before in the original blueprints Rodney unearthed. It was meant to be a storage room for lighting equipment, long since struck from renovation plans. Yet something about the forgotten space had gnawed at him.

He inserted the key, and the lock turned easily, as one frequently used.

The scent inside was faint but telling of dust, oil, aged paper, and something bitter—like the residue of an old chemical compound. Holmes stepped in, closed the door behind him, and lit the gas lamp near the corner, its flame flaring to life with a flicker of pale yellow.

The room revealed itself slowly.

Shelves lined the walls, but instead of light fixtures or tools, they held folders of documents, brittle blueprints, empty vials, and a rusting typewriter on a side table. Holmes approached it at once, rolling the ribbon forward with a practiced hand. The flaw in the "s" type bar was unmistakable. This was the machine used to send the anonymous notes to Victoria, and to forge the documents that put blame on Stamford.

Among the cluttered shelves, he found duplicate contractor manifests, bearing Croft's name. Further down were architectural plans drawn by Trask himself, many with subtle fire hazards marked in faint red pencil—notes only someone with architectural training would recognize. A torn sheet of parchment at the back of the drawer caught Holmes's attention. It was in Brayford's hand. The message read:

He says if we time it right, she won't even know what hit her. The smoke will come from the orchestra pit.

Holmes set the page aside carefully, his expression grim.

A bundle of letters tied with a red ribbon caught his eye. He untied the knot carefully. Each envelope bore Trask's precise, slanted handwriting—addressed to *E.B.* in various flourishes. Holmes extracted the first letter, unfolding the page with clinical precision, though the words within made his brows tighten.

My dearest Eleanor,
You are the only soul who has ever seen the world through the same cracked lens as I do. The theater is our sanctuary—not theirs. When the final curtain falls, we will rise. Together.

Letter after letter echoed the same sentiments: longing, shared vengeance, grandiose delusions about reclaiming the Majestic. The final letter was dated just days before Trask's arrest.

When all is finished—when Holmes is in despair, when Victoria Watson is silenced, and Stamford's memory turned to ash—we will stand at the center of the Majestic, and I will make you my wife. You have waited long enough.

Holmes folded the letters swiftly and placed them back in the bundle just as a sound stirred beyond the corridor. Footsteps—measured, cautious.

Then—another faint sound.

A stair creaked beyond the door. A pause. Then footsteps—soft, deliberate, and drawing nearer.

Holmes quietly locked the door, extinguished the lamp in a single breath and melted into the shadows near the tallest shelving unit, hidden from the door. He heard a key turn in the lock. The handle turned. The door creaked open.

Eleanor Brayford slipped inside, clutching a slim leather folio.

She didn't bother with the lamp. Instead, she moved with the certainty of someone who had been here many times before. Her gloved hands passed over several drawers and piles, hesitating briefly before extracting the small bundle of letters tied with twine. She held them to her chest, her head bowed.

"These precious letters from you, my love," she whispered, barely audible, "mustn't go up in flames."

She glanced around the dark room once, then backed out, closing the door gently behind her.

Holmes remained perfectly still. Only when he heard her footsteps fade completely down the corridor—and the distant creak of a stair descending to the alley entrance—did he move.

He struck a match and relit the lamp. The shadows sprang back into light, and with it, a fuller picture of what had transpired in this room. Brayford hadn't just assisted Trask—she had worshiped him. Her devotion had blinded her to reason and made her complicit in every forged document, every misdirection, every threat.

Holmes gathered the remaining letters and documents, carefully folding and tucking them into his coat. One page caught his attention—an inventory list dated three days before Trask's arrest. The final item was underlined twice: *spare fuse caps—orchestra pit wiring.* It was a detail too precise to ignore.

He extinguished the light once more and stepped out into the corridor, locking the door behind him.

The accomplice was now confirmed.

She had a name. A motive.

And now, thanks to one whispered sentence, she also had a fatal weakness.

The parlor of Victoria's flat was quiet, save for the soft crackle of the fire and the occasional rustle of Daisy's skirts as she moved about. Watson sat in the armchair nearest the window, newspaper folded on his lap, but his attention was fixed on Holmes, who stood before the hearth, arms crossed and expression distant.

Victoria entered the room. Her hair was loosely gathered, and the weariness in her face spoke of a day's worth of strain.

"Well?" she asked.

Holmes looked up. "He wrote her love letters."

Victoria sank onto the settee. "You saw them?"

"I read them," he confirmed. "They were... fevered things. Grandiose declarations, vows of shared destiny. Trask promised her marriage. Power. A future together—once the theater was reborn and his enemies were destroyed."

Watson leaned forward. "So, she believed she was part of some great romantic cause?"

"She believed she was loved," Holmes said evenly. "That's more dangerous than any cause."

Victoria's face showed her concern. "Did the letters reveal anything about Croft's involvement?"

Holmes replied calmly. "Trask referred to him repeatedly, though always with contempt. Croft was useful—a man who had both the architectural skill and the social motive, but none of the resolve to act alone. Trask manipulated him with promises of restored reputation. Brayford was the believer. Croft was the tool."

"And now," Watson added grimly, "the believer is finishing the work."

"Precisely," Holmes said. "Brayford left the hidden chamber with the letters. But her movements weren't just sentimental. She took something else—a folded set of diagrams, newer than the rest, unscorched. I couldn't see the details."

Victoria's face tightened. "She means to carry it out. The fire."

"Very possibly," Holmes said. "Trask's final plan didn't end with his arrest. He left it in her hands, and she intends to light the match."

"But how?" Watson asked. "We've already swept the substage. The gas lines are sealed. You disabled the chemical stockpile. There's round-the-clock patrol."

"There's one place we overlooked," Holmes replied. "The orchestra pit."

Daisy, entering with a tray of tea, froze. "The orchestra pit? But that's where the performers are—where the conductor stands. That would mean…"

Holmes gave a grim nod. "The fire would ignite beneath the heart of the performance. Panic, stampede, collapse—it would achieve maximum devastation. Especially if Victoria were onstage."

Victoria's lips parted in quiet horror.

"I won't be," she said at last. "I'll cancel the performance. Tell the cast we're postponing—"

"No," Holmes said firmly. "You'll do no such thing. That would tip our hand."

He moved toward the table, pulling a map of the theater from his coat and spreading it out. "We let her think she's succeeding, that no one suspects her. In the meantime, we reinforce the pit, place fire-dampening compounds beneath the stage floor, and station men in the wings. I'll take the conductor's position myself. If anything unusual moves—anything at all—I'll be the first to see it."

Daisy set the tea tray down with a nervous hand. "But how would they start it, if no one's down there?"

Holmes tapped the map with his forefinger. "There are several possibilities. A timed fuse rigged in the vent work. A chemical compound that ignites after exposure to air. Or—more dangerously— a pressure-based trigger built into the floorboards."

Daisy blinked. "What do you mean a trigger?"

"A hidden device that activates when a specific condition is met," Holmes explained. "Step on the right spot, and the pressure releases a latch—or crushes a vial. The fire begins before anyone even realizes what's happened."

There was a silence, and then Victoria straightened slightly.

"Today," she said slowly, "during rehearsal... I did feel something strange. Just left of center stage, near the apron. A board that flexed oddly under my heel—too much give, like it wasn't fully braced."

Holmes turned to her sharply. "Did you examine it?"

"No," she admitted. "We were mid-scene. I meant to check afterward, but we were interrupted, and I forgot. I made note of the spot, though. Part of my tap routine takes place on it."

Holmes's expression darkened. "That could be it. A disguised trigger, installed during the final days of construction. It's the sort of thing Croft would be capable of designing—and Brayford would know where to place it."

Watson stood. "So, Croft must be back in London."

"Or soon to arrive," Holmes said. "And if Brayford believes the opening night is secure, they may try to strike before we're ready."

He folded the map and looked to Victoria. "You'll stay here tonight in your flat. Daisy will stay with you in your guest room. Watson and I will be nearby. No one is to know about the trigger—not yet. Let them think the performance will go on as planned."

Holmes exchanged a glance with Watson. "So, we go now."

Daisy looked alarmed. "Back to the theater? Tonight?"

Watson stood and reached for his coat. "We'll be in and out. Quietly."

Victoria rose. "You'll disable it?"

"If there's anything there," Holmes said, already at the door, "we'll neutralize it—without appearing to have done so."

The theater was quiet, the gaslights low. Holmes and Watson let themselves in with the key Victoria had provided.

Watson followed Holmes down the steps, lantern in hand, the air cool and slightly damp.

Holmes motioned to a gap between two braced columns under the main stage platform. "This aligns with Victoria's placement. Help me lift the hatch."

Together they pried up a floor panel used for maintenance access. Beneath, a shallow cavity ran between beams. Holmes crouched and reached carefully into the space. His fingers brushed a set of thin wires secured to a pulley. Following the length, he discovered a small metal housing built into the floor support—a sealed tin cylinder with a trigger arm wedged against the wood.

Watson knelt beside him. "What is it?"

"Simple, but effective," Holmes murmured. "A weight-based ignition. If someone of sufficient size stepped here—during a tap dance, for instance—the trigger would snap, the chemical capsule inside would rupture, and a delayed fuse would ignite whatever's hidden beneath the pit. Possibly soaked rags or flammable powder."

Holmes retrieved his small tool kit and disarmed the trigger with care. He removed the firing pin and fuse, replacing them with a pair of blanks weighted and wired to mimic the original.

"No one will know it's been touched," he said, brushing off his hands.

Watson exhaled. "That would've killed Victoria and half the company."

"And implicated Victoria—if she were standing on the mark."

Holmes lowered the trapdoor and stood. "They meant for it to happen on opening night. A final act of revenge."

They ascended the stairs in silence until Holmes paused before exiting. "The conductor's position places him in view of the audience, but only from behind. Most attendees wouldn't recognize him, but a disguise is still in order."

Watson raised a brow. "You intend to take his place?"

"I intend," Holmes said with determination, "to be where our adversary expects someone else to be. Close enough to the pit. Close enough to strike first."

The sky outside Victoria's flat had begun to brighten to a bruised violet, but inside the warm glow of gaslight gave the illusion of calm. Watson stood by the window, his arms folded as he kept watch on the street below. Victoria paced the length of the sitting room, her movements restless, her hands twisting together. Daisy had excused herself to make tea, sensing the conversation needed room to unfold.

After watching his daughter nervously pacing the room for nearly twenty minutes, Watson said, "My dear, exhausting yourself will not help."

"I can't help it," Victoria said, her voice taut. "What if we've missed something? What if there's still danger—real danger—for the cast, the musicians, the audience?"

Holmes, seated in the armchair nearest the fire, studied her with that rare expression of gentleness he reserved for only a few. "You're not wrong to worry," he said. "But the greatest threats have already been defused. The device beneath the stage is no longer a risk. Watson and I confirmed that ourselves."

Watson turned from the window. "Yes, my child, we found the trigger last night. A cleverly disguised mechanism hidden in the stage floorboards—right where you said something felt off. If you'd stepped there during the performance, it might've set the whole thing in motion."

Victoria stared at him, finally feeling a spark of hope. "And you are sure you disarmed it?"

"We disabled it in such a way that it appears untouched," Holmes said. "Should they attempt to use it, nothing will happen."

Victoria let out a slow breath and sat down on the sofa. "So, the worst of it—"

"Is behind us," Holmes said gently. "Now it is only a matter of catching them before they disappear entirely."

She looked up, her expression still troubled. "And if we catch them mid-performance? What then? Do we end the show? Risk panic?"

"We've planned for discretion," Holmes said. "If the moment comes during the show, Lestrade and his men will act quietly. No scene, no chaos. The audience won't know anything's amiss."

Holmes gave a faint smile. "It's fitting, really. The final act of their plot will play out under stage lights. But it's our performance now."

Victoria shook her head with a ghost of a smile. "You're terrible with metaphors."

"I leave poetry to the Romantics," he replied. "But I promise you this, Victoria—no harm will come to anyone under your roof. The Majestic will endure. So will you. Even so, one can never be too safe, so I will still be in the orchestra pit playing the role of conductor both for the final dress rehearsal and opening night performance."

From the kitchen downstairs, Daisy's voice floated up the stairs, calling cheerfully, "I'm putting in extra sugar, just in case anyone needs fortifying."

Victoria rose, steadier now. "We'll all need it," she said. "Tomorrow, the curtain rises."

Holmes met her eyes. "Yes. But this time, we'll be ready."

The hush backstage at the London Majestic was unlike the nervous quiet of early rehearsals. This silence was sharper and charged with anticipation and thick with unspoken tension. Final checks echoed from the wings, and muffled footsteps moved across the fly gallery above. In the dim light backstage, Holmes stood gazing down at the conductor's podium, his lean frame dressed not in his usual coat and cravat, but in a simple, tailored black suit.

He adjusted a pale brown wig over his natural hair that he had received through the courtesy of Aldous Alcott, the Majestic's makeup specialist. It was light enough to mimic the real conductor when viewed from behind. Morton Michaels, the orchestra conductor had been taken into Holmes's confidence and agreed to the plan.

Watson joined him from the house, tugging his gloves tighter. "Lestrade's men are in place. Three seated on the main floor, two more in the gallery, and one stationed at each exit. All out of uniform, of course."

Holmes gave a single nod. "And the orchestra?"

"They've been told the conductor has a sore throat and won't be giving verbal cues. Rodney's instructed them to follow visual signals only."

Holmes allowed a trace of amusement. "Then let us hope I'm more convincing with a baton than I am with a violin."

From behind the curtain, Victoria emerged, her rehearsal cloak still draped over her costume. Her hair was pinned in soft waves. Despite the early hour, she already carried the air of performance—shoulders high, chin steady—but her eyes revealed the strain beneath.

"Everything's set for curtain?" Holmes asked.

She gave a quiet nod. "As far as the company knows, it's just another final run-through before the opening tonight."

Then her expression darkened. "But what about the audience? And the crew? What if something still happens?"

Watson stepped forward. "Victoria, we've accounted for every potential trigger point. The trap beneath the stage was neutralized yesterday. Holmes inspected the orchestra pit himself. There are no remaining explosives. Even the gas lines have been temporarily rerouted."

"And there's a fire crew stationed just across the street," Holmes added. "Should anything arise, they'll be here in under a minute."

She exhaled, but her brow remained creased. "It still feels dangerous."

"It is dangerous," Holmes said evenly. "But it is no longer uncontrolled. What remains are the accomplices themselves. Brayford and Croft can no longer rely on devices or distractions. If they act, they will do so in person."

Watson's voice turned quiet. "And that's what we're counting on."

Holmes looked toward the back of the theater. "They'll be watching. Perhaps in the crowd, or from a backstage vantage. Waiting for the signal they've rehearsed or the moment they've planned. But tonight, the only performance that will conclude is theirs."

Victoria crossed her arms, then unfolded them. "And if one of them tries something mid-show?"

Lestrade's voice cut in as he stepped from the wings. "If they do, we'll be ready. But unless there's an imminent threat, we wait until the curtain falls. Fewer witnesses. Less risk of panic."

Holmes gave Lestrade an approving look. "Agreed. But I want eyes on Brayford, especially. She's the more likely to act impulsively."

"I've assigned our sharpest man to her," Lestrade said. "He's posing as an usher."

Rodney emerged from a side corridor, waving a folder. "Mr. Holmes, we need to confirm the placement of the pit stand before dress rehearsal."

Holmes gave a nod and followed, but not before giving Victoria a long look. "We are prepared," he said simply.

When they disappeared, Victoria lingered at the edge of the stage, her eyes drifting across the empty house. Watson joined her, taking her hand.

"You've done something remarkable, you know," he said gently. "Even without the danger. Rebuilding this place, leading this cast. It's something I never could've imagined when you were a little girl writing poems in your room."

Victoria smiled faintly, her fingers brushing the edge of the curtain. "Sometimes I feel like I'm just playing a part someone else wrote."

"No," Watson said. "You've written this one yourself."

Footsteps returned behind them.

She turned to him. "Tell me honestly. Are you afraid?"

Holmes met her gaze for a long moment. His answer was not quick.

"No," he said at last. "But I'm very aware."

She said nothing more. The stillness between them said enough.

From the far end of the corridor, the call came: "Thirty minutes until curtain!"

Victoria straightened. "It's time to get ready."

Watson offered his daughter his arm, and she took it with a small smile before heading toward the dressing rooms. Holmes lingered a moment longer, then looked once more towards the pit.

The soft hum of schoolchildren filled the velvet-trimmed house of the London Majestic, their excited chatter rising and falling like waves. Dozens of young faces leaned forward from the edge of their seats, legs swinging beneath rows of velvet cushions. Teachers and chaperones sat interspersed, gently shushing the more restless ones.

It had been Eleanor Brayford's idea to invite them—a "sound test," she'd called it. A gesture of goodwill to the parish school, and a chance to fill the house during the final dress rehearsal. Holmes had approved it reluctantly, seeing the public benefit—but now, he questioned whether it had all been part of the plan.

Lestrade emerged and touched Holmes's shoulder. "We've just had word," he said, his voice troubled. "Trask escaped last night. The prison train made an unscheduled stop near Leeds. Two guards were missing— one presumed dead, the other found unconscious. He likely switched uniforms and slipped away into the fog."

Holmes's shoulders tensed. "Then he'll come here."

Lestrade agreed. "We have men posted at every entrance. A plainclothes officer is already seated with the orchestra."

"I'll be in place momentarily," Holmes said. "Victoria is not to know until this is over."

Lestrade hesitated. "Are you sure that is wise?"

"No," Holmes replied. "But it's necessary."

With a final breath, Holmes stepped down the corridor and into the orchestra pit.

The musicians barely glanced up as he approached. He tapped the music stand lightly, then raised the baton. The overture began.

Above, on the stage, the rehearsal was already in motion. Victoria glided forward in her costume for the opening scene of *The Reluctant Bride*. Her voice rang out clearly, each line filled with vibrant wit and sincerity. The children in the audience laughed and clapped at the right moments, delighted by the comic timing.

Holmes, conducting, let his gaze sweep across the orchestra—not for rhythm or timing, but for faces.

Oboe… cello… first and second violins…

Then he saw it. An unrecognized face- or was it?

A man seated at the rear, occupying a third violin chair—a position that hadn't existed in the original seating chart. The man hunched slightly, his face obscured by his instrument. But Holmes knew the posture. The restless foot tapping. The tension in the shoulders.

W.E. Trask.

The wig was convincing. So were the spectacles. But Holmes had studied this man too long. He recognized him instantly.

Moments before intermission would begin, Holmes shifted slightly on the podium, his gaze sharpening.

Between Trask's feet, beneath the music stand was the violin case. It was not quite closed, as if something inside were keeping it slightly ajar.

Holmes's stomach turned cold.

Victoria's voice continued above him, the scene reaching its final beat of act one. As the children cheered, Trask stood.

It was casual. Almost inconspicuous. He set down his violin, adjusted his jacket, and moved toward the back of the pit.

The case remained under the chair.

Holmes stepped down from the podium, ducked behind the pit partition, and reached for the case. It was heavier than it should have been. He carefully opened the lid to find a slim metal case inside. It was cool-toned and metallic. A wire just barely protruded from the side.

Holmes carried it gingerly through the left side corridor, heart pounding, realizing that the timer was likely set to go off at the start of the second act.

By the time he emerged into the lower hall, Trask was ahead of him headed toward the hidden tunnel he himself had secretly designed during the theater's renovation.

Holmes followed swiftly while carefully navigating through the busy stage wing. The metallic box tucked against his chest; he paused only once—to hand the device to a waiting fireman at the back entrance.

"Neutralize this," he whispered. "Carefully."

The fireman gently took the parcel and disappeared.

Holmes continued into the tunnel, tossing away his conductor's wig.

Holmes shouted angrily. "Trask!"

The fugitive turned; startled, he laughed as he ran toward the exit.

Lestrade and two constables hurried to follow Holmes into the tunnel.

Trask reached for his coat pocket, but Holmes was already upon him.

With a sharp, furious blow, Holmes struck him across the jaw. Trask reeled backward and fell hard against the wall, dazed.

Watson appeared a moment later, eyes wide. "Holmes!"

Holmes stood over Trask, fists clenched, chest heaving. His voice was low, shaking with fury.

"You would have murdered her," he said. "Victoria. And the orchestra and cast. And the children. All of us."

Trask coughed, blood on his lip. "Murder?" He laughed, spitting out a tooth. "No, Mr. Holmes. Cleansing fire. You never understood the beauty in that."

Trask glared at Holmes, a glint of madness in his eye. "You think it ends with me? That the curtain's closed? You're wrong."

Holmes leaned in, ready to strike again.

Trask's smile curled. "You proved you're human after all. I studied you for months. I wanted to break the mind that couldn't be broken. And I did. You love her." He said mockingly, "You hesitated. You got emotional. That's all I needed."

Holmes grabbed him by the collar and dragged him upright.

"You nearly killed the woman I lo—" Holmes stopped short, jaw tight. "No. You're not worthy to even hear the word."

He raised his fist again, rage raw in his eyes.

But Lestrade stepped in. "Holmes—stop!"

Holmes held still for a beat, then delivered one last punch. Trask slumped, groaning.

Lestrade grabbed Holmes's arm before he could strike again.

"That's enough, not that I blame you," he said gently.

Holmes exhaled through gritted teeth and stepped back, looking at Watson.

Two more officers arrived with a young inspector—escorting Croft and Brayford, hands cuffed in front of them, toward the corridor.

"We found them waiting at the tunnel's end," they said to Lestrade. "They were ready to flee."

Croft's face was stony. Brayford's eyes flicked between Trask and Holmes.

"You failed us," Trask hissed at Croft. "Spineless old coward. Couldn't even rig a mechanism without Holmes sniffing it out. I knew you would fail. That I had to come back and finish the task myself."

He turned on Brayford, his voice venomous. "And you—did you think I loved you? I used you, Eleanor. You were leverage. Just another weak mind to manipulate."

His eyes locked with hers as a bloody smile grew across his face accompanied by an almost demonic and growing laughter.

Brayford blinked. Then, in one swift, desperate motion, she grabbed the sidearm of the young inspector beside her.

The shot cracked through the corridor like a thunderclap.

Trask collapsed dead with the nightmarish grin still plastered on his face.

Lestrade gently took the gun from Brayford's shaking hands. She didn't resist.

She stood frozen. "I gave him everything," she whispered. "And he didn't even lo…." She wept bitterly burying her face in her hands.

Holmes exhaled, his hands still clenched.

Lestrade and the officers led Brayford and Croft away.

Holmes and Watson stood alone in the tunnel, Holmes's chest rising and falling, emotion crashing over him in waves. The friends looked at one another, both feeling a weight lifted from their shoulders.

Back upstairs, the cast was preparing to resume the second act. The children, giggling, passed around peppermint drops as their teachers whispered reminders to stay seated.

Holmes emerged into the wings. Victoria stood there, halfway between stage and shadows.

Their eyes met.

She stepped toward him, wordless, worry etched into every feature of her face.

Holmes gave her a single nod.

"Is it over?" she asked.

Holmes nodded slowly. "It's over."

She reached out, took his hand, and held it tightly.

"Thank you, Sherlock." she said.

For once, he had no reply.

And somewhere behind them, the orchestra began to tune for Act Two.

Opening night, finally, was here. The hush of the audience beyond the velvet drapes was like the breath before a confession.

In the quiet of her dressing room, Victoria stood before the mirror, already dressed in her costume for the first scene. The gown shimmered faintly under the warm lights. Her hands rested at her sides, trembling only slightly.

Daisy was behind her, adjusting Victoria's hair.

"You're sure you want to wear it down like this?" Daisy asked, not for the first time.

"It's how I dreamed it," Victoria whispered.

Daisy smiled, her reflection meeting Victoria's in the mirror. "Then it's perfect."

A silence stretched between them, full and understanding.

"I keep thinking of everything that had to happen for us to be here," Victoria said. "All the lies. The fear. The rebuilding. How close we came to losing everything."

Daisy's fingers paused at the edge of her collar. "We didn't lose it. We fought for it. You fought for it."

Victoria turned, catching her friend's hands in her own. "No. Not just me." Her voice dropped. "Daisy, this is your triumph too. If you hadn't stayed—if you hadn't believed—I might've walked away before any of this began."

Daisy blinked quickly, smiling as she looked down. "Well… you're welcome. And you're brilliant."

Victoria turned to her friend and opened her hands. Daisy took them in her own, and they bowed their heads to thank God for His protection.

A knock at the door made them both glance over. A small envelope had been slipped beneath the frame.

Victoria crossed the room, picked it up, and opened it.

In Watson's familiar hand, the note read:

My dearest girl—

Whatever happens tonight, remember this: You have already won. Not applause. Not praise. But something harder to earn—yourself. And I have never been prouder.

All my love, always—
Father

Victoria smiled and pressed the card to her chest. "I hope he knows how much that means."

"I think he does," Daisy said, adjusting the final pin. "And so will everyone out there."

Victoria exhaled slowly. Her heart was steady now.

For the briefest moment, she thought of the first time she had ever seen the London Majestic—how small she'd felt in its towering halls. Her father had lifted her into one of the crimson velvet chairs beside her mother and whispered, "This is a house built for dreams."

Now it belongs to me, she thought. And tonight, I'm giving it a new one.

The velvet-trimmed box overlooking the stage of the London Majestic offered an impeccable view—its sightlines unobstructed, its comfort discreetly sumptuous. It had once been the private box of the theater's founder, Emily Boothe, and tonight, it belonged to her young successor. Victoria was not yet on stage, but the anticipation in the air made her presence palpable.

The house lights dimmed to a golden hush as anticipation rippled through the audience. The air inside the London Majestic crackled with energy—not the chaos of renovations or the tension of danger, but something lighter. Something like hope.

Holmes, Watson, and Mary were seated in the center of the box reserved for honored guests, dressed for the occasion. Holmes wore a dark, impeccably tailored suit and gloves he had not quite removed. Beside him, Watson adjusted his cuffs with habitual neatness, while Mary leaned forward to peek over the edge of the box.

Mary Watson looked radiant and elegant in her blue gown, though there was an unmistakable glint of maternal anxiety in her eyes.

"I still can't believe it's truly happening," Mary whispered, as the orchestra began tuning its instruments below. "After everything that happened."

Watson turned to her with a reassuring squeeze of her hand. "Victoria's earned this moment, my dear. And if anyone can deliver on opening night, it's our girl."

"She's not just opening a play," Mary murmured. "She's reopening a whole world. She brought this place back to life."

Holmes did not look away from the stage, but his voice, soft and even, joined theirs. "She did more than that. She preserved something that might otherwise have been lost." Mary glanced at him, surprised by the gentleness in his tone.

Holmes allowed himself a breath. "I've spent much of my life in places of logic. Courtrooms. Laboratories. Battlefields of the mind. But this theater…" He hesitated. "It reminded me that truth can live in emotion, not just deduction."

Watson arched an eyebrow. "Is that a compliment to the dramatic arts?"

Holmes turned to him, dryly. "Let us not get carried away."

Mary laughed. "Whatever your feelings about the theater, I do hope Victoria knows how proud we are of her."

Holmes glanced down at the house below. The audience was filling rapidly with well-dressed patrons in evening wear, an occasional child whispering in awe. "She will know," he said, "and if she doesn't, she will soon."

The lights dimmed fractionally, prompting a quiet hush across the theater. The chatter softened. The orchestra settled.

Mary leaned closer to her husband and whispered, "Did you ever think, back when you brought her here as a child, that she'd one day be the woman commanding this stage?"

Watson's eyes softened. "I always knew she was a dreamer," he said, "but I never dared to imagine she'd be so fearless. Or so capable."

Holmes studied him for a beat. "She is her father's daughter."

Watson blinked, then chuckled. "Thank you, Holmes. I believe that's the first time you've ever complimented my parenting."

"I was referring to her temperament," Holmes said mildly. "Stubbornness. Independence. A baffling tendency to ignore advice."

Mary laughed, delighted.

Watson gave a mock sigh. "And here I thought we were having a tender moment."

Holmes's lips twitched.

There was a gentle knock on the side of their box. A young usher leaned in, offering a polite nod. "The house is fully seated, sirs, ma'am. We'll begin in just a moment."

Holmes offered a curt nod. "Thank you."

The usher departed, and Mary adjusted the small opera glasses in her lap, though the box needed none. Her eyes returned to Holmes, curious now. "May I ask you something, Mr. Holmes?"

Holmes inclined his head. "Of course."

Mary looked toward Holmes. "So much has happened. Do you think she's all right? Truly?"

Holmes didn't answer immediately. His fingers, gloved in deference to formality, tapped once against the wooden railing of the box. "She stood at the edge of a very real threat and didn't falter. If there are scars, they are beneath the surface—but Victoria Watson is not easily undone."

Mary studied him. "You sound quite certain."

"I am," Holmes said, then added with a trace of reluctance, "Though I would be lying if I said I were unaffected."

Watson offered his old friend a smile that held both warmth and knowing. "You've always had a remarkable mind, Holmes. But hearts," he tapped his chest lightly, "they can be quite a different story."

"I'm aware." Holmes replied.

Mary glanced at Watson, uncertain. "I still don't understand how this Trask fellow managed to do all this right under everyone's noses."

Holmes turned to her, eyes focused and clear. "Trask began long before any of us noticed. He inserted himself into crew rotations, built secret access points into the substage, and created a schedule of controlled chaos. He manipulated individuals, one by one, until he was indispensable and untraceable. A parasite dressed as a partner."

Mary shivered slightly. "But you stopped him."

There was a pause as the curtain rippled slightly in the stage lights. Holmes leaned forward once more, his gaze narrowing as the orchestra pit lit up below.

The conductor stepped into position. Maestro Michaels, restored to his rightful place. Holmes inclined his head in approval. For all his quirks, the man was superb with a baton.

"They'll begin any moment," Holmes murmured.

"Was there ever a moment," Mary asked, "where you thought it wouldn't end well?"

Watson answered first. "Plenty of moments."

Holmes's voice was quieter. "There were times I believed the game would be lost. Not because the evidence was absent, but because the enemy understood us too well. He predicted our methods, anticipated our weaknesses."

Mary tilted her head. "And yet, you still won."

Holmes's eyes fell to the stage curtain. "Barely."

There was something haunted in his voice that made Mary's fingers curl gently around the sleeve of her husband's coat. She asked Holmes gently, "Did Trask say anything to you? At the end?"

Holmes was silent for a moment. "He said he wanted to break the mind that couldn't be broken. That I'd failed to remain detached."

Watson's voice was steady. "You didn't fail. You protected her."

Holmes gave no reply, but the tension in his shoulders eased.

The house lights dimmed fully.

A swell of music from the orchestra pit signaled the overture.

Mary smiled softly, then reached for Watson's hand. "I'm nervous," she admitted in a whisper. "She's brilliant, but—what if something goes wrong?"

Watson gave her hand a squeeze. "Then she'll handle it. She always does."

Holmes added, "Her only vulnerability now is the critics."

Mary looked at him. "And you?"

Holmes blinked. "What about me?"

"Are you nervous?" she asked gently. "For her? For yourself?"

A pause.

Then, almost inaudibly, he replied, "Yes."

The curtain began to rise.

The spotlight warmed the stage, and all other thoughts—Trask, shadows, ghosts—fell away as the first song of *The Reluctant Bride* echoed into the hushed air.

From their box, the three of them leaned forward together, not as detectives or doctors or companions to danger—but as proud loved ones, bearing witness to a dream come true.

The soft rustle of the audience settling in for the final scene echoed gently through the London Majestic. The house lights dimmed to a hush, leaving the stage bathed in a warm amber glow. Holmes, Watson, and Mary all prepared for the grand finale.

The play had been a triumph thus far—clever, charming, and full of heart. Laughter had rung out often, but so too had quiet moments of recognition. The audience had come expecting a light comedy. What they had received was something more refined: a story about choice, dignity, faith, and the courage to defend personal integrity.

A chapel interior was revealed onstage, simple and tastefully arranged. Stained glass shimmered in the painted backdrop, and the leading man in formal attire stood at the foot of the stage—his expression a portrait of hesitant hope. He looked toward the audience, his voice tremulous but clear.

"She said she wouldn't come. That she wasn't the marrying kind. That her heart belonged to only herself."

He paused.

"But she also said… if ever she were to say, 'I do,' it would be because she meant it. And meant it deeply."

He turned to the minister beside him. "So, I stand here. Not as a groom awaiting property… but as a man who loves her, hoping she'll walk through that door."

A hush fell across the theater.

Watching closely, Holmes found his hands still, his eyes unblinking.

The orchestra swelled with a lilting, yearning melody—a waltz that moved like breath, light and slow. The lights dimmed further. The church door opened from the back of the stage.

And then she appeared.

Victoria stood at the threshold in a shimmering bridal gown, delicate and radiant. The bodice sparkled with subtle embroidery, and the skirts moved like mist with each step she took down the aisle. No veil concealed her expression. She walked forward with purpose, her chin high, a quiet smile blooming on her lips.

Gasps rippled through the audience—whispers of admiration and awe—but in the box above, Sherlock Holmes did not move.

His expression shifted, ever so slightly. The lines of calculation gave way to something unguarded. In that moment, he saw neither the actress nor the heroine of a musical. He saw Victoria Watson—brilliant, determined, brave—stepping into the light not as a character, but as herself. Alive. Unbroken. Glorious.

Watson noticed the change in him but said nothing.

Images rose in Holmes's mind without permission: Victoria laughing beside him; her steady hands placing a warning letter in his. Her eyes in that terrible moment when she asked, *"Why would anyone target me?"*

Now she stood, fearless, radiant in white.

She does not belong to anyone, he thought, *least of all to me.*

Victoria reached the center of the stage and faced the man awaiting her as the orchestra started playing the final song softly.

"You asked me once what I was afraid of," she said softly. "I told you I feared cages. Expectations. The sound of a door closing behind me."

She took a breath and began to sing.

I never feared love… only the cost of it—
The silent weight, the price it might demand.
A chain in silk, a vow too tightly spoken,
A life not mine to choose, but one to withstand.

But then you asked for nothing—
No claim, no cage, no key.
You asked for only one thing...
The heart I'd give so free.

The chorus joined her; the stage bathed in golden light. Victoria's voice soared above the harmony—clear, strong, and shimmering with conviction.

For I have chosen joy over silence,
I have chosen faith over fear.
Love, freely given, is no cage...
But a promise I hold dear.

Victoria lifted her face towards the audience—and in that instant, she glanced toward the honored guest box.

Whether it was planned or instinct, Holmes would never know. But her eyes met his.

And he felt, unshakably, that she had meant it for him.

The last note lingered.

A beat of silence.

Then the audience erupted. Flowers were thrown from the front rows. Most stood as they clapped; others cheered aloud. Mary rose immediately, beaming with pride, and Watson stood beside her, joining in the ovation.

Holmes rose last.

His gaze never left the stage.

Victoria stood in the center of it, bouquet in hand, head bowed slightly in thanks. She curtsied once—modest, graceful, and glowing beneath the lights.

Watson leaned toward Holmes.

"Our girl was magnificent."

Holmes replied softly, the words barely above a breath.

"Yes, Watson… she is."

The curtain fell slowly. The lights shifted to soft amber.

And for one long, perfect moment, the applause did not stop.

The corridors behind the curtain swelled with the sound of celebration—cast members laughing, stagehands offering congratulations, flowers being passed hand to hand. But Victoria stepped aside, slipping into the quiet of her dressing room for a single breath of stillness.

Daisy found her there.

"You were brilliant," she whispered, rushing in with tears in her eyes. "You stopped the whole world."

Victoria laughed softly, shaking her head. "We did, Daisy. We did."

They embraced tightly.

A knock at the door interrupted them. A stagehand passed in a bouquet of pale orchids and white violets, elegantly arranged with a small card tucked into the ribbon.

Victoria unfolded it.

In unmistakable handwriting:

Faith is stronger than any cage.
—S.H.

She smiled, pressed the card to her chest, and whispered, "Thank you, Mr. Holmes."

The private room above the restaurant had been decorated with simple charm. White linen over round tables, candles flickering in glass holders, and a modest spread of wine, cheese, and fruit waiting near the back. Someone had even arranged a bouquet of red roses in a silver vase, a subtle nod to the theater and the woman who had brought it back to life, no longer "The British rose of the American stage," Victoria was home.

Victoria stood near the window, dressed in a sapphire blue gown that shimmered under the lamplight. Her hair was swept back but loosely pinned, giving her an air of ease she had rarely allowed herself during the weeks of tension and danger. She accepted congratulations with grace but often seemed more interested in watching the others—her cast, her crew, her family—bask in the moment.

Watson and Mary were seated at a nearby table, chatting amiably with Rodney, who was holding a glass of red wine and laughing heartily at something Mary had said. Daisy lingered near the refreshments, chatting with two of the younger performers. Holmes stood slightly apart from the group, near a glass cabinet displaying old photographs of the restaurant's theatrical history.

"This room once hosted Sarah Bernhardt," said Victoria softly, stepping beside him.

Holmes glanced at the photo. "She was known to command attention with little more than a glance."

"We both know someone else who can do that," Victoria replied, her voice light.

Holmes allowed the corner of his mouth to lift. "Indeed."

Daisy appeared just behind them, clearing her throat with mock solemnity. "Miss Watson, do you have a moment for the important announcement?"

Victoria turned, "I suppose I do."

Lightly clapping her hands with excitement Daisy said, "Mr. Rodney deserves this!"

Daisy called for attention with a playful rap of a spoon against her wine glass. The room quieted.

"Ladies and gentlemen," she said, gesturing grandly, "our leading lady has something to say."

Victoria blushed faintly but raised her glass. "I wanted to take this moment to thank all of you—for your talent, your patience, and your courage. We were tested more than once, and you stood firm. We've made something beautiful together, and I am deeply grateful."

She glanced to Daisy. "And tonight, I have the pleasure of announcing that Miss Daisy Dawn will be officially promoted to Assistant Director of the London Majestic."

The room broke into applause. Daisy flushed pink and looked half ready to cry, taken entirely by surprise. Rodney clapped her on the back.

"You've earned it," Victoria told her. "Every inch."

"Thank you, I had no idea!" Daisy managed. "I—thank you."

"And as for Mr. William Rodney," Victoria continued, "it is my honor to officially name you our permanent stage manager."

Rodney raised his glass in salute. "I accept—with the condition that no one ever asks me to wear a cravat."

Laughter filled the room.

As the party resumed its rhythm, Watson approached Victoria and extended a hand. "May I have this dance, Miss Watson?"

She raised an eyebrow, amused. "I didn't know there would be dancing."

"There isn't. But I've found that when you want to speak with someone privately, asking for a dance is a useful pretense."

She laughed and allowed him to lead her to a quieter corner of the room where soft music played from a gramophone. They danced slowly, turning in small circles.

"You look well," Watson said. "Happy."

"I am. Not entirely at rest yet—but yes. Happy."

"Do you know what you want to do next?"

Victoria tilted her head. "The theater, of course. There's so much more we can do now. But beyond that I'm learning to let the future unfold. One truth at a time."

Watson smiled, touched by her maturity and resilience. "I think your mother would be proud. And your father certainly is."

From across the room, Holmes watched them quietly. Mary moved beside him.

"They're a sight, aren't they?" she said.

"He's always been proud of her."

Mary tilted her head. "And you?"

Holmes hesitated. "Pride doesn't quite encompass it."

"No, I suppose not." She glanced at him sidelong. "You know, Sherlock, there are times in life when caution is wise. But there are others when it's just fear wearing a clever disguise."

Holmes turned his eyes toward Victoria again and said nothing.

"You'll know which it is," Mary said, "when it matters."

The music played on, and outside the tall windows, the London streets glowed with the promise of something new.

The streets of London were quiet by the time Holmes stepped out of the cab and approached the familiar door of 221B Baker Street. The theater had been a cascade of music, laughter, toasts, and color. Victoria went back to her office with Daisy to finish a few details before going home. But now, silence greeted him like an old friend.

He let himself in with a key, his footsteps light on the stairs. A single lamp burned low in the sitting room, casting long shadows against the shelves and scattered papers. The fire had gone out. He did not bother to relight it.

Holmes removed his gloves slowly, almost ritualistically. One finger at a time, he peeled away the formality of the evening. Then his coat, folded neatly and set aside. Beneath it all, he felt older tonight—not in years, but in weight.

From the writing desk, he retrieved a folder. It contained the last of the evidence collected from Trask's secret workroom—schematics, coded schedules, forged letters, and lists of chemicals with precise dosing instructions. Holmes glanced at one of the pages in silence, then closed the folder.

He sat down in his chair, stretching his legs out before him. A long moment passed.

Then came the flashbacks.

Victoria's pale face in the gaslight as she read the second warning note. Her voice trembling in his flat as she asked why she'd been targeted. Her determined steps into the substage. Her laughter over tea. The sound of her final solo, carried on the hush of the crowd.

He closed his eyes.

He had never loved easily. Not in the romantic sense. Not when so much of his life demanded distance, detachment, and control. But somewhere between the letters, the investigations, and the moments fighting to right wrongs together, something had shifted.

He thought of her eyes—both defiant and vulnerable. Of the moment she had stood alone onstage in a bridal gown, looking up toward the box as if she could see him.

He should never have let it happen.

And yet...

He had.

He drew in a slow breath.

"She does not belong to anyone," he murmured aloud. "Least of all to me."

The words hung in the dark room.

The morning light poured through the lace curtains of the Watsons' modest sitting room, gilding the teacups on the tray between them. Mary sat curled in the armchair nearest the hearth, her hands wrapped around her cup, the steam warming her cheeks. Watson, freshly shaved and dressed but with suspenders hanging loose at his sides, sat on the edge of the settee, reading the morning edition.

He lowered the paper, his expression thoughtful.

"Raves," he said. "Every paper. One calls her performance 'a revelation draped in silk.' Another says the play is 'a rare fusion of wit, grace, and authenticity.'"

A pause settled over them, companionable and quiet. Then Mary set her cup down and folded her hands in her lap.

"John… may I ask you something?"

Watson looked up, immediately attentive. "Of course."

She hesitated. "How would you feel if Sherlock and Victoria… if they were to fall in love? Or marry?"

The question hung in the air between them, more delicate than the porcelain teacups, and twice as fragile.

Watson didn't answer at once. He looked out the window, where green leaves quivered on the trees beyond their garden gate. His voice, when it came, was low.

"When she was a child," he said, "I imagined all kinds of futures for her. Some grand, some quiet. None of them involved danger, or mystery, or men like Holmes."

Mary said nothing, letting him find his way.

"But then," he went on, "I remembered that her mother fell in love with a soldier. A man who carried the weight of war in his chest and still managed to write poetry in his journal. So perhaps it's not about avoiding risk but choosing a companion who understands its cost."

He turned to Mary.

"I trust him," he said simply. "More than I trust most men alive. And I trust her. She sees him clearly—not as a legend, but as a man."

Mary's eyes softened. "You'd give your blessing, then?"

Watson smiled faintly. "I already have. Though I doubt either of them has noticed."

They both laughed.

"She's strong, John," Mary said. "But it's not wrong to want her protected."

"No," he agreed. "But it would be wrong to clip her wings in the name of protection. If anyone can walk beside her without holding her back—it's Holmes."

Mary reached for her tea again, her voice light but sincere. "I suppose we'll just have to be the steady ones, when their heads are spinning."

Watson grinned, "As always."

Outside, a sparrow sang from the garden wall, and the morning pressed on—gentle, golden, and full of change.

Watson stepped into 221 Baker Street just before noon, the warmth of the late morning sun trailing in behind him. Mrs. Hudson greeted him at the door with a knowing smile.

"Good morning, Doctor. You've just missed Miss Victoria—she left for the theater not twenty minutes ago."

Watson asked, concern showing on his face. "Was she well?"

"She looked tired. But lighter than I've seen her in months." She lowered her voice. "And Mr. Holmes... he came in late and hasn't stirred since returning home last night."

Watson thanked her and climbed the stairs, the creak of each step somehow both familiar and weighted.

He found Holmes in his armchair, a cup of tea cooling beside him, untouched. He wasn't reading. He was staring into the fire, which had been revived to a low, steady glow.

"Good morning, Holmes," Watson said gently.

Holmes looked up. "Good morning."

Watson held out the morning papers. "You've made the front page again. Well, Lestrade has. But we both know better."

Holmes took the paper, barely glanced at the headline— *"Yard Triumphs in Theater Sabotage Foiled by Quick Thinking"*—and set it aside.

"Let him have it," he said. "He earned it, in the end."

Watson sat down across from him, watching his friend's stillness. "You look like a man still fighting a ghost."

Holmes exhaled through his nose. "You're not far off."

There was silence for a moment, the kind that stretched comfortably between men who had faced death together.

Holmes broke it first. "Watson, he knew how I think. How I compartmentalize. Trask knew where to push."

"He almost won," Watson said softly. "But he didn't."

Holmes sighed quietly, then leaned back and rested his eyes on the ceiling.

"She was never just a pawn in his game," he murmured. "She became the reason I kept playing."

Watson watched his friend, but said nothing, letting the words settle.

"I see the danger now," Holmes continued. "Not just from enemies like Trask—but from me. From what my life demands. The investigations. The risks. If I were killed tomorrow, she would grieve again. I do not wish to cause her pain."

"You think that's a reason to keep your distance?"

"I think," Holmes said slowly, "that love and danger do not coexist well. Not for long."

Watson leaned forward, resting his elbows on his knees.

"Holmes, a life ruled by fear isn't a life. And love... love doesn't promise safety. Victoria already learned that lesson once when her fiancé was killed in New York. But love gives you something worth the risk."

Holmes looked at him.

"You think I should tell her."

"I think," Watson said, "that you already have. Just not in words."

Before Holmes could answer, a sharp knock sounded at the door.

Mrs. Hudson opened it a moment later. "Inspector Lestrade, sir!"

Lestrade entered with his usual energy, though a bit more reserved than usual. "Gentlemen," he greeted them both, then looking toward Holmes. "I thought you'd want the final update."

Holmes gestured for him to continue.

"Croft," Lestrade said, "was found this morning in his cell. Dead. Suicide."

Neither Holmes nor Watson spoke for a moment.

"And Brayford?" Holmes asked.

"Confined to the mental infirmary ward at Holloway. She's… not well. Refuses to speak to anyone. We don't expect a trial."

He shifted slightly, then added with a glance toward Watson, "My wife's been reading all about the play, you know. Keeps dropping hints. Not subtle ones, either. Says she'd love to see Miss Watson's play."

Watson grinned. "I'll pass that along."

Holmes added dryly, "I'm sure something can be arranged."

Lestrade smiled and made to leave, but Holmes stood and extended his hand. "Thank you, Inspector. Sincerely."

Lestrade looked surprised but shook his hand firmly. "Don't mention it."

When the door shut behind him, Holmes sat down again and stared into the fire.

"I think I may have just said goodbye to the last shadow of this case."

Watson studied his friend for a moment. "And what remains?"

Holmes didn't answer right away.

But after a long pause, he murmured, "Hope, perhaps."

The Diogenes Club was as still as a chapel—silent, austere, and governed by the kind of rules only men like Mycroft Holmes considered sacred. No unnecessary speech. No sudden movements. And certainly, no emotional outbursts.

Holmes stepped through the polished doors, the warmth of the spring sun still on his shoulders. He removed his hat and gloves with quiet precision and handed them to the porter with a simple nod. The club steward, recognizing him, gestured with a slight incline of the head toward the far room.

Mycroft was already seated in his favorite chair by the window in the Stranger's Room; a silver teapot and two cups arranged with mathematical symmetry at his side. A copy of *The Times* was spread open on his lap. He didn't look up.

"You're late," Mycroft said.

"You're early," Holmes replied, taking the opposite chair.

Mycroft folded the paper precisely and set it aside. "I was enjoying the latest account of Inspector Lestrade's heroic efforts in preventing the destruction of The London Majestic theater. Truly stirring. Did you know the man single-handedly foiled an arsonist?"

Holmes gave a tight smile. "Lestrade has always had a flair for understatement."

"Mm. Well, never mind who gets credit." Mycroft reached for the teapot. "I imagine the theater will benefit. Any mention from the press can only help it."

Holmes accepted the offered cup with a nod. "Unless you're the one in handcuffs."

"Speaking of which," Mycroft said mildly, "Stamford has been released. Completely absolved. The new statement from Miss Godfrey, combined with your findings and Lestrade's summary, removed all doubt. He's been taken to a private hospital. The stress and confinement did him no favors, but he's expected to recover."

Holmes exhaled slowly. "Good. He deserves peace."

"And your gratitude, I presume."

"Immeasurably," Holmes said. "He introduced me to Watson."

"Indeed," Mycroft mused. "And if not for that meeting, you'd never have met Watson's daughter."

He stirred his tea without looking up. "Which, I assume, is the real reason for your visit."

Holmes did not answer at once. He stared out the window instead, watching the wind rustle the green leaves of the square below.

"She was nearly destroyed by this," he said quietly. "And she emerged stronger than I expected."

"She emerged," Mycroft replied, "because she is not a porcelain figurine, but a woman of exceptional intellect and spine. A fact which you appear to be struggling with."

Holmes's lips twitched. "Perhaps."

Mycroft sat back, fingertips pressed together. "Tell me, then—what do you want from me?"

Holmes considered. "Perspective."

Mycroft arched an eyebrow. "How delightfully vague. Very well. Shall we begin with the facts? You are a man of danger and precision. She is a woman of vision and heart. You fear that your world will ruin hers. That she will suffer by association."

"She nearly died because of it."

"She nearly died because of a madman, not because of you. You did not summon Trask. You defeated him."

"But what if the next one is smarter? Quieter?"

Mycroft studied him. "You are not asking me whether you should love her. You already do. You're asking whether you can allow yourself to."

Holmes looked down into his tea. "Yes."

For a moment, neither brother spoke.

Then Mycroft said, "Do you remember our parents?"

Holmes blinked. "Of course."

"Brilliant," Mycroft said. "Cold. Exceptionally private. And entirely incapable of showing affection."

Holmes tried to defend them. "They believed sentiment was distraction."

"They did." Mycroft's gaze softened slightly. "Which is why I find it fascinating that both of their sons ended up craving something they never offered."

Holmes looked up.

"I've spent my life watching from a distance," Mycroft said. "You've spent yours leaping into danger. But neither of us has found someone who makes the world feel... bearable."

"Until now," Holmes said softly.

"Until now," Mycroft echoed. "And that brings us to Aunt and Uncle Vernet."

Sherlock smiled faintly. "You always said they were anomalies."

"They were," Mycroft replied. "French. Passionate. Hopelessly in love. And somehow still productive, respected, and entirely unruined by domesticity. Of course, being French that was in their blood."

"You sound almost envious." Holmes observed.

"I am envious," Mycroft said simply. "But I'm also practical."

"And your verdict?"

Mycroft set his cup down. "The question is not whether she would distract you. The question is whether her absence would."

Holmes was silent.

Mycroft stood, adjusting his coat. "I don't need to meet her to know she's extraordinary. But I would like to. When will that happen?"

Holmes stood as well. "Soon – if the lady will have me."

Mycroft gave him a rare, approving smile. "Then go to her. And for God's sake, try not to overthink it."

As Holmes left the club, the air outside felt less weighted. The world, for once, did not need solving. Only choosing.

The London Majestic stood quiet in the morning light, its grand façade catching the sun like a monument to resilience. Inside, the remnants of the previous evening's triumph still lingered with bouquets in the wings, programs left tucked in velvet seats, and the faint scent of dust and roses.

Victoria stepped onto the stage alone, her heels echoing in the empty house. She paused at center stage and took a slow, centering breath. It no longer felt haunted. Not by Trask. Not by shadows. Only by possibility.

Behind her, Daisy and Rodney emerged from the wings with a set of architectural diagrams and a measuring stick.

"The back wall's still not quite aligned," Rodney said. "But nothing structural. We can fix it."

Victoria turned to them, her tone decisive. "I want the hidden passages gone. Every one of them."

Rodney frowned slightly. "That'll mean tearing out quite a bit of paneling. Some of it original."

"I don't care," she said. "They were designed for secrecy. For control and evil. I want transparency now. Light. Safety."

Daisy stepped forward. "What if… we repurpose them instead? Keep the structure but open them up. Make them usable for crew movement, quick changes, extra storage. We reclaim them."

Victoria considered this. "Transform what was hidden into something helpful."

"Exactly," Daisy said. "No more secrets."

Victoria gently smiled. "All right. But we document everything. And I want every entrance and exit clearly marked. No more shadows."

As they turned to gather their supplies, Rodney paused near a small storage closet tucked behind a faded velvet curtain. It had once been sealed shut, but Trask's tampering had left it slightly ajar.

"Something's in here," he said, kneeling to pull free a dusty box.

Victoria felt a shiver. "Be careful! It might be another hidden explosive the fire brigade missed!"

"Nah," Rodney grunted, "There's years of dust covering this old thing."

Daisy came to look, and together they opened it.

Inside were faded theater programs, old tickets, clippings from yellowed newspapers. One caught Victoria's eye—a brittle page from a forgotten publication.

"Emily Boothe's Bold Vision for the London Majestic"

There was a photo—a woman in a high-necked gown, standing on the very stage they now occupied. Her eyes were proud, her posture certain. Beneath the headline, a quote was circled in pencil:

"Theater is not escape—it is revelation. A mirror in which the heart may recognize itself."

Victoria stared at it for a long time. "She was so young," she whispered. "And fearless."

"She reminds me of you," Daisy said softly.

Victoria touched the edge of the page with reverence. "We're not just building on her dream. We're continuing it."

They stood in silence for a moment before Daisy glanced around. "If she's watching, she'd be proud."

Victoria laughed quietly. "Then we're doing something right. Mr. Rodney, can you build a simple display case in the lobby so visitors can see these treasures of our history?"

Rodney checked his watch and cleared his throat. "I'll start measuring. It shouldn't take very long to finish."

"Thank you, Will" Victoria said. "Truly."

He gave a nod and disappeared backstage.

Daisy lingered, then brightened suddenly. "Oh! This came for you while you were upstairs. A boy dropped it off. Said it was urgent."

She handed Victoria a small, cream-colored envelope sealed in red wax.

Victoria opened it carefully.

"Would you join me for dinner this evening?

– S.H."

Victoria smiled despite herself.

Daisy leaned closer, reading the signature upside down. "Is that who I think it is?"

Victoria folded the note and slipped it into her pocket, trying to hide her smile. "Yes."

"About time," Daisy said, grinning.

Victoria looked out across the empty theater once more. "Yes," she echoed. "It is."

The sun faded gently through the lace curtains of 221B Baker Street, casting dappled patterns across the sitting room floor. The scent of fresh tea and warm scones wafted in the air, though the plate on the sideboard remained untouched.

Mrs. Hudson moved quietly through the hall, dusting cloth in hand, though her eyes were far more curious than her cleaning was urgent. She paused at the threshold of the sitting room, peering in just enough to catch sight of Holmes, his door slightly open.

He was standing before the small mirror on the wall, adjusting the collar of his charcoal coat. Not with haste, but with care. His dark hair was neatly combed, his shoes recently polished, and he wore a clean white cravat—not his usual, but one folded with intention. From the corner of the room, his violin case rested shut, untouched for days.

Mrs. Hudson watched him a moment longer, surprised by how… almost nervous he looked. Not in the way he appeared before a case—brisk, calculating, methodical—but something gentler. Something unsure.

He caught her reflection in the mirror and turned, a faint look of amusement crossing his features.

"You're going out?" she asked with polite nonchalance.

"I am," Holmes replied, reaching for his gloves. "Dinner engagement."

"Oh?" She tilted her head. "Not a client, then?"

"No," he said. "Not a client."

She smiled to herself. "Well, it must be important. You haven't touched your scones."

He gave a faint smile. "Some things outrank scones."

She stepped into the room, pretending to dust the bookshelf as she spoke. "She's a fine woman, Mr. Holmes. Brave. Sharp. Kind. And far more patient than most would be."

With a subtle smile Holmes said, "Are you implying that extra patience would be required?"

"Well, perhaps a bit," Mrs. Hudson replied with a bit of a giggle.

Holmes turned to face her more fully, his tone softer than usual. "What are you thinking?"

Mrs. Hudson considered her words carefully before speaking. "I think you've spent most of your life believing that solitude is safer. And maybe it is. But it's a colder kind of safety, isn't it?"

He didn't answer at once. Then he said, "I used to think love was a distraction."

"And now?"

He glanced toward the door. "Now I think perhaps... I was distracted without it."

Mrs. Hudson watched him walk to the door and retrieve his coat from the rack. As he opened it, he paused.

"When did you know?" he asked.

"That you cared for her?" She smiled warmly. "The day you let her try to play your violin."

Holmes chuckled softly. "You always did know too much."

She shrugged. "Housekeepers hear everything."

He gave her a nod of gratitude and proceeded down the stairs and out into the street.

Mrs. Hudson stood in the doorway for a long moment, her arms folded gently. Then she looked around the room, at the tea left untouched, the violin case unopened, and the soft afterglow still lingering from Holmes' rare smile.

"Well," she murmured to herself, "it's about time."

The hush of early evening had settled over London as Holmes stepped from the cab outside the London Majestic. The streetlamps glowed like sentinels along the pavement, and the last wisps of pink and gold from the sunset streaked the sky above the theater's graceful marquee.

He adjusted his collar and stepped through the front doors, nodding politely to the doorman, who recognized him at once and gave a slight bow.

Inside, the theater bustled with quiet energy—stagehands securing props, costumers sorting garments, a technician adjusting lighting cues. It was the controlled chaos of a building preparing for the next night's performance.

Rodney spotted him first. The older man smiled broadly, wiping his hands on a rag as he crossed the lobby.

"Mr. Holmes. You're expected. She's just wrapping up a few things. Come with me."

As they walked through the corridors, Holmes took in the sights and sounds with quiet admiration. This place had changed—not in structure, but in spirit. It was no longer haunted. It was alive again.

Rodney led him through the door and escorted him onto the boards themselves. Victoria stood at center stage, speaking with Daisy and a pair of dancers. She wore a hunter green dress that caught the golden light in flattering flashes, her hair pinned with the faintest suggestion of stage flair still lingering.

When she turned and saw Holmes, her expression brightened—not with surprise, but with warmth.

"Mr. Holmes," she said with a smile, "you're punctual."

Before he could answer, something unexpected happened.

A smattering of applause broke out from the wings. Then from the rafters. And then from the stagehands, costumers, and performers gathering nearby. Within seconds, the entire staff and cast had joined in—not raucous or theatrical, but heartfelt.

Holmes stood frozen, startled.

Victoria stepped toward him, clearly moved, and gently took his arm. "They insisted," she murmured. "They know what you did—what might have happened without you."

Holmes gave a small nod, the faintest smile twitching at the edge of his mouth. "They're overly generous."

"Not at all," said Daisy, stepping up beside him. "You're not much for curtain calls, I imagine—but you've certainly earned this one."

Rodney added, "You helped save this place, sir. That's no small thing."

For a moment, Holmes stood quietly, his gaze moving over the faces in the theater—the crew, the cast, the women whose lives had been targeted, and those who had helped to protect them. His usual reticence faltered just enough.

"I am grateful," he said, "and honored to have played some small part in this theater's return to life."

The applause swelled again for a final beat before fading.

Seeing his discomfort, Victoria gestured toward the stairs. "Shall we?"

Daisy reached out and adjusted a thread on Victoria's sleeve. "You two have a lovely evening. Try not to solve any crimes at dinner."

Rodney chuckled. "Your carriage is already waiting."

With a final wave, Holmes and Victoria descended the stage steps and crossed the lobby. Outside, the carriage stood polished and ready, the driver tipping his cap in greeting.

As they stepped inside and the door clicked shut behind them, the theater's golden lights faded into the distance.

Holmes sat back against the cushioned bench and studied Victoria beside him.

"You didn't tell me there would be a standing ovation."

"You didn't tell me you'd look so uncomfortable," she replied with a teasing smile.

He arched a brow. "I consider it a character flaw."

"I consider it endearing."

The carriage turned onto the boulevard, the clatter of wheels soothing and rhythmic.

They said nothing for a while, letting the city roll past. The night, like their journey, was just beginning.

The restaurant Holmes had chosen was tucked discreetly between two stone buildings near Covent Garden, marked only by a burnished brass plaque and a small set of stairs leading to a velvet-curtained entry. Inside, candlelight danced along the dark wood paneling, and soft music drifted from a string trio nestled in a corner. The air smelled of butter, rosemary, and wine.

"I'd have brought you here long ago," Holmes said quietly as he helped Victoria out of her coat, "if not for all the—activity."

She smiled as she handed her coat to the attendant. "I rather like that word. So vague. So… accurate."

They were shown to a table near a large arched window where ivy curled along the pane outside. The silverware gleamed. The china was pale with an ivy motif not unlike the one outdoors. It was elegant without being ostentatious—clearly a place Holmes frequented when he wanted calm without spectacle.

They settled in. Holmes ordered wine. Victoria ordered a pear salad and pheasant; Holmes requested the fish special without asking what it was. She noted it with amusement.

"You come here often enough to trust the chef implicitly?"

"I've never been poisoned here. That's all the trust I require."

The corners of her mouth lifted. "What a romantic sentiment."

Holmes glanced toward their waiter, who had just discreetly set down a carafe of wine.

"New to this establishment," he remarked once the man departed. "American, by the accent—Midwestern, I'd wager. Likely involved in theatre himself. His hands show calluses where stage ropes bit in."

Victoria tilted her head. "You read all that from a wine pour?"

"A pour. A voice. A pair of worn shoes." He sipped his wine. "The world announces itself to those who choose to see."

Their first few minutes were filled with pleasantries—how the orchestra had improved since rehearsals, the delight of hearing actual laughter from the box office staff, the return of the costumer's missing cat. But beneath the words pulsed something deeper. Something unsaid.

After the wine was poured and their meals arrived, Victoria leaned in.

"Do you think my father will write about all of this? The case, the arrests, the traps? He is, after all, your Boswell."

Holmes studied his fork for a moment before replying.

"That might prove difficult," he said at last, voice low.

She looked at him, puzzled.

"The story isn't complete yet."

Victoria gently nodded her head, understanding something unspoken. "No, I suppose it isn't."

They ate in thoughtful quiet for a moment.

"Have you thought about what comes next?" she asked, turning her glass slowly by the stem.

Holmes looked out the window. "I'll continue my practice, as usual. London has no shortage of mysteries. I'll likely find myself tangled in another within a fortnight."

She smiled. "I wouldn't expect otherwise."

He turned his gaze back to her. "And you?"

Victoria's face brightened. "The theater is still so filled with potential. It wasn't just about restoring it, but making it shine. I want new productions, fresh talent, even some outreach to schools. It will be a benefit to the community. I want it to become something alive again. And because of you, I have that chance."

"You would have done it without me."

"No," she said, gently but firmly. "Not like this. Not safely. Not in time."

Their eyes held for a moment, a long moment, filled with shared memory.

Holmes cleared his throat. "Perhaps we should take some air. There's a garden out back. Quiet, less overheard."

Victoria rose. "Lead the way, Mr. Holmes."

The garden patio behind the restaurant was quiet now, dappled in moonlight and the perfume of roses. The lanterns swayed gently in the breeze, casting golden light across stone benches and trimmed hedges. Holmes and Victoria strolled without speaking, the rhythm of their steps finding easy harmony.

Holmes held the wrought iron gate open for Victoria, and she stepped through, her silk skirt whispering with each movement. They walked in silence for a moment, the quiet between them no longer filled with tension, but with the weight of possibility.

A soft violin melody floated out as the string trio still played from within the dining room.

At the far end of the garden stood a stone bench beneath a blooming magnolia. Holmes gestured toward it, and they sat side by side.

"I can see why you like this place," Victoria said softly, glancing up at the moon between the boughs. "It's peaceful. Hidden."

"Few people know it exists," Holmes replied. "Which is why I come here when I need to think without interruption."

She folded her hands in her lap. "Is that what we're doing now? Thinking without interruption?"

Holmes gave a faint smile. "Something like that."

There was another pause. Then Victoria said, "Daisy told me I should let you speak first."

Holmes turned toward her, eyes narrowing just a little. "Did she?"

"She said I'd be tempted to fill the silence just to ease the moment. But you—you need to arrive at things in your own time. She said if it was worth hearing, I'd wait."

Holmes exhaled a quiet laugh. "She's rather astute."

Smiling, Victoria said "She's earned that title."

He leaned forward slightly, resting his elbows on his knees. "Watson said something to me. That a life ruled by fear is no life at all. That love doesn't promise safety, only meaning."

Victoria watched him, sensing the effort it took to say the words.

Taking a deep breath, he continued "I spent so long convinced that distance was protection. For others. For myself. That detachment was strength. But that never stopped danger. Or pain. It only dulled the moments that might have made it worthwhile."

She reached out, placing her hand gently over his.

"What are you afraid of, Sherlock?"

He didn't answer right away. Then, in a voice lower than usual, he said, "Failing you. Bringing ruin to something good."

She held his hand a little tighter. "You've never failed me. You never could."

They sat together for a long moment, the breeze tugging lightly at her hair.

"I used to come to gardens like this when I needed to think," she said quietly. "Before the theater. Before Trask. But tonight… I don't want to think. I just want to – feel."

He reminisced out loud "I keep remembering the first time I saw you at Baker Street," he said. "Your hair and clothes in disarray as you stood on that ladder."

Victoria smiled saying, "First impressions are the most important, they say."

The smile on Holmes's face faded. "I also remember the day you placed that first warning note on the table. Your hands were shaking, but you pretended they weren't."

Victoria gave a small laugh. "And you pretended you didn't notice."

"I noticed everything," he said, his voice barely above a whisper. "But I didn't yet understand… what you would come to mean to me."

"I won't ask you to say anything you're not ready to say," she said gently. "But I am here. And I'm not going anywhere."

Holmes turned to her, his expression open, unguarded for perhaps the first time in her presence. His voice barely above a whisper: "I have never loved anyone the way I love you. And I never expected that I would."

She drew in a quiet breath, her eyes shining.

She looked down at their joined hands. For a long moment, she said nothing. Then—

"My heart," she began softly, "was so broken, I didn't believe I could ever love again. Not truly."

She looked up into his eyes. "Until you."

Holmes's expression didn't change at first. But something in him eased. The careful reserve, the shield of control—lowered, if only for her.

No more words followed. He reached for her face, cradled her cheek with one hand, and leaned in.

Their kiss was not rushed. It was quiet, reverent—an answer to every unspoken question, every brush of fingers, every look that had lingered too long.

Holmes reached for her hand. "You've undone me, Victoria."

She softly replied, "And you've restored me,"

They sat there as the music faded, the warmth of each other's presence settling like a promise in the night.

Later, the carriage let them out early, at Victoria's request. They walked the rest of the way arm in arm, the gaslights throwing long shadows across the pavement.

The London Majestic rose ahead, its elegant façade softly aglow. The posters for *The Reluctant Bride* still gleamed in the display window, and one of the upper windows remained lit. Somewhere inside, a janitor moved through with a broom and lantern, oblivious to the quiet pair outside.

They stopped at the front steps, gazing up at it.

"It used to feel like it belonged to my past," Victoria said softly. "Now it feels like it belongs to my future. To our future."

Holmes looked at her—not just with affection, but with a depth of admiration he rarely allowed himself to show.

He didn't speak.

He didn't need to.

Victoria stepped closer, smiling as Holmes held her in his arms on the empty street.

And together, they stood in the glow of what they had built and what was yet to come.

Holmes studied the building for a moment, then turned his gaze to her. He said nothing.

Victoria looked at him, smiling. "You always do that. Say everything without a word."

He gently shrugged his shoulders. "A skill hard won."

She gave a contented sigh. "What are you thinking?"

He paused just long enough that she knew the answer mattered.

"I'm thinking," he said at last, "that some beginnings... are worth the cost."

Victoria's smile deepened, as she rested her head lightly against his shoulder.

And together, they walked on into the London night.